SQUIRE of SOL II

First paperback edition September 2024

Book design by Terminally Unique Books, llc

979-8-9904722-0-4 (paperback)

www.ollydee.com

Hey Jacob! Look at me, dedicating my book to you. Love you. <3

Dear ⧉⧉⧉,

It's always been just a true, unavoidable fact that one day I'd have something that could kill everyone you know planted next to my heart.

I didn't think I had a choice. Not until I met you.

I'm sorry. I have to do this.

Love,

Drew

ONE

YEAR

EARLIER

Blow Out the Candle

Drew's stomach — as well as a few other vital organs — were trying to climb out of his body. *'Nope,'* they seemed to be saying. *'Don't wanna be part of this anymore.'*

Drew understood where they were coming from.

He knew, distantly, that Teach was talking. Was saying all kinds of reasons for why this was happening, and Drew, frankly, couldn't hear said reasons because of the alien standing ramrod-straight and still at the front of the class.

It was a lush summer's day. Sun caught the dust in the air and sparked; a small galaxy of swirling grime. The treetops outside the window whispered bright green leaves together in a hush. The clock ticked. The students were all silent. Many were gaping, as Drew knew he must be. Teach was glaring pointedly at them, though, and still speaking, and—

And—

There was an Emni at the front of the class.

"Anyway," Teach snapped out, and Drew quickly closed his mouth. Shrunk into his cushion, trying to surreptitiously vanish behind his squat desk, heart hammering. "I expect nothing but your kindest ways

in helping Riis adjust."

The alien—Riis, apparently, okay, *what*—shifted then. Bowed his head slightly, and maybe it was out of respect, but Drew only saw the four thick horns atop his head suddenly pointed towards them, ram-like curls on either side and sharp jutting points front and center. Because of the slope of the classroom, the squat desks with cushioned seats all swelling up around the center where Teach and this new addition to the class stood, it felt for a moment like Drew might fall forward into those points.

'Riis' spoke clearly in rough, slightly whistling Standard, making Drew jump. "Thank you, Teach. I appreciate the introduction. I'm grateful you have welcomed me so graciously," then he peered out at all of them all and—Drew couldn't help flinching—blinked, a second pair of eyelids flashing over liquid dark eyes before the first. "Let us all do our best this year."

After class Riis was swarmed, because of course he was. Drew wasn't part of that, even though Amy yelled, "Drew!" after him from the center of the fray at the front row, where the alien seemed frozen, blinking quick and stunned around at his new classmates.

Drew didn't make eye contact with any of them as he burst out the door and down the hall, an entire percussion group crashing about inside him, barrel drum reverberating in his gut.

He could feel the alien's eyes long after the thick wooden door had slammed behind him and he was down the hall, skipping the elevator and storming down the great marble stairs, out into the green courtyard. When he collapsed on a bench, shaking in every part of himself, trying as hard as he could to contain each quake. Drew pinched tightly at his kneecaps until his fingers hurt, knuckles whited out and bent backward, and tried to breathe.

The day had started relatively normal. Get up, brush teeth. Poke hard at the mole on his cheek and squint at his buggy eyes. Get slapped upside the head by Amy for using her hairbrush in a mad attempt to make his flat dark hair do something other than flop down over his forehead. Try and slap Amy back upside the head. Get dodged, easily. Get made fun of. Get toenails painted sparkly maroon by Amy, who'd clucked that he'd spent the summer totally limiting what she had to work with, in terms of nails. True. *"Stop biting your toenails, Drew, christ."*

Put socks and clunky boots over feet, hiding toenails. Put his nice chainmail over his black turtleneck, and feel small, even in this barest amount of the clunky armor customary for his caste.

Upon checking their schedules, they'd learned they were in the same first class and ducked gleefully out their window onto their dinky little balcony, sprinting down the great metal fire stairs and across the narrow-sloping parking lot, up to the street and the corner store. There they grabbed coffee and grub. The drowsy warmth of a fading summer had pressed a bright heaviness against the top of his head. A cool, briny breeze had been whispering from the direction of the sea, which could be glimpsed in a glare of turquoise between the sloping spires marred with harsh lines. Old-Earth-style and modern built buildings smushed together. They'd caught the trolley—a common thing Amy had turned him onto when his bike had broken down—and munched comfortably on their respective corner store grabs on the way to school, sharing bites here and there.

It had been so normal. Such a normal day. And Drew hadn't realized he'd *needed that* until suddenly he didn't have it anymore. The summer before had been stuffed to bursting with interviews, attention, forced smiles and the omnipresent question: *"Now that you're 20, how do you feel, Squire, about being Knighted at the end of next summer?"*

"How do you feel about receiving the switch?"

"How"

"Do"

"You"

"Feel—"

"'Sup." Amy's hand came down solidly on his head, scritching once, whipping him back to this fresh new reality. He spasmed.

"Whoa," she said, eyes widening, plopping down next to him on his bench. "It's just me."

"I know," Drew said. His heart was still pounding in his ears.

"Well, why freak out, then?"

He didn't dignify this with a response.

"It is weird," Amy responded anyway. "I mean. I didn't even know they could survive off their moon. Isn't the atmosphere way different over there?"

"Humans are over there, too," Drew said. "Otherwise how would their population be controlled?"

Amy shrugged. Popped gum he hadn't realized she'd been chewing. "Robots?"

Drew glared. As a tactics-caste Enseeo, she knew perfectly well about the situation over on Drune, the moon of their neighboring planet. At the very least he knew she knew the basics: since the end of the war with the Emni over 180 years ago, the creatures weren't allowed to leave. Their planet was closely monitored—if not outright ruled—by the same militarized monarchy that ruled Earth II. They existed as a race of casteless, facing all the consequences of being 'alien' on their own homeworld, with none of the freedoms afforded the humans that chose to reject the caste system.

Amy rebelled in a strange, small way that scared him, though: casually pretending she was stupid in the face of everyone, even him. She was the only Enseeo he'd met at Americas University who talked like the Grunt-castes he'd grown up surrounded by, as they'd acted as guards of both King Admiral and his mother, the current Knight of Sol II. While it was normally almost heart-clenchingly comforting to hear flippancy rather than the practiced snide politics of Earth II's young elite, today it annoyed him.

"You know damn well it's not robots," he eventually settled on.

"Would be easier if it was, though, right? Then we could just bomb 'em without thinking much about it, if that time comes."

"That time won't come."

"Well. You would know."

Drew's blood was hot in his ears. "It's been generations since the first *and only use of*—"

"Yeah," she said quickly, "you're probably right."

"I am."

She rolled her eyes.

Quiet between them, for a moment. A merchant was selling tsousou fritters across the street, and the hot, buttery smell wafted over, mingling with the scent of freshly-mown grass and the sea. Grunts snorted and slapped at one another at the squat bar next door, sloshing warm beer in pitchers. The ocean at the end of the street glittered. The day wore on, and none of these outside people seemed to know it—that a living, breathing alien was right inside the hallowed halls behind them.

"Do you think he lives in the dorms?" Amy asked casually.

Drew stiffened. "He can't possibly."

She shrugged one bony shoulder. "I mean," she said, "before, like, an hour ago I would've said him being here at all is a 'can't possibly.' Aren't they not allowed off their little moon?"

"They're not," Drew snapped. And then froze. Chewed on that.

"So how… Drew, for shit's sake, I'm *talking to you!*"

He'd already risen and started jogging fast across the green, back through the great stone halls of the school.

Students were milling about. Most in the camo-printed Enseeo casual garb, little ribbons or interwoven threads implying their caste within that, though some staff, of course, wore blue Teach coats, gleaming with buttons that did that job more officially.

As per usual, his very presence supplied a path between them all before he reached them, clunking forward in his black Knight's mail and boots. Drew knew he looked like a weird, scrawny Grunt, dolled up as something more important. Knights normally studied at the Grunt academy across the street, though they were a higher caste than your average foot soldier. It'd been an exception for three generations now though: that the Knight of Sol II attended this school. Was elevated above Grunt status, above even Knight status. That's what they called it, anyway. "Elevated."

Whose bastard he was probably only helped that status.

The halls were wide, so it wasn't too odd, the way the students and staff would scuffle quickly to the sides before him. It was still intentional enough that it made him grind his teeth. Made him barrel through, like he was supposed to. Inherit his roughness and—ideally

—live up to it.

When he'd pounded all the way up the five flights of stairs—soul too hectic at this moment for the stoic stillness of an elevator ride—and reached Shrink Kanak's office, he froze. Glanced around. A few med-caste Enseeos were gathered in an alcove across the hall, sharing a snack between class and gossiping. They didn't look up at him until he rapped his knuckles lightly on the wooden door.

"Just a minute!" Shrink Kanak bellowed from inside, and he flinched.

Pointedly ignored the med-castes who were now staring openly at him. Re-stocking their gossip glasses, most likely.

It wasn't so odd. They were all required to speak to Shrink Kanak once a quarter.

He kind of did it more often than that, though.

There was a muttering inside followed by Shrink Kanak's short lilting laugh, and then a strange sound—the distinct clack of claws on wood, and it took him barely a second to realize what was about to happen before it did and he shrank, eyes darting down the hall, but then the door opened, and there he was.

Drew had always figured Emnis were huge, enormous, double the height of a man, but this creature blinked its bizarre eyes down at him from just about a head above, and Drew let out a hiss without meaning to, stepping back.

Riis stared. He looked, even through all the alien weirdness, exhausted. His black eyes drooped, and he stood with his shoulders tight and his dark gray horns pointed forward, even though nothing else in his stance suggested a threat. He even, in fact, pointedly clasped his hands behind his back after a moment of staring down at Drew, as if submitting to an imaginary restraint. Casual.

"You are the Knight of Sol II, correct?" the alien said after a moment, and the words whistled roughly, but were clear, understandable. So strange. Drew had known, distantly, that they could speak, but it was beyond uncomfortable to hear proof right before him.

"No!" he barked out on instinct, and Riis stiffened.

"Okay." Shrink Kanak was behind Riis, and Drew instinctively recoiled as she dropped her hand lightly against the Emni's arm, which he immediately lowered, opening a clawed hand and holding hers as well. He was wearing a *button down*. This was *insane*. "Okay, Drew, great. Come on in, kid. Riis—it was lovely to speak with you, please come and visit if you need anything."

"Thank you, Shrink Kanak," Riis whistled out softly, and glanced back at Drew, hard, before he turned and trotted away, clawed feet clacking down the hall.

No shoes. Somehow that was comforting. But still—

Drew could barely breathe.

"Drew? Kid? You okay in there? Drew?"

Drew turned and gaped down at her, and then pushed forward into her office. He barely caught her rolling her eyes skyward before she shut the door. Then, in a flourish of soft pink (dangerously bordering on non-standard) robes, she came around her squat wooden desk—batting a drooping branch of one of her many potted plants out of the way as she did—and plopped down on the cushion behind it, gesturing loosely at the cushion in front.

There was still an indent in the center. Drew remained standing.

"What can I do for you, Drew?"

"What the *ever loving fuck*—"

"Okay, calm it down. Until you're knighted I'm still in charge, kid —"

"How is he even here?! There are *laws against this*, you know! He's just—he can't—I mean—"

"Blow out the candle."

"Huh?!"

He knew what she was on about, but glared, breathing hard. She held out the omnipresent candle from the raised corner of her desk, though. He took a deep, tight breath. Held it. Blew out the candle.

Sat down on the cushion.

It was still slightly warm beneath him, and he flinched.

"What's this really about?" Shrink Kanak spoke bluntly, replacing and then re-lighting the candle swiftly before pushing a bowl of spiced nuts across the table towards him. He gritted his teeth. Took one of the nuts.

"It's not enough just being what it is?" he snarked. Crammed the nut in his mouth. Tongued the salt from it before biting into it, hard.

"I mean, yes. It could be. Given the circumstances and your rather personal involvement, though, I'd say maybe no."

Drew snorted, looked away. Chewed. Swallowed.

"This must be strange. I know it must be. Suddenly you're faced with it, right? You, the future host for the weapon aimed at Emni homeworld, quite abruptly in front of a member of that species, I'm guessing for the first time in your life. Remember, though, this is what you wanted. Just last quarter you were going on about Emni rights."

Drew stared. "...I was not."

"You said, and I quote, 'If we're going to learn to live together, we should learn to live together.' End quote."

Drew clicked his tongue against the roof of his mouth and glared down at the nuts. "I didn't mean like this. I meant—"

She rolled her eyes, cutting in immediately, "Where? On Drune? Humans already live on Drune."

"No, I meant *here*, just—"

"Not where you can see them? Not where you can be *reminded?*"

Drew flinched. That was it, though. As usual, she'd cut his bullshit to the quick immediately.

Shrink Kanak's eyes narrowed. "So tell me, Drew. In your own words. What's this about?"

Drew breathed shallowly. Took a breath and blew out an imaginary candle. The real one fluttered on her desk. "It's just weird timing."

"For you, you mean? Because it can't be for the political state of things right now. The war is over. Has been over for nearly two centuries now, in fact. To quote a precocious young man I know: if we're going to learn to live together, we should learn to live together."

"Yeah, but… isn't it dangerous?"

Shrink Kanak's face didn't change, but her voice was a tad crisper when she spoke next. "Riis is barely more than a child, carefully selected from a slew of applicants with—essentially—*one* thing in mind: is he dangerous? He's not. Folks higher up than you have decided. Your… eh, the King Admiral was even involved. He's not dangerous."

Drew flinched. "I didn't mean that," he said quickly.

She stared at him. Something softened in her steely eyes. "You mean it's dangerous for him?"

Drew's breath hitched.

"How? You don't even have it yet. Even if you did—"

"Forget it," Drew snapped, rising. "I knew you wouldn't understand. Just forget it."

"You're not gonna flip the switch yourself just by seeing him, you know."

"Uh-huh. Bye."

Shrink Kanak snorted as he barreled back out the door as chaotically as he had arrived. He heard her call out before the door clicked shut, though. "Bye, Drew! See you soon."

****

The rest of the day passed with a frankly shocking lack of fanfare.

First the relief of Physics with the total lack of alien life, along with the blessing of Amy as his lab partner. Evidently, they would spend this semester learning about the differences between the laws of physics between Earth II and Earth, as if Earth prime wasn't just an old story told to scare the children at this point, the original King Admiral's ship having escaped to Earth II almost three centuries ago now. "As if physics has strict laws, anyway," Amy had chortled into his ear, and he'd rolled his eyes and snapped out the word 'nerd,' and that had been physics.

After that was P.E. though, and the Emni was already there, looking bizarre and awkward in the gym uniform. Just painting a totally surreal picture: long, oddly joined legs sloping out from beneath the black shorts and t-shirt stretching over his broad chest.

17

Drew was immensely grateful they didn't Game or Fence today. Just sat in the cavernous gymnasium on the gleaming wooden bleachers and listened to Teach Sir speak passionately about the importance of doing things like Game or Fence, regardless of caste. How there was *a history! A pride!* In fencing in particular, considering their origins. Drew didn't quite know what this meant. It was a well-known fact that the original Military of the Americas had not actually included Knights, and that the original King Admiral had just *liked* the idea of Knights, and had also been in charge. A dangerous combination, as it turns out, three-ish centuries later with castes like his still in existence and a 'King' before the admiral's title.

Teach Sir seemed to be of the mindset of 'just ignore this' when it came to the Emni. While most of the students stared at Riis the whole time, Teach Sir punched on, passing a ball back and forth between his hands and pacing, gesticulating wildly with his hunched shoulders like it was any other first day.

The Emni sat primly on the lowest bleacher and watched with rapt attention, and Drew sat in the highest one with Amy and blew out seven imaginary candles, at least.

Then lunch, which was participated in everywhere; a caf provided and food trucks crowded before the green outside. The skewed nature, therefore, meant it didn't have to include Riis. Drew saw him in an alcove, though. He looked almost like he'd tried to hide, but failed, and was currently crowded by students who were asking him questions, leaning in too close, one even poking at one of the topmost two horns peeking out from behind the crested gray mound of his forehead, and Drew flinched. The alien looked like he was trying to shrink stiffly into his own bones, a sandwich untouched before him.

The Emni looked his big, bizarre eyes up at Drew like he'd heard that flinch, and Drew walked quickly away.

He found Amy where he knew he would, at the dark bar next door to the main campus building. She was nursing a hot beer — a strange drink for an Enseeo, another tiny rebellion of hers — and watching the news bulletins flash across the cracked TV mounted in the corner. The bar smelled sour and damp, and the seat when he sat down clung to the fabric of his pants stickily, the hem of his black chainmail clinking obnoxiously on the metal rim, and Drew kind of hated her.

"Have a fun therapy session?"

Drew grabbed her beer and downed it in one, choking only slightly. It burned in several ways. She laughed, raised her hand, and ordered another. The barkeep nodded, whipping out a filthy glass and beginning to dry-wipe it with her equally dirty cloth in preparation.

Even after just the one beer, the whole world felt dewy and spiced. It was too easy to blur his eyes at his own reflection in the mirror behind the rows of bottles, and he saw Amy's focus sharpen as his own face went slack. As she waited for him to speak.

"It's just… not fair." Drew said, finally.

"Hm."

"I mean, the publicity alone is going to be bad for him." Drew hesitated, and then said, as harshly as he could get the words out, "It sure as hell was for me."

Amy looked up at him then. He shivered, looking away. Blamed the beer.

"There hasn't been any mention of it, actually," she said after a moment.

Drew blinked. "Huh?"

Amy jutted her chin towards the television. Sure enough, the bulletins flashing by contained nothing more interesting than the influx of lobster from the north in their southern seas. Get your forks and butter out, by the way this is who won sportsball, blah blah blah whatever.

"How?" he snapped. This felt—to him, at least—like a burning ember of pure *news*. It was actually beginning to seriously stress him out that no one else seemed to think so.

"Well," she said, "I've been thinking, and the way I figure it, they don't want folks to know."

"Amy… that's the stupidest thing I've *ever heard*, I mean *what*, we all have tablets, so many people must've at least posted pictures on their facepage, I mean—"

"No, you can't. I tried."

Drew blinked up at her. "Huh?"

She rolled her eyes. Opened up her tablet and selected a picture of the Emni she had taken, it seemed from right before the creature. Drew felt himself shrink, the Emni's big dark eyes staring directly out of the image at him, and Amy dragged the picture to her facepage and attempted to drop it in.

"WARNING" Facepage immediately declared.

"INAPPROPRIATE CONTENT IS PROHIBITED."

"I can't even post it," she said casually. "I can't send it, either. I tried to send it to you. And this is, like, the third picture I took. The other two have already disappeared. This one probably will soon, too."

Drew stared at her. "They're keeping us from sending proof."

She snickered into her beer. "Yup. Now he's just an urban legend. A myth. Oooh, is there an Emni at Americas University of Enseeos? There's no proof. Just students gossiping. Probably just a rumor. And you know even that won't last long; no one's gonna want this to reach home. They don't want anyone to really *know.*"

"I mean," Drew stammered out, "they do know, though. We all know. He was just… *in our P.E. class, like…*"

"Well, yeah. But they didn't announce it beforehand, and isn't that odd? When you came here we had a whole ass assembly. Last day of the year before."

Drew flinched. "It doesn't matter though, because everyone at Americas University *knows.* They didn't even tell us not to say anything! Just… made it impossible to send proof, but still, we could tell our parents, and they didn't tell us not to…"

She grinned at him then, toothy and wry, and her dark eyes danced. "Exactly."

He stared. "What?"

"What better way to ensure it's not the very first thing everyone does? I'm not saying they're trying to keep him a secret or anything. Just saying they're trying to be a li'l coy about it. Soften the blow, maybe. Let it be a rumor, and then confirm later once no one's been mauled by the beast. I mean. The parents aren't going to be happy.

Have you told your mom yet?"

Drew flinched with his whole body, and Amy laughed. "I don't see why she needs to know," he replied in clipped tones.

"Yeah, 'cause she'd throw a fit. Probably send a Grunt, which would be *especially* humiliating for you *especially 'specially*, oh future Knight of Sol II. See? They're counting on us to not say shit 'cause we don't wanna be pulled from school. Or worse—get Grunts assigned to protect us," she said bluntly. "Like, I get it. We're precious Enseeo babies, aww, so important! The littles of society's elite, yes. But they're banking on us to just be young, too."

"What do they even have to gain, then?" Drew snapped. "It can't be a publicity stunt if they're not being public. Seriously, why even do this?"

Amy shrugged, grinning. Furious, Drew drank her second beer, choking with far more sincerity this time halfway through and slamming it down with a thump and a slosh, much to her amusement.

Later that night, Drew and Amy were sitting out on their little fire escape balcony with their books, enjoying (as much as he could, he was *enjoying*) the final breath of summer whispering through the city from the sea. Their apartment was quite a few blocks away from the surf and from Americas University, but it was possible to see two sloping spires of the school and the glimmer of water from the balcony, so they called it their 'view.'

Drew's tablet between them blipped, then, and began to buzz, and he knew from Amy's cackle who it was before he picked it up, hissing at her to "Shut up, please."

He answered quickly. "Hey, Mom."

His mom, golden and curly-haired and not at all like him besides the mole on her cheek, beamed out at him. "Hey honey. How'd the first day go?"

Drew shut his eyes so he wouldn't have to see Amy's smirk as he said what he knew he'd say all along. "Fine. Nothing really new."

They chatted, briefly, about which professors he had. Whether or not she remembered them from her University days. About the ride to school, and whether he'd made any friends. No. No, he hadn't. He didn't need more friends. Thanks, though, Mom.

When they hung up, he tilted his head back against the rusted metal rail of their balcony and breathed, slow. Blew out the candle.

"Man, Drew. I know this must make you… uncomfortable. Like, it's not cool how they did it. I feel like they should've told *you*, at least. But. I don't get why you're so upset about this, to be real." Amy said finally. A wind whipped heartily across them and she shivered delicately, shutting her eyes.

Drew batted her stringy dark hair out of his face and glowered, pointedly. "I'm not."

She raised her eyebrows high at that one.

He looked away, something twisting deep inside. "I'm not. Why would I be?" Then he swallowed, staring dully out at the setting sun, the twin moons rising high over the ocean now as the sky sank into a gentle dusk. "It's not like I'm ever gonna be the one to flip the switch."

She cackled at that. He swore and kicked at her lightly.

2

Big Feelings

The night started relatively simply. Say goodnight to Amy, make his ablutions in the bathroom, brush his teeth. Use her hairbrush again, sneakily. Lie down. Enjoy a frantic, guilty self-love ritual. Clean up. Shut his eyes hard and think determinedly, "I will not dream tonight."

He'd been having dreams recently. Scary ones, often. Almost as often, sexy ones, of the sort that wasn't quite acceptable for a Knight of Sol II, considering the shape (muscle-bound, strong, bigger than him, *hng*) and sex (hint: not female) of his romping partners in such dreams. So he'd set out another part of his nightly ritual where he blew out the candle and thought, as willfully as he could manage: I will not dream tonight.

He dreamed anyway.

In the dream, the switch was literally that: a switch, protruding from his chest. He walked through school that day with arms outstretched, legs shaking, terrified he'd move wrong and it'd flip up. He knew in the dream he contained not just the switch, but the weapon. It rested in his gut with a crackling, toxic weight.

Riis stared at him, blinking those strange eyes, when he stepped into class. He tried to hide the switch, but Amy leapt up and crowed delightedly, "Look at you! Finally Knight of Sol II." Then she laughed at how it rhymed and tried to hug him. The scream ripped through him as the switch flipped against her breasts.

He woke up sticky with panic sweat, the blankets damp and clinging to him like a wet cocoon. Flopped back down on the bed shaking.

****

"Did you have another sex dream last night? I heard you yelling; must've been good."

Drew glared at Amy. She waggled her eyebrows. "Anyone specific?"

"Shut up."

She cackled. "Not my boyfriend, right? He's cheated on me enough with you in dreamland… I'm gonna have to tell my mom to get me a new apartment if that keeps up."

"Ha. As if you would. You wouldn't tolerate living alone."

"No," Amy immediately snarked back, *"you* wouldn't tolerate living alone. That's the only reason your Mom lets us live together. You know, before *marriage*," and she snickered.

Drew flinched. She glanced at him, and then thankfully left it alone.

Upon their arrival at school, it was clear someone had tripped the fire alarm. Possibly there'd been a real fire. The lazy way in which students were lounging on the green beyond the hedges told him no, though. So they slipped through the gate and joined the buzzing frey. Amy immediately sidled up to Jas, who slung an arm brazenly over her shoulder and kissed the top of her head before flashing a bright grin Drew's way. Drew glared back.

Amy's boyfriend Jas was muscly. Had sharp, gleeful green eyes that never looked away first when eye contact was initiated. He was also bigger than Drew. *(Hng…)*

"Hey Drew, you talked to our newbie yet?"

"No," Drew snapped, flopping down against a tree, flipping open his physics book to a random page, and glaring down at the text.

"He's all in a tizzy about it," Amy, the traitor, said coyly.

"Oh yeah, you *would* have some complicated feelings about this one, wouldn't you?"

Drew scowled down at his book.

"Why don't I help," Jas said, coy as Amy, and too much like in one of Drew's dreams, and he felt a flushed heat spill across his face before Jas turned away and bellowed across the green, "Hey Riis!"

"What the *fuck!*" Drew tried to leap up. The ground below was slick from a quick rain last night, though, and he slipped backward and fell with a wet smack.

It didn't make any difference. The Emni was there in a flash, far quicker than any human would have made their way across the green, and Drew groaned, flopping his head back.

He could barely breathe. Jas was laughing, explaining something, but Drew could barely breathe. He tried again, fruitlessly, to get up.

Then a shadow cut across the clouds and the sloping spires of Americas University, and the Emni was blinking down at him.

Drew froze.

"Anyway yeah, Drew has some real big feelings surrounding you, so I figured! Maybe you two could talk, clear the air," Jas was saying bluntly, and Drew absolutely hated him. Amy was shifting nervously beside her man, and threw Drew a cringing, sympathetic look, but didn't say jack-shit to stop this, and Drew felt like his tongue was choking him.

"Oh," Riis whistled quietly. "Well."

Quiet. It took Drew a good second to realize the green had gone silent as well. That their fellow classmates, basically the whole school was staring, and he saw Riis shrink slightly before a look of purely universally recognized determination seemed to sharpen in his strange eyes. He glanced around the crowd, and then turned to Drew and said, in the most diplomatic tone Drew had *ever* heard, "Are you injured? Do you require assistance in rising?"

Drew hissed, without meaning to, as a clawed hand was offered.

The hand recoiled.

"Oh come on, Drew," Jas said, with no small amount of amusement.

Riis stared down at him. His four horns cut a shadow made of spikes and slopes, strange to look at.

Amy was quickly there, though, and he saw her shoot a glare up at Jas before reaching down and grabbing Drew's arm, "I've got him," she snapped, and Riis shrunk back.

She hefted Drew to his feet. His legs were shaking, and he stilled them quickly.

Everyone was still staring. He saw Riis especially though, eyes so wide and dark he could see his own peaky face grimacing back, and Drew looked away first, hot blood rushing in his ears.

"It is understandable, I suppose," Riis said after a moment, still looking at him. "That you feel complex ways about my arrival."

Drew shrugged. Though he felt an odd relief. So bizarre that the first one to freaking fully acknowledge that would be the Emni himself. Of course he felt strange. This is who he would be sacrificed to get to. Not literally, but basically, yeah. An Emni. The enemy, the one he'd be killed to kill.

Then Riis continued, "I feel complex ways about your existence, after all."

Drew grimaced. Definitely did not comment on that. Because like, same.

"Whoa there, wait, what does *that* mean?" Amy cut in harshly though, and Drew turned quickly to her, trying to communicate *wait SHUT UP* as much as possible without actually speaking, but she was off. "You don't get to feel 'complex ways' about him; he's from here. You're not. You gotta admit it's… weird."

Drew shut his eyes. His heart was hammering. "Amy…" he started.

Riis cut in though shortly, prepared it seemed for this immediately, "Arguably, I am more 'from here' than you yourself," he said lightly, and Drew's eyes snapped open.

He had said something of the same sort last semester in Shrink

Kanak's office. She had nodded, smirking at him. Had this already been in the works at that point?

It didn't matter how true a statement that was, though. Only that the Emni had said it. The crowd shifted. The energy made a plummeting leap from curiosity to something far more intentional.

"Alright!" Shrink Kanak threw open the main doors with a slam and stood before them at full four-ish foot height now, in lime green today, the rebel. "So—it appears to be safe to go back inside, if you'll all form a—"

Drew didn't wait to be told to do anything in an organized fashion. Instead, he bolted for the entrance, leaving the dust of the Emni's social life in his wake.

****

"What right does he *have*, though! 'I'm more from here than you,' honestly. Earth II is ours. First King Admiral's ship arrived here almost three centuries ago. We're the ones that built this place into what it is today! There were no *cities* here before! No castes to organize the population! People just made bad choices all over the place before we got here. Even if the Emni did have a few scattered settlements here before that, they're formed on that dinky moon, and Earth II—while maybe not where humans were made… I mean, hell, even with that shitfuckery, it's where *I* was made. My parents definitely fucked on Earth II."

"*Jeezus*, Amy," Drew said through gritted teeth. "Can we please just focus on the experiment?" The science lab was all a-tizzy with whispered conversations about this very subject. He could smell the gossip in the air, mingling awfully with the sharp bite of chemicals and disinfectant.

Amy sucked her cheeks in and snatched a vial out of his sweating hand. Dumped it into a kind of flask thing, and then flipped on the burner before stirring in some strange gray sand, plopping the whole mess down on the burner, setting a dinky egg timer, and rearing on him. "Drew, I don't get it. First, even looking at him makes you shrivel up. Then, Jas is—admittedly—a jackass, and you snap out at him. But now… why are you defending him?"

Drew shrunk in his seat. "I'm not!"

"You are. You normally love shit-talking with me. Hell, if my *boyfriend* had said it—"

"Stop. Please."

She let out a huff, but stopped.

The rest of the class, on the other hand, continued, whispered conversations overlapping into one damning theme. *"The nerve of that Emni," "he really said we didn't have a right to our own homeworld,"* and, over and over again: *"why's he even here, anyway?"*

Drew glared down at the experiment. It was starting to bubble. The timer went off. Amy moved quick and smart, clicking off the timer and turning down the burner before splashing a stone into the center. The stone fizzed and then turned translucent as glass, bubbling only slightly after. Done.

"It's just not fair," Drew said eventually.

She looked hard at him. "What do you even mean by that?"

He shut his eyes and curled his painted toes in his shoes, sucking in a hard breath through his teeth. "It's not fair. He doesn't know any better. He just… they just *dropped him into the lion's den*, and—"

"Hey, hey," Amy interrupted, "that's your own people you're talking about. 'Lion's den,' what."

He shot a glare at her. "It's not my people, though. It's Enseeos. I'm not."

Quiet, at that. Then: "You might as well be, at this point."

He actually laughed. That was laughable, after all. "I'm not, though. Knight of Sol II still has the word 'Knight' in it. I'm a Grunt. I'm expected to be a *Grunt*, just a… fancy one. Y'all are supposed to be composed, tactical, a little sneaky, whatever," she snorted at that, but didn't correct him, and he continued in a semi-frantic whisper, "I'm supposed to be… to be…"

"A willing sacrifice," she said softly, and that was that, and true.

He shuddered. "Patriotic. Charismatic. Rough in a way that charms people." he said tightly.

She snorted. "You are kind of rough. Just not in a particularly charming way."

"Exactly."

Amy shrugged one bony shoulder, like it didn't matter. He felt a sudden swoop of love for her through all the annoyance and despair. They stared at the completed experiment in silence.

"So…" she said eventually. "That's it, then. You're both outsiders. That's why you're defending him."

"I'm not *defending him*—"

"What I don't get, though, is why you're also being a tool to his face. I was just following suit, really. Out of loyalty to you more than anything," and Drew flinched.

"I don't mean to be," he said tightly, after a moment.

She smirked at him. "Well. Don't, then."

Drew glared.

Later, though, after a P.E. class that contained all the awkwardness in the world—dodgeball today, and the ball had literally *popped* on one of the Emni's horns when someone had whacked it hard at him—Drew couldn't shake the notion of that. Of just. Not being a tool, maybe.

Evasive Techniques

Drew managed to avoid Riis, by and large.

It was relatively easy, as Riis seemed to have decided to do the same. Just. Don't look at him. Just don't sit near him. Just don't respond when Jas or some other douche started ragging on him, even though something in Drew always clenched at that. Also—at the space that seemed to have formed around the Emni since his comment about who rightly belonged on Earth II. The crowds of the first day had for sure dispersed, and whether in relief or agony, Riis now walked and ate alone.

Drew saw him less and less, in fact, as the days wore on. Riis would walk head down into the caf or up to a food cart. Order, grab his food, and bolt for… wherever he would go.

His dorm, probably. He did indeed appear to live on school grounds.

Drew remembered being new.

Being not only new, but important. Not only important, but different. Not only all of the above, but frankly: a disappointment.

Riis was not only new and important in terms of developments, but strange in a way that folks absolutely found disappointing. He was not the looming monster they'd expected of an Emni. He did not have horns longer than their forearms. While he moved pretty quickly for such a stocky creature, he could not phase through solid material or transcend space and time (that they knew of). He also didn't seem to eat anything except pickles. That was just a super strange factoid that Drew picked up on one day when someone said near him, "alien boy only eats pickles, what the fuck."

Then Drew literally couldn't help but notice it. Sauerkraut. Pickled radishes. Baby pickled cucumbers. Pickled lobster, even, when the slop in the caf ended up being that one day. The Emni had been the only one—quite literally, *the only one* who got the main dish. He'd even stuck around that day, practically *inhaling* the concoction before trotting back for seconds.

Not only that, Riis ate a *lot*.

Which was. You know. An accomplishment on Earth II, where long winters had essentially trained the planet's fresh human inhabitants to consume a minimum of four meals, and snacks were carried by all to share amongst friends.

Riis didn't share his pickles.

Not that anyone shared anything with him, but still. It just seemed *wrong*. If anything, as a guest, Riis should make the first move. That just seemed like it should be right.

It might not be right, but it *should be*.

Drew was agonizing over this on the way to history. He had missed homeroom after missing the trolley, as he was wont to do on the nights Amy slept over with Jas and wasn't there to force him to obey his alarm. So he barrelled in late, musing on the pickle thing, and absolutely froze in the doorway at the total lack of seats.

No seat. Except for two. One on either side of the Emni.

Amy visibly cringed at him. She made no move to help, though, pillowed as she was against Jas on a cushion by the windows.

The Emni blinked at him, and then seemed to stiffen.

Drew took a breath. Walked as casually as possible to the cushioned seat that was maybe a few inches farther away than the other one, and plopped down half off the cushion in an attempt to *not sit any closer to him than necessary, oh my god.*

The room was silent at first. Stares all around. Drew—as well as Riis, he couldn't help but notice—staunchly ignored this. Then someone snickered and the silence collapsed into whispered conversation, only the occasional glance thrown back their way, and Drew dumped his backpack out on the squat wooden desk before him, flipped open his physics book again, and stared at a random page.

"It's upside-down." The Emni's voice was a soft whistle.

Drew startled and flipped it quickly.

Riis stared at him, openly. Just no sense of social decorum at all. *Stared.*

Drew was seriously about to say something. He was absolutely going to say something.

Teach saved him by switching on the projector.

Or at least, Drew thought he'd been saved. Then the image stuttered from Teach's desktop to the first slide, though, and everything in Drew *clenched.*

THE EMNI WAR

Every head spun around. Some turned back as Teach began to speak, but many more stayed focused on Riis. And on Drew, who was. You know. If anything, even more of a key player, if one got real specific and individualistic about it.

"So," Teach said, and her voice was staunchly neutral, "we're beginning today the next section on the history of our settlement here. We've covered the plagues and war that forced us to leave Earth prime, as well as the original King Admiral's formation of our current society aboard his militarized vessel. We've covered what we found here on what we called, in a *burst* of creativity, Earth II. It's time to focus on… the reception we received."

Beside him, Riis' hand shot up.

Drew seriously resisted hiding his face.

"Eh… yes, Riis?"

"Can I ask for clarification on what you mean by 'reception?'"

Dead, still silence.

"... We will get into that during the class." Teach settled on, eventually. Very diplomatically, in Drew's opinion. "Anyway. I know this is, to put it mildly, a *controversial topic*, and... yes, Riis?"

"Is it considered controversial on Earth II?"

Dead, still silence again.

"Well," Teach said, trapped and Drew didn't envy her. "In the way that war is always a sensitive topic. Yes. Yes, I'd say it is."

Riis nodded. He did it in a way that looked odd. Practiced, almost. Two short bobs of his four horned head.

"Anyway," Teach continued, and flipped to the next slide. Riis didn't comment further as they went through the show, very neutrally now outlining the syllabus for this semester. The only reaction he had came when Drew was at a disadvantage to noticing it, though he still did, hyper–aware as he was of the alien beside him.

"...Thus, it was decided that in an effort to connect us emotionally with the sheer force of damage inflicted by the weapon, there must be one willing human sacrifice to pay the price for the loss of life that would be sustained if the weapon were to ever be used again. This sacrifice will hold the lone switch to launch the weapon in their body, beside their heart, so it will be impossible to activate without killing them. So, yes. We will discuss the Knighthood of Sol II. I'm sure you'll have plenty to say on that, Drew," she said lightly, and Drew flat out wanted to kill himself.

Chuckles, chortles in the classroom. Drew shrugged. Bared his teeth and grinned in his own practiced way; shrugged again. Glared down at the table.

Riis, beside him, stared.

****

"We're not even gonna get to the good bits if the alien keeps interrupting," Jas snarked, loud enough for Riis to hear, on the way out of class.

Beside Drew, Riis dropped his book.

Drew bent to pick it up. It was an instinct, really. Book fell. He was kneeling next to where it fell, gathering his own shit with shaking hands, admittedly rather distracted. He picked it up.

Handed it back to Riis.

Realized what he'd just done.

Absolute silence.

Riis blinked at Drew. "Thank you," he said, rather curtly, and then grabbed the book and, in under a blink, he was at the Teach's desk and muttering something, and Drew didn't hear it because he'd pushed past Jas and bolted from the room.

Leaned against a wall a few hallways over. Shut his eyes. Blew out the candle.

Blew.

Out.

The.

Candle.

"Hey!"

Drew jumped out of his freaking bones. "What?" he glared at Amy. He was shaking. He was still shaking.

She leaned against the wall next to him and said nothing, though. Just leaned there.

He wanted to cry.

He didn't want to cry.

But he kind of wanted to cry.

"You handled that class really well," she said eventually, and he snorted. She grinned at him, nudging him slightly, and then said, "C'mon. Physics should be chiller. Maybe that's the end of today's BS."

It would've been great if that was the end of today's BS.

Instead, however, not twenty minutes later, while they were engrossed in an unrelated conversation about sportsball (more specifically: sportsball *players*) over their half-finished experiment of the day, the television in the top corner of the room blipped on.

It was static for a moment, and then the screen went blue and a swift beep, and they all paused. It wasn't so odd. Announcements happened every now and then.

But then…

Prince Sebastian of the House of the King Admiral came on screen, teeth stark rows of white and bared like he'd bitten into the beating heart of joy itself.

The world narrowed.

Amy slapped his arm, like he wasn't already paying *very* close attention. Perhaps he wasn't, though, because Seb lifted his hands in greeting and Drew imagined for a moment those hands digging into his chest, peeling him open to get at the Switch, because it would be *him*.

It would be Seb who did it.

Next in line. Same as him.

"Huh?" Drew said, and his voice was someone else's, far away.

"Shhhhuddup listen!"

He swallowed. Shook his head. Listened.

"So, in a gesture of good faith," the words that were coming out around those teeth were lilting, amused almost, calm, not a murderer, but, "I have decided to pay a visit to the Americas University of Enseeos. I look forward to getting to know *all of you.*" and then the asshole winked, as he continhued, "Especially you, Drew."

It took Drew a solid ten seconds to realize he hadn't imagined it.

The fat popping on the bunsen burner suddenly spat out at him. It'd sizzled beyond what they'd been trying to do to it, and it spat a burning coil of heat directly at his chin, mere millimeters below his mouth.

He blamed that for why he retched.

****

"He did not *puke* he just *sounded like he was gonna*, lay off him!" Amy bellowed at top volume across the green and Drew groaned, throwing himself backwards onto the grass. The first years snickered, looking quickly away from them.

"Must you?"

"Course, buddy. Someone's gotta set the story straight."

"They weren't even talking near us."

"Even worse."

"Yes. Yes, you did indeed make it 'even worse.'"

"Oh, fuck off Drew, seriously," she snapped. "I'm trying to *defend you*. Say 'thank you darling' and move on."

Drew rose as fluidly as he could. Bowed. "Thank you, darling," he said through his teeth, and then turned and stalked back across the green, slamming open the tall and solid main door. He could hear her laughing. What did she even think she was doing—at the end of the day, she was no different than them. He was a joke to her, too.

It was with little to no attention paid that he skulked through the grand foyer and stepped into the elevator, stopping it right before the doors closed and sliding in.

Which is how he ended up in the elevator with Riis.

Elevator

Drew froze.

Riis' eyes widened and he blinked in his freakish way, and for a moment they just stood there, both inside the elevator. Then the doors closed behind Drew and the elevator didn't move.

Drew jumped. "Uh," the singular dumb syllable shook in the air between them. "What floor?"

"What? Oh. Eh, fifth." The Emni's whistle was especially prominent on the 'fth.'

"Right. *Fifth.*"

Drew pushed the five. Then, because it seemed like the right thing to do, the third. Not the second. That would've seemed lazy. Not the fourth. That would've seemed like he was just trying to get out before Riis (which was, you know, true). The fifth—where Shrink Kanak's office was, where had actually been intending to go—was taken. *So.*

Unfortunately he pushed the three exactly at what must've been the wrong moment and the ancient, faulty elevator made an absolute bitch move and groaned to a halt, beeped once, and then went totally dark and silent.

For a second, there was just their breathing. The emergency lights flickered on. One of them, anyway. It stuttered to a dim red glow right on the edge of the ceiling, basically useless except to make them into soft shadows rather than just *pitch black nothing*.

Then. Well. Drew couldn't help it. He laughed.

He jumped practically out of his skin when a strange belting bellow joined him, and Drew found himself clinging to the back wall of the elevator.

Riis, just a horn-headed shadow before him, was saying, "Oh my, I laughed, I just laughed, too, I didn't…" and then another, softer little whistling belt, this one a little more swear-shaped, and there was a solid *thump* as Riis leaned back against his own respective wall.

Silence.

Drew's heart was in his throat.

"I just laughed." Riis' whistley voice was very soft. The shadow of his shoulders hunched up by his ears. His head was bowed, hands lifted to his face, all of him tense and defeated, and Drew let out all his air in a slow, shuddering breath.

Fuck. Well.

"Oh!" Drew finally blabbed out. "Interesting. I, eh. Wasn't sure you could… I mean…"

He could tell, even in the dark, he was being glared at.

Drew let out a strangled noise and fell back against the dark wall of the elevator. It made a kind of terrifying *kathunk* but didn't, like. Plummet. So. "I don't know, ok! I don't know anything. I'm a know-nothing. Just. Jeezus christ, it's funny, you're right. You're right. I laughed, too."

Silence.

"It is funny." Riis' voice was very quiet.

"Nice. Yup, glad to see we both… have a sense of humor."

"Sense of humor. Yes. Perhaps this shall be what brokers a true peace and understanding between our people." Riis deadpanned. His horned shadow was absolutely still.

It took Drew a minute to realize it was a joke. Quite before he did, he snorted, though, and then Riis let out the bellowing, almost bleating sound again and Drew found himself laughing harder, half out of actual amusement and 110% out of a very real fear.

"It could happen," Drew said eventually.

"Ah. If only it were as easy."

"Ahaha… yeah."

Quiet.

"Is that what… what you're here for, then?"

"Eh?"

"To broker peace and understanding. I mean, I'm sorry. You're probably just here to… to attend university…"

"I'm here as an envoy of sorts, yes," Riis said finally, and his words tripped with amusement.

"Ah. Interesting."

"I wish it was."

"It's not? It… sounds interesting."

Riis let out a huff. "It is exactly what we expected it to be. I don't know why I'm still surprised. I suppose I expected less from myself, though."

Drew scrunched his face. Considered just adding a simple, "Hm," but in the end did say, "what do you mean by that?"

"Less anguish."

Drew froze. Let out a faltering chuckle. Riis didn't laugh, this time.

"That, uh… sucks." Drew finally said.

"Yes," Riis agreed. "I am personally devastated by the lack of understanding. I was warned, but I suppose I was naive. Which adds humiliation to the mix."

Drew let out a hard breath. "Wow," he said after a moment.

"Indeed."

"Not many people would just… say that."

Drew could practically *hear* the Emni blink. "Why?"

Drew laughed, shortly. Something in him was twisting hard, like a part of his soul was being wrung out. "Well… it's just not done. You know. It's kind of considered polite here to like… waffle around heavy emotional stuff like that. Be harsh rather than blunt. But to call the harshness 'bluntness.' I dunno."

That practiced double nod again. "Interesting," Riis said after a moment. "I am not sure I understand. We have few secrets in virtually all Emni cultures. It's considered rude to hide your feelings."

"Oh! Well… that's probably better, to be real."

Silence.

Finally, Drew spoke again, haltingly. "Is there a restart button in this elevator?"

"I pushed it."

"Okay. Okay, great, uh. Nothing… seems to be happening."

"Why do I make you so uncomfortable?"

Drew sucked in a breath, hard. Blew out the candle. "Uh," he said, figuring they were pretty far past denying it. "Well. I—"

"I actually had the gall to assume you would be the most understanding of my cause, yet you seem to be the most uncomfortable."

Something there pricked like a pin to the chest. Drew spoke quickly, "Why would you assume I would be the most understanding?" It seemed an insane assumption. Drew was basically shitty little royalty. Even not counting who *everyone knew* his biological father was, he was the future Knight of Sol II. A symbol, at the very least, for their world, for their society, for *humanity's* tenuous peace and survival.

The elevator abruptly started again as electricity was restored. Thrown into a fresh harsh light, it was suddenly very awkward to be so close to Riis, to hold his stare as Riis said, calm and blunt as ever, "You are the only guaranteed victim of any future act of war against my people. It just makes sense to me that you'd… feel something about that."

The doors opened. Third floor.

Drew didn't move. He was having trouble even breathing. After a moment, the doors closed.

"Are you having a… I don't know the word in Standard. A *grunt, hiss* a, eh… are you upset?"

Drew shook his head, slowly. Squinted his eyes closed, hard. *Blow out the candle. Blow out the candle...*

"Blow out the candle."

Drew's eyes popped open.

Riis was looking at him intensely. He held up a single claw—long, tapered, only slightly curled. Drew let out a surprised exhale, honestly kind of floored, though he'd known Riis went to see Shrink Kanak too. Riis nodded, satisfied, as the breath hit his hand.

"Goodbye, Drew." Riis spoke softly as the doors opened again, and he exited. Drew watched him walk carefully, somehow *elegantly* down the hall. The doors closed.

The elevator didn't move.

Well, shit.

****

"Hello, Drew." She didn't look up from her tablet until he plopped down in front of her, but then she glanced up, smiling slightly before closing the tablet's case and steepling her fingers.

"Hey, Shrink Kanak..."

They sat in silence for a moment. Drew opened his mouth and closed it again. It had become oddly difficult to speak.

"...So," she said eventually, "are you just here to sit quietly and waste my time, or..."

"Riis isn't doing so hot."

She blinked. "Huh. Well. That's to be expected."

Drew gritted his teeth, glared down at her stupid nuts. "So? That doesn't seem fair, that he—"

"I'll be honest, Drew, this is a big change."

Drew shot an incredulous stare her way. "For him? I mean, yeah, obviously, like—"

"No, obviously for him," she rolled her eyes, "I meant for *you.*"

Drew stared at her. "...uh?"

"What happened to my next chapter of The Drew Saga?" and he groaned as she let out a sharp, barking laugh, continuing, "Where is my play by play retelling of something Amy said that pissed you off? Where is—"

"Okay, haha, very funny, fuck off."

"Seriously. The fact that you came to me to talk about another student is frankly *growth.*"

"Seriously." His face prickled with heat. "Fuck off."

"I can't help but wonder, though—what concern is that of yours?"

Drew swallowed, glared over her shoulder at the treetops out the window, scraggly blue-green branches swaying in a gentle breeze. "Well, I mean. Shouldn't he… be sent home? It's like. He came here to foster peace and understanding…"

"Uh-huh."

Drew stared at her. She raised her eyebrows. "That's not how it's working out," he snapped, finally.

Shrink Kanak smirked then, sitting back, "I would argue it is."

"How?!" Drew's stomach was a churning vat of acid, "People don't sit near him, don't talk to him, definitely don't listen to him. Everything he says is *mocked,* mercilessly. At best! He's gonna get hurt if—"

"You seem to be understanding him pretty well," she shot back immediately.

Drew breathed. Stared.

She smirked, opening up her tablet again and flicking her finger over some note, "I know you were trapped in an elevator with him for a hot second—"

Drew shook his head, snapping back to reality, "Okay, how—"

"Unimportant. I know you got to talking. Did he say he wanted to go home? Or are you just supposing that?"

Drew's teeth clicked closed. He swallowed.

"I think the solution is less us or him taking further action, and more something that rests pretty solidly at this point on *your* shoulders."

"Ugh," Drew said, slumping back into a hunch.

"Yes. Ugh. Anyway, I have been curious—how do you feel about

Prince Admiral Sebastian coming here to visit you?"

Everything in Drew turned to ice.

"Drew… that wasn't meant to—"

"I know. I just. I know. I just…" the words were fumbling puffs of untethered cotton, not coming out right at all, spilling thick and fuzzy from his lips, and…

"Blow out—"

"—The candle, got it, cool." Even his breath came out in a stutter. He didn't look at her. Looked instead at her enormous potted avocado tree, most leaves strong but some a curling brown. Even inside, avocado trees resisted the terraforming that had allowed old Earth prime life to flourish on this foreign world. He stared at the stupid tree. Breathed.

"There. So I recognize you must be feeling a way about this. It's… complicated, to say the least."

"No," he said quickly. She blinked.

"No?"

"It's simple," the words were distant, far off, *true*, "I'm the future Knight of Sol II, and he's the future King Admiral. Someday he'll be in charge of killing me to get at the switch if war is declared again. Both of us have a duty and an honor and a destiny and… all that shit."

Shrink Kanak shut her eyes for a moment. Opened them. "Hm."

"It makes sense, I mean, that he wants to meet me," Drew's voice was reaching a new octave, and he cleared his throat quickly, narrowing his focus to a single crinkly, dying leaf on her dumb terraforming-resistant plant. "He's been away at school all his life, and I've just been, like… living with my mom in his dad's house." He let out a choked laugh; shut his eyes. "We're also supposed to basically live *together* there once we're knighted and crowned, too, and he probably has to make sure I'm not a giant tool. Which. You know…"

The corner of her mouth twitched. "You're not a *giant* tool."

"So, yeah, he wants to meet me, whatever. I'll meet him. It's simple, see."

Kanak's eyebrows shot up. "Hm."

Silence.

Drew swallowed. "I gotta get to class, I guess, I mean–"

"Yes, you do. Okay. Bye, Drew." He shot up, grabbing at his meager belongings and not making eye contact with her as she continued: "Also… remember my suggestion, in regards to Riis."

"Yup. Sure. Bye."

****

Drew had a lot to think about, and for the first time, it was easiest to focus on the Riis situation.

P. E. was next.

He got there as quick as he could, late though he found himself, and sat down hurriedly next to Amy on the bleachers. He glanced quickly at Riis, who seemed tense and distracted. Teach Sir was already speaking, and Drew's head spun as he tried to catch up to what was being said.

"—won't be happening until the first day of next semester, so you'll really get a chance to strategize and prepare! I'll choose the team captains out of a hat, and then they can alternate and choose their team members. And remember—we aren't here to pick our friends— we're here to form the best possible team. Some of you have gotten… real loyal. That's great, outside this class. Outside this section, even. But for Wargames, I think it's smart to—"

Drew's brain short-circuited. Wargames.

Great.

So great and not politically charged at *all* jeezus *christ*…

Teach Sir pulled the first name out of the hat. It was Jas (because of course it was) and he punched the air, whooping and smacking a kiss atop Amy's head as he rose. Amy rolled her eyes, but seemed pleased. There was general cheering; Jas was almost offensively popular.

Riis was stock still across the room.

Drew realized before perhaps anyone what had happened when Teach pulled the next name. When Teach Sir faltered, froze for barely a moment, and glanced up. Then decided to ignore it, not draw more attention to it maybe, and instead called out casual as ever, "Second team Captain will be Riis."

A collective intake of breath. Riis' eyes were wide. With more clumsiness than Drew had seen in him thus far, he slowly rose. Came to the front.

Utter fucking silence.

"Ok, so now our captains will alternate, choosing their teams from amongst the rest. I'd like to remind y'all this is a *game*... uh, yeah. Go ahead."

Jas went first. Every freaking hand rose and waved as he looked over the crowd, folks all beyond eager to be on his team. He chose Amy right off the bat, totally ignoring Teach Sir's insistence they choose based on tactical skill rather than favoritism. She all but *pranced* up next to him, grinning toothily out at the class.

Then it was Riis' turn.

No one raised their hand.

Eyes turned away. Students shrank on the bleachers. The space around Riis' eyes tightened. In frustration, but also something Drew recognized, something *far* more wounded, and he hated it, and-

The Emni's eyes widened and he spoke quickly, "Drew."

Drew slowly lowered his hand. A hand that had shot up on instinct, betraying him utterly.

Rose, and came to stand behind Riis, heart hammering.

Everything was silent for a moment. His classmates were gaping. Jas' eyebrows were high up on his head. Amy looked utterly flabbergasted.

Riis' eyes shone with relief though, and he looked back at Drew and blinked, slowly. Drew felt a strange swoop through his gut, and suddenly, he knew.

He'd done the right thing.

Cool.

Okay.

He smiled at Riis and nodded once, briefly. Patriotically.

Whatever. Then turned and glared out at the rest of the class, positively daring them to *(please don't, though)* say jack-shit.

5

Companionship

You basically committed social suicide."

Drew let out a huff. They were in an isolated courtyard near the back of Americas University grounds, lushly overgrown and beautifully neglected, leaning against a great stone half-open walkway of the school. He was currently attempting to balance a pencil on his upper lip, and was frankly legitimately pissed Amy wasn't letting him focus. Also. Other reasons, too. "Don't I know it."

"Seriously. Jas would've picked you next; I would've made sure of it. It's not like you would've been *last*, you frankly didn't need to raise your hand *at all*, and—"

"He didn't have anyone to pick."

"So! Let him pick some rando. Or even you, sure. Just. Not with you raising your hand like that," Amy said tightly. She chewed her bottom lip. Looked away, out over the empty expanse of trees and vines.

Drew did her least favorite thing and shrugged, widening his eyes. The pencil fell to the ground. She glared.

He didn't know what to say.

Their team had ended up being frankly ridiculous. After him, Riis had picked Lara, who was a round and sweet Biotech Enseeo known for her Medic's notes letting her skip phys ed. Then Duncan, who was basically the lowest of all the Enseeos, his family lineage being Stitchers, of all things. Then they'd really lucked out and gotten Fay, who probably would've been a Grunt if choosing your destiny was at all a possible thing. As it was, she was a Mechanics Enseeo.

With the exception of Fay, whose face rarely changed, the others had all cringed at being chosen, though Duncan had tried to save face by raising a hand to high-five Riis when he awkwardly jogged up to join them. Riis hadn't, apparently, been taught about high-fives.

They'd all cringed first, though. All except Drew, who had done a lot of that internally, despite literally asking for it.

"Pardon me, may I speak with you?"

The voice came from an opening in the arched walkway behind them. It was whistling, rough.

Amy gaped as Drew slowly rose from his place slumped against the wall. "Sure," he said. Did not make eye-contact with her as he walked, following Riis away across the courtyard.

The space around Riis' eyes was tight. When they'd reached a private alcove by some trees he stopped, turned, and stared inscrutably at Drew. Who tried—and failed—to maintain eye-contact. Instead, he looked at the horns above his eyes. The dappled light through the trees danced on the points, making them look almost soft, somehow.

"Why did you volunteer?"

"Eh?"

"For my team. For the wargame."

"I know what you're talking about," Drew said haltingly. Then sighed, picked at the hem of his chainmail, and looked away. "I felt bad, I guess," he said finally. He suddenly felt awkward about having something less declarative to say and added, "I didn't want you to be, like, socially devastated or humiliated or whatever."

Riis seemed to chew on this for a moment, blinking slowly at him again. It was unnerving, the way that those second lids came sideways over his big black eyes before the next. Unnerving how slowly it happened, sometimes. Other times, how fast it happened.

Less unnerving than it used to be, but still.

"So, it was not interest."

Drew positively shrunk in his skin. "Huh?"

"Interest in… companionship."

"What! Oh my god, no, I mean… I guess…" he laughed, nervously. "Uh. Just so you know, you probably shouldn't phrase it that way."

"Why?"

"People will get… the wrong idea."

Riis blinked again, a little quicker. "What idea?"

Drew seriously wished the ground would just open up under him and suck him down into the depths of hell where he belonged. His ears were on *fire*. "Just… the words 'interest' and 'companionship' combined like that normally mean… something, eh… else."

"Other than the step before friendship?"

Drew laughed; he couldn't quite help it. "Uh. Yeah."

Riis snorted. It was clear what he thought about *that*. "Okay. Well, I do not need your pity, is my point."

Sharp and to the quick. Drew flinched. "It's not pity."

"Isn't it?"

"I just. I dunno." Quiet. He was hyper-aware of Amy staring openly at them from back where he'd been sitting across the courtyard. "I remember being in your position."

Riis blinked one of the faster blinks and then pointedly glared. "You remember being an 'alien' envoy socially infiltrating the ranks of your colonizer's young elite?"

"Jeezus," Drew swore, staring skyward. "You can't just… just *say things* like that."

"I can. It's a part of my culture to be, as you humans like to put it, 'blunt.'"

"But yeah! Ok. Not exactly. But I'm not exactly… I mean, I'm kind of a different… status, socially. Than the Enseeos."

Riis considered him. "You are a living sacrifice, rather than one whose worth is measured by developed—and, your people argue, *inherited*—skill." he said eventually, almost hesitantly.

Drew laughed. It came out cracked and crazy. Riis didn't react, though, just looked at him. "Well," Drew said eventually. "Yeah. I guess, yeah. But I mean. Status is… everything, over here…"

"Your caste system. I am aware."

"Yeah. So, I'm both a higher and lower caste than, like, everyone here. As a Knight caste I'm lower, but I'm also the Knight of Sol II specifically, which is, you know, high, and then there's the fact I'm a bastard—low, but there's also the *breed* of bastard, eh… I'm basically in a caste of my own, and it… makes people uncomfortable. I guess that's all I'm saying. I remember making people uncomfortable."

Riis blinked. Mid-range, slightly slow blink. "You appear to still make people uncomfortable."

Drew groaned. "Thanks," he snapped. "My ego needed that."

"Indeed."

Drew blinked, surprised, and then found himself grinning slowly. He felt oddly bright and calm, all of a sudden. Like if Amy was ragging on him, and Riis squinted, blinked very slowly. "Anyway," Drew said awkwardly. "I guess I'll see you soon. When's our first wargame meet, Captain?"

"Eh? Oh… we are supposed to have meets?"

Drew laughed, "Well, yeah. Gotta have meets if we wanna win."

Riis nodded his quick double nod. "Winning would be preferable, yes?"

Drew stared up at him. "I mean," he said, and then really thought about that. "Maybe?"

Silence. After a moment Drew shrugged. Riis mirrored it, shrugging back with one sloping shoulder.

They said their goodbyes; parted ways. Amy immediately accosted him, basically interrogating him for all the 'juicy deets,' as she put it. She seemed frankly unnerved by his lack of comment on the matter. He didn't quite know what to say, though. The late afternoon light shone lazily down into the courtyard, the four walls locking in the heat and blocking out the wind. The sinking sun cast glowing embers on their faces through the trees. He was purposefully coy, teasing her relentlessly with information which became increasingly more vague every time she asked. Eventually, with a huff, she surrendered, and they ended up studying half-heartedly for a physics test.

He found it difficult to pay attention, though. In the dappled sunlight he couldn't quite stop remembering how that same sun had softened the Emni's harsh features.

Wargames Meet

—RIIS created the group 'Wargames Meet'—
Riis: Greetings.
Drew: Hey Riis
Lara: Hello !!
Duncan: Sup y'all
Fay: right let's get to it
Riis: Indeed. Getting to it, I would like to schedule a time for tea and discussion.
Fay: what's tea gotta do with it we should be training
Duncan: I won't say no to some freaky alien tea time
Lara: Is it safe for humans?
Drew: Guys jeezus christ
Riis: It is tea from the caf… I assume it's safe for humans.
Riis: I was intending us to meet in the common area of my dorm. However, if this is not possible or makes you too uncomfortable,

we could of course meet elsewhere.
Lara: I dunno maybe the caf…
Drew: the caf is gonna be noisy af Lara wtf.
It doesn't make us uncomfortable we'll be
there.
Riis: Let's try and be civil.
Drew: Right. Sorry.
Duncan: LOL. Drew being civil. Shock.
Fay: i just don't get why the tea we could at
least be drinking muscle milk we should be
beefing up
Drew: ok word you bring fucking muscle milk
then Fay. We're counting on you. Jeez.
Duncan: MMMM mm carbs
Fay: ill bring enough for all of us how much
will we drink? I know i normally do like four
in the morning
Lara: Oh wow is that safe??
Drew: I'm DYING
Riis: ????
Drew: not really
Fay: ill bring twelve
Riis: Yes, of course. Feel free to bring your
own food and refreshments if you wish. I
shall supply tea. And, for those interested,
I will make a pastry often eaten on Drune.
Drew: Oh nice
Duncan: Huh!
Fay: how many carbs
Lara: Is THAT safe for humans…
Riis: My human teachers on Drune ate it often
for breakfast.
Lara: ok…
Riis: I have never heard this word, 'carbs.'
What does it mean?

Drew: not important.
Fay: im not dieting or nothing im only asking cuz im trying to bulk up
Drew: no, REALLY??
Duncan: aaahahahahaha this is gonna be fun. Where's your dorm, Riis?
Riis: I am located in the Southwestern spire. Mine is the only 'suite style' dorm above the atrium.
Lara: Wait really? I thought they decommissioned those dorms. Aren't the environmental controls broken?
Riis: No; in fact, I tend to keep my living quarters at a much warmer temperature than you might be comfortable with. I shall turn the setting colder for this meeting.
Drew: don't worry about it we'll wear tanks
Duncan: you'd like that wouldn't you Drew
Drew: shut UP
Duncan: I got a mean tank bod
Drew: doubt it
Lara: OK fine, fine, we'll meet there. I'll bring cookies, if we're bringing something.
Drew: I'll bring beer
Riis: Isn't alcohol prohibited on campus grounds?
Duncan: I'll bring da beerDREW JINX
Riis: Let's meet tonight after the evening seminar. Please, I must insist, do not bring anything that could risk my expulsion.
Drew: right ok for sure
Duncan: ok SURE *wink wink* no beer here *wiiiiink*
Riis: … Okay??
Drew: jeezus. Right. See y'all then.

Don't Say

"Yeah, I dunno… stuff?"

Drew's mom let out a huff, soft eyebrows raising on the screen, all of her clearly finding this response so *very* far below adequate. "Oh really? What kind of 'stuff?'"

"You know. Uh. Physics test—got a solid B. Didn't even cheat off Amy this time. There's—"

"Is Amy still with that *boy?*"

"Mom, it's fine—"

"You two were declared to one another over a year ago. You'd think by now she would've… tied up loose ends, is all I'm saying. I mean, how must you feel!"

Drew cringed. "I feel fine. It's not like *I* wanna be making out with her."

She blinked. Her glossy pink lips thinned. Then she continued rather pointedly, "I mean, is it your intent, once wed, to have an open marriage? That would… also be inappropriate, given our standing."

"Also? Meaning what?" Drew snapped out. He couldn't quite help himself.

"You… you know what I mean." She got out. Her eyes flicked to the side, and he knew what she was about to do before she did it, "Anyway, King Admiral has returned. I have to go, kid. Love you."

She lowered the tablet before she flicked it off. For a second, he saw it, and felt everything in himself go cold, as it always did—the faint glow of the switch buried in her chest.

****

Drew had figured out he was gay when he was eleven. He hadn't learned the word for it until he was a dumb fourteen and had met Amy at a wise fifteen. That was when she'd introduced him to both that glorious three-letter word and a banned erotica serial zine she'd gotten her hands on a few copies of. Then it had really been off to the races.

He'd mentioned his feelings about boys to his mom before then, of course. It used to be like that. He had, at one point, told her virtually everything there was to share about his young life. That pretty much stopped when he told her this, though. She'd gone tight-lipped and told him not to mention it again, and not to worry, he'd probably grow out of it.

He hadn't.

At first it had been confusing. Disheartening, to say the least. Honestly, it still kind of was. The saying surrounding homosexuality on Earth II, and especially in the city around Capital Hull, was a distinct, "Don't say and we won't sway."

Don't say it out loud. Fuck who you want, in secret. Keep it dirty and quick. Don't be open about it, and you'll stay within our good graces.

There were, of course, other gay people. He knew of a few. Had even had a fumbling tumble or two with a waiter at a diner on the southside. A diner he could no longer go to, as said waiter had, to put it mildly, wanted less of Drew than Drew wanted to give him.

There were even gay couples living openly. The women who ran the bar, for instance—Bernie and Paige—who dressed like Grunts and lived like wife and wife above their bar.

The higher up you got in caste, however, the less acceptable it was; the more that awful maxim applied, like a too-precious cattle brand to the ass: *don't say and we won't sway*. You have my loyalty, you pervert, as long as you don't remind me of your deviance.

Drew was not exactly low in caste.

Beyond that, he was in the public eye. Even now, as Squire of Sol II, he was often asked to do interviews over the summer. Usually, they were just about his mom or the Knightly lineage or whatever, but occasionally they were about other things, about *himself*. The first time he'd been asked if there was a 'special lady in his life' his mom had cringed so hard off-camera, he'd had to shut his eyes. Grin, shrug. Shrug. Grin.

Don't say. Then, maybe, they won't sway.

Drew hated it.

He needed to get laid.

"I need to get laid," Drew snapped out at Amy on the way to school the next day.

She flung herself dramatically back on the trolley seat, practically on top of an older Enseeo on his way to work, "TAKE me, Drew!" she bellowed, and Drew swore loudly, hiding his burning face.

"But really," she said softly as they were walking from the trolley stop across the street towards the school. "I think... maybe Duncan?"

Drew froze before the gate. Stared. *"Duncan?"*

She flinched.

"He's not quite your type, I know..."

"I don't think I'm *his* either. He's always making fun of me. And always talking about... girls."

"Exactly," she said testily. "I know he's kind of gawky. Not as *athletic* as you like 'em. But he's... you know... probably..."

"Probably, huh?" Drew snapped as they started forward again. "Probably what."

"Oh, shut up, Drew."

"Hm. Duncan. You're gonna get me killed."

"No," she snarked back. "*You're* gonna get you killed. *If* you go about this wrong. Just… talk to him. Let him make the first move. You'll see."

Drew huffed.

But he stared at Duncan later, though, in History. Duncan sat on the cushion in front of Drew, so it was pretty easy to do without, like. *Being gay about it.* He had nice ears, Drew decided. They were slightly folded. Biteable, maybe. He'd do.

Drew glanced around, feeling slightly flushed. Caught Riis' eye. Riis was staring *right at him, fuck.*

Could Emnis read minds? They couldn't.

They couldn't.

… Right?

Drew bolted from class as soon as Teach dismissed them, realizing abruptly he had totally missed the entire lecture, which had mostly been about the first settlement on Earth II—before the official first contact, thank christ, so therefore less controversial than *the entire rest of this section was sure to go.*

He made his way to the caf, heart hammering.

How was he going to do this? *Should* he do this?

"Drew!" Drew jumped. Amy was bolting down the stairs towards him, and he almost groaned and looked away, but there was an intensity about her that stopped him; a focused gleam in her eyes, and then the television in the corner of the room blipped on and the static jolted before a face came into focus, teeth straight white lines, and—

"Hate to interrupt your day, but my schedule has shifted. I'll be here a little earlier, now… actually, I already am here!" and Seb suddenly jerked the camera around and yes, wow, that was—

That was—

The front of the school.

He was literally live vlogging from the green.

Seb swung it back around, grinning at them all, the whole image was made of teeth, and then he said, clear as day, "See you soon!"

Blip. TV went back off. Excited chattering.

Amy had reached him, frozen. "Uh," she said, "yeah, history Teach told us after you, uh… are you okay?"

"I'm fine." Drew said. He took a breath. Held it. Did not blow out the candle until it hurt. And then he said, mouth full of teeth, "Excuse me. I'll be right back."

He bolted.

****

Drew ran to the atrium first, because it was almost never used, and so would be safe, right? Wrong.

Students started crowding in twenty minutes into him hyperventilating and dry-heaving in the corner by the curtained stage, and he slipped backstage and around to a currently-vacant but sure-to-soon-be-buzzing hallway. *"Wonder what Prince Seb's gonna do a presentation about, let's get good seats, okay—"*

Drew didn't have enough candles to blow out.

Shrink Kanak would most likely *present* the Prince Admiral. Leaving the school seemed decidedly too much of an act against what was expected of him, and the idea of exposing himself to the sky made him positively quake in his boots.

Where was there to go? Where was the *last place* Seb would look?

It hit him all at once.

He was, after all, right under it.

And heading there later today, anyway.

It wouldn't be so odd.

"Nope," he said anyway to himself as he bolted up the stairs behind the atrium, a winding circle staircase for a section of the school that was so removed it even lacked an elevator. "Nope."

Nope.

He thought it again, silently, as he knocked—a tad frantically—at Riis' door.

Riis startled, inside. He could hear him in there. *Fuck.* Part of Drew had been hoping Riis just wouldn't have come back here yet, that Drew would just have to hide outside his room like a creepy little gremlin.

It would've been so easy. When Riis got back he just would've been like, *Oh, I just got the time wrong, whatever, then I fell asleep,* real casual like.

Riis paused before the door for barely a moment. Drew felt like he could feel him breathing over there, and then the door opened and Riis blinked at him.

"Uh, I got the sleep wrong—" Drew started, and then Riis stepped aside and beckoned inside quickly, and Drew dove into the room.

Breathed.

Blow out the candle.

Blow out the... *wow.*

Riis was apparently a fan of home decor.

"I was not expecting any of you for quite some time. Please excuse the mess." Riis said quickly, shutting the door softly and stepping forward, grabbing a blanket off the floor before placing it delicately on a squat, plush sofa that was *definitely* not something that had come with the dorm itself.

"What mess?" Drew asked blankly. Riis gestured to the blanket, and Drew started laughing, breathlessly. "This place is *gorgeous.* Did you do this?"

"Oh," Riis said, jumping slightly. He squinted, reaching up and scratching at the base of one horn. Drew blinked, suddenly distinctly reminded of his mom primping at her dark honey curls. "Yes. I... have found myself rather homesick. My pack sent me gifts in order to help ease my life here."

"Wow," Drew said, looking around with a new appreciation. There were multi-colored wooden beads hanging in every door–the doors themselves, he couldn't help but notice, removed delicately from the hinges and leaning up against the window. Two rooms sat empty, but he could see the corner of Riis' carefully-made bed in the room closest to the bathroom. An enormous ornate orange and red semi-circle rug lay splayed on the floor in the main room. A plush olive-green couch was only one of the pieces of low-lying furniture, though Drew saw that the beige stock dorm sofa had been pushed around the stone table in the center, probably in preparation for their meet tonight. The room even *smelled* interesting and precise, a sharp salty woodsy smell.

There was a small gas *fire* burning in the center of the table.

"Ok wow, is that real?"

"What? The table?"

"The *fire*, Riis."

"Oh. Yes." he seemed amused, and did not elaborate.

Drew's eyebrows were in his hairline. "Is that, like, allowed?"

Riis' eyes narrowed. "Religious discrimination is not allowed, so I assume yes, it is." he said curtly.

Drew blinked, felt a prickly heat come to his cheeks. "Oh. Okay. Cool."

They stared at each other for a moment. Then the Emni sighed, turned away. "Would you like some tea? I could brew a bit now. I would like to save most for the meet tonight, but I believe I have enough."

"Yes. Please," Drew said quickly.

"Please sit."

Drew sank down on the plush green couch. It really was *very* low.

Riis busied himself at an enormous darkly stained wood cabinet for a moment—also not standard for a dorm—and then returned to the table with a couple of teabags and what was clearly a squat, cast-iron kind of teapot. He filled this with water from a plastic jug he pulled out from under the table, and then placed the pot directly on the fire before returning the water and sitting back onto the sofa behind with a plop.

Right next to Drew.

He didn't sit like Drew, though. Instead, he curled his legs in, sitting cross-legged with strange feet up and under his knees on the couch. Drew quickly toed off his shoes and copied him, and was instantly relieved to not have his knees up by his head.

Silence.

"I'm sorry about—"

"—I suppose you're—"

They both froze. Stared at one another. Drew looked away first as Riis blinked slowly at him. "You first. I dunno," Drew said haltingly.

Riis blinked again. Nodded twice. Then said, "I suppose you're trying to escape your potential murderer."

Drew choked on nothing.

"Uh," he got out eventually. Riis was looking at him with what seemed to be genuine concern, and also like he was crazy, like *Drew was crazy*, as if Riis wasn't the one who'd just said— "That's, uh... not how we say it."

"I am aware."

"Okay. Great. So long as we... both know that."

"Hm."

"Well..."

"What were you going to say?"

"Oh," Drew flinched, looking away. "I'm sorry about the chat. Everyone was just... being really ignorant. I dunno."

Riis shrugged. "You have no right, really, to apologize for anyone but yourself. And, I suppose to some extent, Duncan."

Drew stared.

Riis blinked back at him. Then continued, haltingly, "Or perhaps not? You are mated with Duncan, correct?"

This time Drew legitimately couldn't stop coughing for a good long minute, and Riis slapped him hard on the back in one swift jerk, and then Drew was outright laughing, hysterically, like a crazy person, and Riis said, "Oh my," and Drew abruptly felt a very real swirl of affection for him.

"No." he got out after a minute. "Um, no. Where... why do you think that?"

"Pardon me," Riis said haltingly. He seemed not even slightly embarrassed, just confused, and crouched again next to the fire, removing the now silently steaming pot with two careful claws and plopping it on the stone table before opening the lid and shoving the teabags—*inside their paper wrappers?* Drew cringed—into the pot. "Your mutual reactions to one another confused me. As did your discussion in the chat. You must understand, we are far less, as your movies put it, 'casual' than you are. We do not often mate or even 'flirt' without… guidelines in place."

"Wait, what do you mean 'mutual reactions?'" Drew asked quickly. Did Duncan look at him, too?

"Your arousal." Riis stated flatly, staring at him quizzically like, duh.

Drew gaped at him. "Hold on hold on hold on," he said after a minute. His brain might very well be short fucking circuiting. "You can… sense that?"

"I can smell it."

"Oh jeezus." Drew dropped his head into his hands. Against his palms, his face *burned*.

"It's perfectly natural. I am honestly confused by the human reaction to sexual matters. You seem both more casual and less casual than us, by a longshot in both directions." Riis huffed.

Drew stared up at him through his fingers. "Okay, well… wait, you said he… uh, I mean, you 'smelled,' jeezus, I mean—"

"He watched you closely in physical education during the game 'dodgeball' and became aroused, yes."

Drew stared. And then cackled, delighted. "Amy, wow. She can really call it."

"Well," Riis honestly seemed kind of amused. "Are you going to mate with him, then?"

Drew absolutely blanched. He had never felt blood rush to and from his face so quickly in his *life*, jeezus. "Uh. I dunno. Maybe?" he said, stiltedly. "I just… it's kind of different. For us."

"Indeed."

"I mean. Specifically for like, me and… and Duncan."

"Oh?"

Riis poured him a cup of tea. Handed it to him carefully, and Drew took it. Laughed, rather shakily, and looked away. "Yeah, I mean. I guess I kind of *need* to tell you this, now… for gay people, it's hard. To, uh, live."

"Gay?" Riis asked, face scrunching slightly.

"Oh! Uh," Drew said shakily, half expecting the sex police to drop out of the ceiling and arrest him, to be real, "you know, gay. Same gender with the same gender. In this case, men. Who, like, have sex. With other men?"

Silence.

"Do you not… have that?"

"No," Riis said. "We don't."

Drew didn't know quite why he felt that like a stab to the heart, but he did. It was unique, then, perhaps. It was not natural to want this kind of thing. Certainly not a universal anomaly, at the very least.

"We don't have 'men.'" Riis then continued, and Drew shook his head after a stunned moment.

"Wait, but… aren't you…"

"I have sperm, if that is what you are asking," Riis said, utterly brazenly, and Drew's face heated and he flinched. "I also have ova."

Drew stared.

Riis stared back. Daring him, perhaps, to comment.

So he said, "Okay. Cool." and Riis relaxed, minutely.

"It is a common misconception that we are *all* men, when the idea of 'men' is not even a concept we hold. Accepting for the moment the unlikely assumption that sex and gender at all correlate: while some of us have strictly sperm or ova, it is almost impossible to tell without testing, and the norm is both. Another misconception is that we are a sexist society, keeping our 'women' locked away," Riis continued, and Drew flinched. He'd heard that one before. "We do not do this. In fact, if I were to go by your baseline standard, I am both male and female. And no part of me is 'locked away.' So."

"Both," Drew said, shakily. "I mean, yeah, okay, I can get behind that. Would you rather… I mean… probably gonna be confusing… but… eh, pronouns?" He had met exactly two people, ever, that had talked to him about 'pronouns,' and now certainly seemed the time to bring that up.

Riis clicked his tongue. Drew suddenly felt like he was being clucked at by a matronly grandmother. "The 'male' pronouns you have used so far are fine," Riis said. "I'd like to blend as seamlessly into this school as possible, and it is not strictly wrong, referring to me as you would a man. It is simply… irrelevant to me."

"Ah," Drew said. He stared down at his cup.

"So, I should not mention yours and Duncan's mutual arousal?"

Drew tried very hard not to frantically descend into giggling, "Um," he got out, "you probably shouldn't mention… *anyone's* arousal, mutual or otherwise."

"Noted. Thank you."

This time he did actually giggle a bit madly. "No worries."

They sat in companionable silence for a moment, and then Riis —totally wordlessly—whipped out a tablet and pushed play on a movie he seemed to have just begun watching before Drew interrupted. Drew watched over his shoulder until he set it up on the table. He was shocked to recognize it—a human movie called Sisterhood, about, well, sisters. Experiencing sisterhood, and all its torrid ups and downs. It'd been a big hit like a decade ago.

They watched it until it was halfway through and one of the sisters was getting married to the other sister's beloved, at which point Riis whistled something very swear-shaped and pushed the tablet aside and whipped out a series of cooking implements. He then proceeded to quickly prepare small flat donut-like things over his dinky little fire with Drew's pretty incompetent help. When they'd finished this they sat back on the couch, farther away perhaps than Drew would sit with, say, Amy. Closer than they'd been before, though. A sugary, smokey smell hung in the air from preparing the weird donut-things, and Drew found himself actually looking forward to eating them.

Soon there was a timid knock at the door and they both jumped. Riis opened the door. On the other side was a very nervous and— Drew was shocked to realize this—only slightly early Lara, a small tin of cookies clutched in her hands.

The sun had already set. He'd done it; he'd escaped Seb for the day.

It had all gone by so quickly.

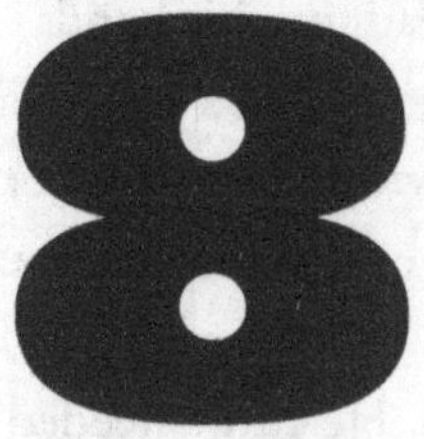

Teaching

"R ight," Fay huffed, taking a swig of her muscle milk. It dribbled slightly onto her knobby pale chin, and she licked her tongue down and collected it, crassly. "I know I'm most comfortable in defense. Who here is slight and quick?"

"I am relatively fast," Riis said sagely. This was a very modest statement.

"Yeah, it should defo be Riis," Duncan cackled. He shot a glance at Drew like they were in on the same joke. Drew, knowing what he now knew, just raised his eyebrows. Maintained eye-contact as he licked a bit of donut grease from his thumb.

Duncan flushed so hard his freckles went pale and looked away rather quickly.

Nice.

"I'm not fast or slight," Lara said softly. She was the only one sitting on the stock dorm furniture, and seemed to feel awkward about being higher up than all of them, though was making no move to change seats. Just was sitting, thick sloping shoulders hunched down slightly. "I don't think I'll be very good in *any* position, sorry…"

"No, I chose you because of your adeptness with command," Riis said, and everyone froze.

"Wait," Duncan said, "you're saying you actually… thought about it? Who you were picking? I kinda just assumed it was whoever made the mistake of making eye-contact first…"

"Duncan," Drew snapped. "Don't be rude, jeez."

"Right, except for Drew, who, like. Wanted it."

Drew dropped his head into his hands.

"I was tactical in my choices, yes," Riis responded, "at least in terms of how *my* people view what benefits a war."

A very awkward silence followed this statement.

Drew sipped his tea.

It was absolute water. He really needed to pull Riis aside and tell him teabags were wrapped, and could therefore be unwrapped.

"Eh," Lara said eventually, "And. What would that be?"

"Strength," Riis said immediately, gesturing at Fay, who nodded rather fiercely. "Supplies," this time he gestured to Duncan, who gaped. "Negotiation," pointing to Lara, who blinked her big dark eyes in surprise, "and… Drew."

Drew shut his eyes, barely stifling a groan. Duncan let out a mad cackle. "Wait, so just 'Drew.'"

"He… seemed to desire teamship with me." Riis said, and Drew blinked; Riis seemed flustered.

"And what do you mean 'supplies?' They 'supply' us with our lazer guns. And it's not like I… *have guns*. My family sews. Sure, we sew the united military uniforms, but still…" Duncan continued, haltingly.

"Ah," Riis said, performing his quick double nod. He paused then, and a line formed between his eyes. His next question was decidedly focused, and Drew felt for Duncan, who was having a turn at being the target of that focus. "So you are saying we are playing at battle, rather than war itself."

"Well," Duncan stuttered, "I mean *yeah*…"

"Interesting."

"You thought we were staging a whole war?" Drew asked, feeling a tad frantic about it.

"Well, yes. 'Wargames.' It implies something more than a simple fight," Riis said, rather tersely to be honest.

Silence. Not a kind silence, at that. Drew quickly laughed awkwardly, breaking it as thoroughly as he could, "Well, yeah, I mean, you're right."

"So wait," Lara said haltingly, "you chose me because…"

"You seemed most capable of brokering peace," Riis said curtly. "Yes."

"Wow," Drew said, a little shrilly at this point, "I mean, that'd make more sense, yeah!"

"Not for P.E." Fay cut in bluntly, "that's some sociology shit. With gym it's about the *exercise*."

Riis waved a hand, clicked again, "My apologies. You must understand—we do not traditionally separate subjects of study like this on Drune."

"Wait," Duncan snapped, "you just, like, learn everything at once? How does that even *work?*"

Riis paused. Seemed to be chewing on something before speaking, and when he did speak, it was rather short. "No. It does come more naturally for us to combine subjects, is what I meant. In our own schools we do just that. However, I attended a traditional human school for six quarters before I arrived."

Everyone in the room was now gaping. "With other humans?" Lara finally squeaked out. "The schools on Drune are… eh…"

"No." Riis said quickly. "My presence here is the first instance of an Emni learning *amongst* humans. This same situation on Drune would be illegal. While we have certainly integrated to some degree, schools, prisons, and hospitals are kept stringently segregated. I simply meant that I attended a human-run school. For Emni." Silence. And then Riis added, rather quickly, "I had to. We all do."

Quiet.

Then Fay belched loudly, and things got a little less intense. Duncan and Lara giggled, commenting brightly on the *power* of the burp. They both seemed beyond relieved to have a distraction. Drew stared at Riis though, who caught his gaze and held it.

He stared back unblinking until Drew looked away.

****

"That was *so weird*. He seems okay, but, like… *so weird.*" Lara said hesitantly, glancing around as if Riis might hear her from the school far behind them.

They—Lara, Drew, and Duncan—were currently waiting for the trolley across the street from the green. Riis had bid them all goodnight almost a full hour ago, now. Fay had bolted for the gym, declaring a need to 'train.'

The trolley was abysmally late.

"He's alright," Drew cut in quickly, feeling strained. Also oddly elated, though. Strangely light, as if nothing could touch him.

Duncan had been staring at his ass on the stairs. Just blatantly staring. Practically licking his lips.

He really wished Lara would fuck off. God, he was just… so ungodly ready for Duncan to do something other than salivate and stare.

"He's rude is what he is," Duncan snapped. Drew flinched. It'd also be nice if he stopped talking.

Suddenly, as if answering his prayers (most of them, anyway), a bright purple car pulled up. Another Enseeo classmate—a friend of Lara's—cried out the front window, "Hey girl, you want a ride?"

She shrieked and giggled. "Yes! Ugh, I don't know what's up with the trolley, I was about to give up and walk! Oh no, wait," Lara turned back to them quickly as if embarrassed, "Oh, do you, I mean… if it's not far, I'm sure she can—"

"Nope, I"ll walk." Drew said quickly. Casually.

"Yeah," Duncan said. "I could use a walk."

You could use a lot more than that, Drew thought gleefully, positively overbrimming with confidence at this point.

The car pulled off and they started down the street.

It was dark.

Nary a soul in sight.

Duncan was really, *really* not that bad to look at. Tall. That was really the most important part, anyway. Tall.

What's more, he thought Drew was nice to look at, too. Apparently. This was frankly the most exciting thing. Duncan getting aroused, watching him fumble around playing dodgeball. Duncan maybe playing out a fantasy later, alone in his room…

"So, what do you think about *mmMMF-!*"

Drew ate the rest of his words, slamming his mouth against Duncan's as they passed under an awning, pushing his whole body hard against the taller boy's, and Duncan… punched him.

Drew staggered back. Rose, blood sparking a freshly split lip. Froze.

Duncan, similarly, seemed unable to move.

"I—" Drew started, and then Duncan pushed him back against the wall of the shop and *stuck his tongue down Drew's throat.*

They made it back to Drew and Amy's apartment. Barely. Kind of.

Duncan was desperately, gut-wrenchingly eager, shoving him against every surface they passed pretty much, and by the time they got in Drew was gasping, light as a freaking feather, and hard as he'd ever been in his life, hands skating down his back, a mouth on his neck, bristled shadow rubbing against his jugular, oh jeezus—

He was very, very grateful he'd had the wits to shoot Amy a quick message of 'CLEAR OUT NOW SEX INCOMING.'

Also grateful she had, you know. Listened.

"I've never, I mean," Duncan was stuttering against his ear, his breath short gasps, evidence of his excitement pressed hard against Drew's stomach, and Drew grinned into his neck.

"I have," he said coyly, and shoved Duncan back, hard. Duncan fell flat on the couch, disheveled and delicious, "I'll teach you. Don't worry." Duncan swallowed. There was a dab of blood on his chin from kissing Drew. His Adam's apple dipped, his whole face was flushed, and Drew dove heartily into him, determined as he ever had been to see how far that flush went.

Sex

Drew liked sex.

He really, really liked sex.

Duncan seemed flat-out addicted to it, though. Which was. You know. Kind of almost a nice change of pace from Basil the waiter, whom he'd done the deed with a few times and then gotten ghosted by, and then flat out told to fuck off by when he confronted him about said ghosting.

Duncan, Drew was pretty sure, would literally *never* tell him to fuck off.

Whether or not Drew would have to tell Duncan that was another, quite larger issue.

"I mean," Amy was positively snickering, curled against him on their balcony, both of them woozy with the shitty pink wine she'd brought home, "it's kinda *good* though, right? What's your problem? 'This boy doesn't like me waah,' I can get. 'This boy likes me *too much,* waaah,' though… I don't get that one. Especially since the other one is like, your *natural state.*"

"He just *can't get enough of me*," Drew snapped, "I had to tell him you didn't know and couldn't be convinced to leave just so he wouldn't show up tonight. For, I might add, the fourth night in a row this week. Never mind *last week*. Last week it was like, *every night*."

"Oh, I know. I'm the one getting kicked out all the time."

"Exactly!" Drew huffed, taking another hearty swig. "You *are* getting kicked out all the time. It's flat out rude. Not to mention… exhausting."

"Oh, poor Drew. Getting too much sex."

"Shut up."

"It's honest to god astounding how little it's calming you down."

Drew shut his eyes and leaned his head back. "I just like… a bit of a game, you know? A question? Some angst and some longing. I love a good pine. Is that too much to ask for?"

"You sound like one of my mom's romance books."

"Well *alright*, I want some *romance*, then!" Drew bellowed, and she cackled, shushing him quickly. He let out a huff. "Seriously."

"Hmm. Maybe make dinner for him."

"Absolutely not."

"Eh. Can't really complain then, can you?" she snarked, and he rolled his eyes.

****

"Is this normal?" Riis asked, tightly.

Drew glanced up from his tablet. "Huh?"

He'd been (hiding from Seb and now, also, Duncan) visiting Riis virtually every day since they'd all first had their Wargames meet. It was convenient. No one really even came into this wing of the school, unless they were going to the atrium downstairs. Riis had also turned out to be pretty fair company: quiet, a tad deadpan in his delivery, and almost brutally honest in a way Drew frankly found endearing, at this point.

"He hurt you."

Drew blinked. It took him a second. "Oh!" he laughed, touching his lip. "Yeah, nah, I dunno. I took him by surprise." It'd been healing pretty well. Evidence of the split was almost gone, at this point. Drew didn't quite know why it was being brought up *now*.

"Not that. I didn't know he'd done that. That is also, though… is that normal?"

"…uh?"

"… I was referring to the bite mark on your neck."

Drew flinched. He'd thought his collar hid it. Apparently not, though. "That's just a hickey, I dunno."

Riis stared blankly at him.

Drew cleared his throat. Reminded himself that this was another reason he liked hanging out with Riis; no secrets. No topic off-limits. "A hickey is like… eh, sucking. You suck on someone's… neck, normally. Until it bruises." He felt a feverish swoop then, remembering what else Duncan had been doing while giving him a freaking hickey, and—remembering the smelling thing—quickly thought of less exciting things. Very quickly.

Riis blinked. "Ah. Yes. We do that. I suppose we just… bruise less easily."

"Eh. Cool." Drew said, trying not to laugh.

"What about the hitting? I'll admit, that is rather taboo in my culture."

"What? Oh. No, ours too, I just. I kissed him without warning. I dunno. I hadn't done it before, and he hit me. I guess on instinct."

"Ah. That seems… unnecessarily violent."

Drew shrugged. Looked away. Riis was still staring at him. So he spoke, hesitantly. "I mean… I dunno, I can be abrasive to some people. I mean. I like when people are a bit abrasive. I guess *obviously*," he laughed, gesturing at Riis, who blinked, and Drew quickly backtracked, "but yeah! It freaked him out. But he's not freaked out now. Definitely *not*." He did, admittedly, snark that last bit out a bit, glaring up at the window and slumping haughtily.

"Ah," Riis nodded twice, a little slower than he usually did. "You wish to end your sexual relationship."

"Oh my god, jeezus."

"Well, you do."

"Ugh."

"Is this not normal for humans? Humans begin and end sexual relationships often. I knew that even before arriving here." Riis said, honestly pretty testily, and Drew rolled his eyes. Riis continued, though. "If anything, based on my observations, it would be bizarre if you did *not* end it eventually."

"So, wait," Drew cut in, mostly out of curiosity but also just because he wanted to switch the subject, "so you guys, like what, mate for life?"

He expected some explanation, but Riis simply nodded his customary two short practiced bobs of the head. Also, did the clicking noise Drew was beginning to recognize was as good as a nod to Riis. "Yes. We do."

"Oh," Drew said, and then silence. "I mean, I guess I knew that. I heard y'all like… uh…" he faltered. He'd heard they killed the wives of those who were dead. Buried them along with the fallen one alive. All kinds of terrible things that couldn't be true, right?

"We are born. In our lives, we find our pair—our lifemate. We live as one in that pair. And when the time comes, we die as that pair." Riis said quietly.

Drew blinked. "What?"

"My parents, for instance. They partnered when they were young. My 'mother,' I suppose, got pregnant with me. Then, they were separated. She died birthing me. My 'father' most likely perished as well, either before or as she did."

Silence.

"Wow," Drew said after a moment.

"Indeed."

"That… that's terrible."

"It is not," Riis said curtly, and then rose. Walked over to the window, peering out as if expecting someone. "It was not, anyway. It was simply… how we were. We feel… very deeply. It's a source of pride. Our trend towards deep connections. The sturdy tie between the emotional and physical. It's only in war with humans we have found it to be a disadvantage."

Drew let out a hard exhale, shaking slightly. "I mean… I can see how that… how that would be a disadvantage. In that case."

"For every one soldier killed, another always perished," Riis said quietly. "For every casualty, count it twice. For every captured prisoner, even. It is rare we survive great distances from our mates. Many died. Through ignorance if not malicious intent. My mother birthed me in a camp, for instance." His shadow was a sharp cut against the light, his shoulders tense, and Drew felt a sudden, deep-seeded ache, imagining a small Riis growing up alone. In a *camp*, too, jeezus. Even in history class the war camps were taught as a moral error on their part. "I can only assume my father died as well."

"I…" Drew shut his mouth. He didn't know what to say. He *didn't know what to say.*

Riis nodded. Didn't click, this time. Bowed his head afterwards, and spoke softly, in his blunt and starkly vulnerable way, "I grieve them daily, though I was adopted by and raised in a strong pack. There has always been something… absent."

Drew rose. His own limbs were fumbling and foreign as he slowly came up beside Riis.

Drew didn't touch Riis. Wasn't brave enough to. But he stood there, hands in his pockets, and looked out over the green expanse of the tops of trees. Felt Riis' presence like an ember at his side.

"We should get to class," Riis said quietly.

Drew blinked, shook his head. "What?"

Riis glanced at him, and then away. "Physical education."

"Oh," Drew said softly. "Right."

They gathered their things. Went to class. Didn't quite acknowledge one another out in public, as per usual. Walked just as far from one another as they ever had. For the first time though, Drew felt hyper-aware of the distance rather than the closeness.

Homebrew

D rew! You have *got* to *stop flinching!*" Fay bellowed, still pelting balls hard at him from across the gym.

"Jeezus, stop hitting me then!" Drew squealed, dodging yet again before stumbling and falling over his own feet and to the gymnasium floor with a smack. He felt a ball smack similarly against his shoulder.

"Alright…" Riis cut in, hesitantly.

"Lara! You too! Eyes up! Retaliate!"

"Ohmygod ohmygod ohmygod!" Lara was shrieking, ducked half down behind the bleachers and holding a ball in front of her face like a shield.

"Ok, that I believe is sufficient—"

"And Riis!" Fay snapped out, "Stop *babying them!* You are supposed to be *Captain!*"

Riis stiffened. Fay chucked a ball at him. It bounced off his face. He didn't move.

"Okay," Duncan said nervously from over by the bleachers—he'd gotten hit out early in the game. "I think everyone's out except you now, Fay…"

"You're right! Everyone *is out.*" Fay slammed her final ball down, hard. It bounced high before barreling off towards Lara, who shrieked, ducking again. Fay just sat down with a plop on the shining wood floor, though, glaring up at them all. "We have a *lot* to work on."

"I believe," Riis said, rather tersely, "this is a problem that can mostly be solved via devotion to… a tactical plan of attack, rather than, eh. Dodgeball."

Fay considered this. Riis blinked rather quickly at her. "Nope," Fay said after a moment. "Nope, like, it's definitely just brute strength and skill you're all lacking."

Drew groaned, throwing himself down on the bleachers with enthusiastic disdain. Duncan grinned eagerly at him, and he shut his eyes.

****

"Y'all over on Riis' team are, like, waaay more devoted to this than we are," Amy said flatly over dinner.

Drew shrugged one shoulder, shoveling fried rice into his mouth. They were having a night in at home together, seeing as she was fighting with Jas and Drew was 'standing by her side' (aka avoiding Duncan). Their apartment was dimly lit and they'd gotten takeout for the occasion.

"I mean," Amy continued, "that's, what, your third meet this week?"

Drew flinched. He had not done more than imply his visits to Riis' dorm were all wargame meets, but it still felt like a lie. "Not that many," he said truthfully, to make up for it.

She snorted. "It totally has been," she said, and he looked away, cringing.

\#

"I, uh. Really dunno how to talk supplies, Riis," Duncan said awkwardly. They'd decided before the Fay debacle to give each member of the team a chance to strategize based on inherent and learned skills. Post-Fay debacle, it was kind of a relief to only have Duncan and Lara on the horizon. Drew was seriously hoping Lara would bring a craft for them to do as the main event of her meet or something like that. She seemed the type.

Riis shrugged. "Speak on what you feel is pertinent, then. While here on Earth II you have a predestined path; on Drune and amongst the Emni people your worth would be earned through individual action and thought. As I am Emni as well as the team captain, I intend to Captain us in this fashion." Dead, still silence in Riis' dorm.

Drew sipped his tea water.

"Uh," Duncan said, obviously feeling cornered, "Well. I recommend everyone wear their gym clothes for this, as they're more, eh, comfortable. And wick away sweat. And, um. We have to. For sports…"

Silence again. "Thanks," Drew finally said, "True facts, all of that."

Duncan brightened. Drew barely contained an eye roll.

"Well," Riis said, seeming a tad irked, "What else do you have to offer?"

Duncan shrunk in his low seat. "Uh," he said. "I can… mend?"

"Ooh! Can you cross-stitch a heart on my gym shorts?" Lara burst into the conversation.

"Ooh, same!" Drew said, cackling.

"Well, if this is to be our team signifier, perhaps on mine as well," Riis said casually, and Drew couldn't help it, he burst out into a mad fit of giggling.

Fay fumed in the corner, glugging her muscle milk.

****

"I believe I have offended Fay," Riis said quietly that night during episode thirty or so of an ancient Earth of Old show called *The X-Files*.

Drew blinked, coming back to reality. "Huh? I mean, yeah. Probably. So?"

85

Riis blinked rather swiftly and looked away. "It concerns me, what others think. A feeling that is perhaps not ideal for my current situation, but is true nonetheless. I do not wish to be her enemy. I would like for her to at least… feel neutral towards me, if 'liking me' is not on the table at all."

Drew let out a huff. "I honestly wouldn't have guessed that," he said after a moment.

"Eh?" Riis said, blinking quickly at him.

"Well," Drew said, hedging, "it's like… You always speak your mind. You always say what's right to say, regardless of how it's bound to be received, I mean. I dunno. I don't associate all that bravery with being a people pleaser. Like, of the two of us, I would've said I'm more… more like that. But I personally couldn't care less if I offend Fay, so."

Quiet, for a while. Then Riis spoke very softly, "I did not say I will change in order to lessen her rage at me. Merely that it bothered me, that she had these feelings at all. I sincerely wish to heal the hurt between us."

Drew looked away quickly. He could feel those eyes still staring at him, black wells under an iridescent film. "Oh," he said awkwardly. "Well."

In their show, a man was being led down a dark hallway. Led to a chair, where he was strapped down. Drew shut his eyes, realizing what was about to happen before it did, the man now shouting some religious stuff, the kind of stuff people shout when they're about to die, anything to make it worth it, and–

Blip.

He opened his eyes. Riis had turned off his tablet; placed it back on the table. He pulled out the tin of cookies Lara had brought before from under the table and held them out. "Would you like these?" he asked, deftly skating over the conversation Drew obviously didn't want to have, "They are rather cloying to me."

Drew laughed. "Sure," he said.

For a while he just munched on the cookies. Riis swiped up his tablet again and went into some book or something in a language that was full of loops and squiggles, reading it carefully. After a moment Drew spoke, "I would just like, tell her what you told me," he said, finally. "Fay, I mean. Like. I'm beginning to see the value in all this truth about your feelings… stuff."

Riis clicked twice. Nodded like an afterthought. "Perhaps I will."

"Though I'll be real, now that I actually think about it, she probably *doesn't* see the value."

"Eh?"

"Yeah. Yeah, I take it back. Don't be honest. Be like… surreptitious?"

"… Ah. Alright. I shall do my best."

****

"So." Shrink Kanak was sitting back on her cushion, head tilted slightly, *staring him down.*

"Soooo?" Drew responded when the silence went on just barely too long.

"Wargames, huh."

"…yeah? So?"

"What? I mean, that's what you're doing, right? Wargames? Meeting at least once a week, from what I hear." *Jeezus, why did she seem so coy about it?*

"Hm." Drew managed to get out.

She squinted. "You having fun?"

"What do you mean?"

"I dunno," she shrugged, smirking at him. "It's important, you know."

"To have fun?"

"Oh yeah."

"Is that, like. Your official shrinkly question?"

"Absolutely."

"Okay, fine. Yeah, I guess."

"Nice! Nice."

A long pause. Drew glared.

She smiled, oddly soft. "I'm glad he has you," she said finally, and he felt his face heat.

****

Lara did not bring a craft for them all to do, though it seemed like it at first when she burst breathless and uncharacteristically late into Riis' room, arms laden with papers, books, a small parcel like bag, and multi-color pens.

It hadn't been a craft, though. It had been something else. Something very hyper-fixate-able, Drew discovered with glee.

"Are you guys sure you haven't done this before? Really? Cuz this is pretty sweet! Very good! A lot of long-range, but we have a paladin, a monk, a bard, and… what are you again, Drew?"

"Warlock," Drew said immediately. He had put a lot of energy into his character sheet. Lara pursed her lips looking down at it. That was good, right? That must be good. His character sheet was utterly fabulous.

"Okay, cool!" Lara handed them back their sheets. "Okay. Everyone download the dice app I told you about, and we'll get started."

"Wait," Duncan said nervously, "just like that? We're just… getting started?"

"That's good, we gotta learn on the battlefield!" Fay bellowed.

"I'll help you guys! Just let me know when you're confused. It's okay, I always go easy on DnD babies," Lara said briskly, opening up a bizarre three tiered cardboard shield thing that looked worn, decorated with a plethora of dragon stickers and sparkles.

"I believe I have a firm grasp on the rules," Riis said, closing the book she'd passed around. "I must say, I am impressed. This is a fascinating method you've chosen."

"Thanks!" Lara said brightly. "You don't have a firm grasp on the rules, though. Just, like. Preparing you…"

"I don't?" Riis blinked quickly.

"Anyway!" Lara continued. "You all wake up–"

"Wait, we were sleeping?" Duncan said worriedly.

"I wasn't sleeping. I was knocked unconscious during a fight! Which I still won!" Fay bellowed.

"Indeed…" Riis said.

"You all wake up!" Lara interrupted with a snap. Fay was glaring around at them all, especially Riis, challenging him. He stared back, unblinking. "You're in the middle of a dark, spooky forest. Upon opening your eyes, you see around you… eh, each other…"

The story continued just as haltingly at first, but once they really got into the riddles and the mysteries Drew realized Lara had seriously put a lot of thought into this. She also hadn't been joking when she said at the beginning, *"There will always be more than one way to solve any problem."*

"I roll to punch the lock," Fay said bluntly.

"Oki-day. Go ahead."

"Nat six."

"Okay, so again, 'nat' is really just before—"

"I punch the lock."

"Okay, fine. You punch the lock. It gets punched. I dunno what you really want me to—"

"I would like to play a song on my lyre," Riis said suddenly.

Silence. Lara blinked. "Eh. Okay? To what end?"

"I would like to strengthen Fay's will in punching the lock," Riis said immediately. He blinked slowly across the table at Fay, who looked startled and then nodded sagely.

"Alright. Go ahead, roll," Lara said.

Riis rolled. He blinked quickly at his tablet, and then—with all of them at this point leaning forward—he turned it around. "I believe this is a situation in which you say 'nat,' yes?"

"Woooo!!" Duncan bellowed, and then slapped Drew on the back like it was him who'd done it.

"Alright! That's some *fierce* teamwork!" Fay shouted.

"Let's get the fuck outta this cage, y'all," Drew deadpanned. He had already attempted spelling the lock open and failed. Certainly no one had helped *him*.

It was, however, oddly sweet. Oddly fitting and right. Fay actually shot one of her rare, furrowed-brow smirks across the table at Riis, who squinted, clearly quite pleased.

Drew felt a strange flutter in his chest.

Blamed the warmth of the room.

The Notorious Winter Break, Part I

The sky was winter-pink. It was crisp and cold out on their balcony, but Amy was all warm limbs curled against Drew, both of them huddled close under the thick blanket they kept by the window for exactly this purpose.

It was the first day without classes. Soon, most everyone would be going home for the holiday. Drew, however, was where he'd be already. His mom had called yesterday—some situation on Drune, because of course there was. She and the King Admiral were already headed that way, because of course they had to. He could, of course, come home. Spend Xmas with the Grunts and the servants. He'd politely lied and told her he just might spend the holiday with Amy.

She had been thrilled.

Because of course she had been.

"You sure you don't wanna *really* come home with me?" Amy said suddenly in one hard exhale. Her breath puffed in a cloud against his face. Drew glared.

"And Jas, you mean."

"Yes. I mean, he's nice to look at…"

"And your parents."

"I mean, duh, it's their house."

"Who I'm going to be hanging out with, primarily. Who are, like, nice enough, *sure*, but who are going to be asking me all about wedding plans, babies, and other *marrying you* related topics, all whilst you and Jas run around trying to find nice private places to get nasty."

"Jeez, you make it sound like torture…"

"Amy."

"…What?"

Drew sighed, leaned heavily against her. "Amy… why not just… *marry Jas?*"

She stiffened immediately against him. "I dunno about that," she said after a moment. "Like, even if the caste shit wasn't an issue—"

"It *shouldn't be*. I mean, christ, it should even be *less of one*, with him you're both Enseeo caste, even if he's—"

"Just. I dunno. Even if it *wasn't*. He's kind of… dumb. So, bone-achingly hot. But pretty dang dumb."

Drew snorted. Refused, though, to fall into her trap of 'rag on my hot boyfriend,' much as that game ordinarily appealed to him. "Okay," he said. "But you like that about him."

"I dunno, Drew. He's like… I dunno. You're more… safe."

"Jeez, thanks."

"It's a compliment! Like, sure, we're never gonna mash bits," she said, and he swore, leaning back immediately in only slightly feigned disgust, "but!" she was cackling. "That's honestly even better. That's safer. You're my best friend. I *know* I'll always love you. I don't know that about Jas."

Drew considered this.

He wasn't opposed, was the thing. He was supposed to get married anyway. Get married to a girl, obviously. And frankly, the notion of being bound to Amy for life was pretty nice, truth be told. He often wondered what exactly she got out of their farce, though.

"Besides," she said coyly, "I'll still fuck Jas, if I want. I'll just… make all the eternal vows and stuff with you."

"Well *goodness me*, aren't I lucky."

"Yeah! Yeah, you are. Maybe we can even get Jas a ritzy apartment," she giggled. "Duncan, too, if he's still hanging on. Maybe they could live together; why not. Save some money. You and me can head over there when we wanna get laid, and not be there when we wanna do, like, *anything* else."

Drew rolled his eyes. "No," he said, finally.

She blinked, staring at him, a nervous hurt flashing in her eyes. "Huh?"

"I'm not going home with you for winter break," he said quickly. "Enjoy your holiday with Jas. Jeez."

She immediately looked relieved, but pouted dramatically all the same. He poked her protruding bottom lip and she laughed, ducking forward and trying to chomp down on his finger.

****

A few hours after she had left, Drew had already danced around the apartment naked, jerked off in the living room, watched two movies Amy hated, and jerked off in the living room for a second time.

He was bored.

Beyond bored. Something else, too. It felt almost like he'd misplaced his tablet, or like everything in their apartment was slightly askew.

He got dressed. Went out on the balcony. Stared at a few great blue-horned gulls who had wandered far from the sea and were perched on the shipping container stack across the street. Sat down on their little balcony and shivered.

It was colder without Amy.

Drew considered, for one gut-wrenching moment, calling Duncan. Duncan had also gone home to visit family, but he only lived a short way outside the city proper. He would be there, Drew knew in his heart, within the hour. Then at least he'd be warmer.

Instead, he found himself thumbing open his tablet and doing something just *wildly different*.

Drew: Riis? Are you still at school?

Drew flipped his tablet back away after sending it. He shivered. Almost immediately his tablet buzzed and blipped against his hip, and he took it out again quickly.

Riis: Yes. You as well?
Drew: yeah. I mean no. I'm at my apartment a few blocks from the school. Just a trolley ride away, really. Super easy to get to.
Riis: Alright.

Conversation halted. Great.
Drew took a deep breath. Blunt. Emnis were blunt. Right.

Drew: anyway yeah i'm just bouncing off the walls by myself do you wanna come over my place this time?

Utter fucking radio silence for an hour.
Then...

Riis: That's an utterly insane suggestion, given the circumstances. That being said, yes. I am 'bouncing off the walls' as well.
Drew: awesome!! Cool!!
Drew: I live at 78 United Ave
Drew: Capital Hull proper
Drew: across from this fish place and above

this corner store you'd like has lots of
pickles
Drew: anyway yeah
Drew: call me when you get here.

Drew swore and *forced himself* to stop typing. Considered throwing his tablet off the balcony. Stared at the rolling '…' instead, though, which eventually blipped to a single one-word response.

Riis: Alright.

****

It wasn't until Drew had dropped his tablet down on the charger and turned to face his living room that he realized it was literally disgusting. Vile. Atrocious. Just seriously the worst thing, and Riis was *clean*, wasn't he?

First thing he did was change into a shirt without stains. Then take out the trash. The elevator, when he went into the core of the building, turned out to still be broken, so he did his and Amy's usual thing of running down the fire escape stairs. A practice he actually rather liked, ordinarily, as it really felt like they had their own house rather than a unit in a shipping container stack.

By trip number three of taking out the trash, he was literally wheezing, each breath like an icy dagger to the chest, and Drew collapsed on the lowest step after cramming the final bag into the dumpster. Distantly, from four flights up, he heard his tablet start to ring. Drew swore, glaring up at the stairs, readying himself for yet another unwelcome serving of *exercise*, when—

"Drew?"

He froze.

Riis stood—distinctly alien despite the scarf wrapped tight around his face, the hoodie pulled low over a sock hat, and the (Drew literally had to bite his cheek to keep from bursting into hysterics) wide-rimmed, extra-dark sunglasses attempting to block what remained of his face. Riis hung up his tablet with one gloved hand which looked just *extra long and weird*, the claws contained awkwardly.

"Riis… hey."

They stared at each other. Riis let out a huff. "It is rather cold, and I am rather conspicuous, so—"

"Right!" Drew leapt up. "Right this way, c'mon." With a new vigor, he began pounding his way back up the fire escape.

Riis followed, barely making a sound beyond the light clack of claws only slightly hidden under long pants, though he kept pace easily.

"So," Drew said, slowing as they neared their destination, "it's, uh. Not exactly as clean as you're used to…"

"I assumed as much."

"Hey! Rude!"

"I did not mean—"

"Buuuuut here we are!" Drew leapt through the wide window and into the apartment, flinching immediately.

The trash was gone. That had been a good start. His and Amy's clothes and jackets were still heaped on the chair, though. Books and various puzzles and about half their jewelry and beauty tools were scattered across the coffee table, much of it spilling onto the surrounding floor. Shoes were flung in every random direction next to the window. In the kitchen in the corner of the living room, it was obvious plates and cups were overflowing out of the sink.

Riis crept delicately over the shoes. Turned and smartly closed the window. Turned back around.

Drew chewed on his lip and tried not to just burst out apologizing.

Riis picked up a blanket off the floor, placing it neatly on the couch.

"Great," Drew said, absolutely deflating. "Okay. So. Yeah, as you can see, it's very much *my* home."

"Indeed," Riis said softly. He pushed down the hoodie, pulled off his hat, plucked off the sunglasses, and began unwinding the scarf from around his neck. Drew looked away. "Would you like my assistance?"

Drew blinked. "What?"

"In cleaning. That was what you were doing when I arrived, correct?"

"Oh," Drew felt a hot spike of embarrassment turn sharply to anger. "No thank you," he said primly, and, suddenly just a tad defensive, walked around Riis and plopped down on his sofa. "I was pretty much done."

"...Were you."

"Yes," he snapped.

"It appears to be *very* disorganized in here still, Drew," Riis said bluntly.

"Jeezus christ, maybe I like it that way, Riis! Listen, around here you don't just... come into peoples' apartments and tell them their home is *gross.*"

"I didn't," Riis said, blinking quickly at him. "I offered to help."

Drew barely contained a scream. "Okay," he said through his teeth. "Thank you, but no thank you."

"You're welcome, and alright then."

Drew huffed. "Okay, whatever. I dunno. Do you wanna watch something? We subscribe to, like... everything, so we don't even have to pirate."

"Alright."

Drew whipped out his tablet, turning on the TV and skating his finger through the Flix app, trying to find something... something *neutral.* Riis delicately sat on the very edge of the couch. Jeezus. This was such a stupid idea.

This had been such a stupid idea.

This was so *awkward.*

"Thank you," Riis said suddenly, "for inviting me here."

Drew blinked. Squinted at him, suspicious.

Riis' eyes widened. He looked away rather quickly, leaving Drew wondering if this had been the wrong thing to do, he'd only *squinted*, but then Riis spoke: "It has been very solitary, my existence here. This is the first time since my arrival that I have even left the campus. My only socialization comes from classes and… from you, when you visit. I was quite sure I was facing a two-week period of total isolation. The thought left me rather despondent."

There it was again. That honesty.

Drew swallowed. "Oh…" he said. "Don't mention it. I, uh. I was lonely too."

Riis nodded, sagely. As if they'd just agreed the weather was awful.

Suddenly, a solid gold nugget of abso-fucking-lutely brilliant idea seemed to bellow forth from Amy's instincts to his brain.

Drew leapt to his feet. "Wine!"

Riis startled. "Pardon?"

"We're not on school grounds, so we can have *wine*. Can you, eh… Drink? Wine?"

Riis blinked. Fast, and then slow. "Yes," he said, sounding amused.

Drew leapt over the coffee table and barreled into the kitchen, only slightly colliding with the fridge this time. Whipped out two mugs and poured them each some wine.

Eventually they settled on some older movie about a little boy in a big house who could go inside paintings or make paintings come to life or whatever. Kid shit, Drew thought. Then it took a decided turn towards the kind of cheesy horror you just don't get anymore —bad CGI, jump scares and screams, and soon Drew was giggling and tipsy, Riis even relaxing back against the couch, legs curled under his knees, squinting at Drew across the middle cushion, which they'd both left vacant.

The small painting hopper was, for reasons that made no sense to Drew and Riis—they agreed—now in Capital Hull Central's famous art museum. They were only half-watching at this point,

Drew leaning sideways on the couch, drunkenly telling Riis about the Amy engagement farce, when Riis glanced at the television and stiffened.

Drew turned quickly to see what it was, expecting some more jump scare shit. What he saw was frankly far more terrible, and he sucked in a harsh breath through his teeth, making a mad fumble for his tablet, which appeared to have vanished.

Riis sat very still and stared at the television.

The boy had happened upon the 'Portrait of Interplanetary Peace.' It sat regal and huge at the end of the hall, the original King Admiral shaking hands with the Emni leader. Slowly, though, the CGI Emni leader depicted in it turned, maw opening to reveal jagged, pointed teeth, horns busting through the surface of the painting like it was tearing at flesh, and a hissing, belting roar emanated from the—

Blip.

Drew's hands shook on his tablet. His thumb still pressed the power button so hard his nail whited out in the center.

Riis said nothing. After a moment, he sipped again at his wine. He wasn't looking at Drew.

Drew wondered, frantically, what to do. If he should say something? Ignore it? If the first option, what, exactly, was there to say?

There was then a sharp knock at the door. Drew immediately took advantage of this, rising and swaying for a moment—okay, perhaps not tipsy, perhaps just drunk—when Riis hissed suddenly, "I'm not supposed to be off school grounds."

Drew turned back to him, blinking dumbly. "What?"

Riis had risen and swayed, also rather drunkenly, eyes abruptly wide and rather frantic. He spun his head around like a cornered animal, hissed again through his teeth, "I am *not* supposed to be off school grounds; it can't be discovered that I disobeyed this condition of my attendance! The consequences, not just for me, but for the future of the *program*, for—"

Drew jumped again over the coffee table, narrowly avoiding crashing into the wall and making a beeline for his room. He flung open his bedroom door, beckoning quickly. Riis all but dove into the room, and Drew quickly shut the door, heart hammering.

"Drew? Kid, you okay? I just heard a thump. I guess you didn't go to Amy's?"

He absolutely cringed with his whole goddamn body. His mom. His *mom* was here.

The Notorious Winter Break, Part II

You seriously need to be more careful, honey, honestly, tripping over the *coffee table?* Did you not *see* it? It's a coffee table!" his mom clucked, smiling golden and soft at him.

Drew cringed. Shrugged, flinched. Just the. Whole range of uncomfortable body movements. Tried very hard not to glance at his bedroom door.

She had come to drop off a present and visit before her departure. She'd invited herself in, presenting him with his carefully wrapped and enormous Xmas present—it was absolutely something sportsball or fencing related, she sure had hopes, that one—before plopping down on the couch, picking up Drew's cup of wine, and taking a careful sip. "You really shouldn't drink alone, honey," she'd said then, smiling at him. And he was fucked. They were fucked.

His room was on the innermost side of their container and lacked a window. He normally liked it fine that way. It was kind of like a cave. But in this moment he was furious that he hadn't fought Amy at all over the bedroom with a window that opened onto their fire escape. That nice, escapable bedroom. Then he was also furious he hadn't considered that and just shoved Riis in *her* room.

"Is something wrong, honey?"

Drew snapped his head back around, facing her quickly. "Nope! Nothing. I'm good."

Silence.

Her eyes narrowed.

He had barely a minute to suck in a breath and let out a whimpering, "Mom, no!" before she was up, storming quick and steady across the living room, slamming open his bedroom door with a thump and standing there, golden and tall and angry.

Drew leapt forward, "Mom, mom wait—"

"Where is he?!"

His heart was exploding out of his fucking chest. Somehow, Riis had managed to hide—there were no immediate signs of him behind her in the bedroom. Drew had to act quick, though. "What? Eh, who?"

"You have company. Two wine mugs—*mugs*, really Drew, at least use wine *glasses* I mean—and you're just, what, sitting in your nice shirt in the middle of your apartment in the middle of the day alone? *That's* why you decided not to go with Amy? There's... there's a *boy here.*"

Silence.

He ground his teeth together behind his lips. Shut his eyes. "Mom..."

"Where is he?"

Silence.

"Tell me, Drew."

"Why?" he snapped out, something hurting *deep* in him at this point, "You wanna meet him? You've never shown any interest *before* —"

"Interest? *Meet* him?!" she reared on him, gaping at this point, "Drew, this is *serious*. If we were... were... bakers. Taxi drivers. Newsies or mechanics, even, sure! You know I love you regardless! But you are the future *Knight of Sol II*. You have an *honor*, a *legacy to uphold.* You—"

"Okay," he snapped. He couldn't quite meet her eyes. There was a shift in the room behind her, and he shut his eyes quickly, not quite wanting to meet that pair of eyes, either. "I get it. I get it, Mom."

"Do you? Because whoever this… this *boy* is, he could talk! It's not exactly a sacred act, you know."

"I get that."

"Can you imagine the fallout if this… this *hobby* of yours came to light?"

His mind went utterly static white noise blank. *"Hobby?!"* he found himself shrieking, before he clamped his hands over his mouth, staring at her.

She stared back at him, lips so tight against her teeth they quivered. "I'll leave you to it, then," she said brusquely. Turned to the room and bellowed, "Enjoy yourselves," before storming swiftly back out to the living room, grabbing her coat, and flinging open the door. He heard her let out a hollow, guilt-trippy sob before it shut.

Drew held his face in his hands. Breathed.

Blow out the candle.

Blow out the candle.

Please don't cry…

Opened his eyes.

Riis stood right before him, eyes wide, whole form still. Drew swore, leaping out of his fucking skin for a moment, and then laughed, forcefully. "Wow, she did… not see you. Where did you hide?"

"I managed to duck under the bed in time. You have… quite a lot of potentially misplaced items down there; I thought I should inform you. It is unimportant now, though. What was the context of that… interaction? Are you alright?"

Drew flinched. Right to the fucking heart of it, then, as usual. "Uh," he said, voice wavering. He looked away. "Remember how I told you about… about being gay?"

"Yes."

"Well. I am."

"I assumed as much," Riis said, blinking. "Context clues and all."

Drew let out a choked laugh, biting it back quickly before it became something else. Riis was looking at him with utmost focus. A line had formed between his dark eyes, and while he was pretty hard to read, there was a tangled energy between them now that felt strange, charged and uncomfortably raw.

Drew turned away. "But yeah! It's like. Not considered great, not considered proper, and I'm supposed to be those things. I'm supposed to be the Knight of Sol II. All… Knightly, and not-gay and stuff." He wandered over to the couch, plopped down and took an enormous glug from Riis' wine mug. He couldn't quite bring himself to sip from his own. His mom's lipstick had left a smudged pink kiss on the rim.

Riis was very quiet. Then, "I do not wish to be culturally insensitive, but that sounds utterly ridiculous." And with that, he let out a huff and plopped back down on Drew's old side of the couch. "Anyway. I believe we were switching the movie?"

Drew blinked. "Oh," he said. Then let out a laugh, surprising even himself. "Yeah… yeah, we were switching the movie."

"Something romantic, please. No more of this… surprise monster stuff."

"Fine."

"And, I think, low stakes. This has been… an exhausting hour for both of us."

"…For sure, Riis."

****

They ended up binge-watching a show about an almost-too-witty-to-tolerate mother and her studious daughter. Heartily, they debated which boyfriend was the right fit for the daughter—who got around—and came to agree that they staunchly *didn't agree*. Riis liked the sarcastic twink who read a lot and talked like a giant tool. Drew was personally a big fan of the charming rich boy. They agreed, though, that the hometown hick with the flippy hair was a *last choice*. If any choice at all.

Soon the room was spinning dizzily and the TV had long since asked if they wanted to keep watching and Drew was well and truly drunk now, but still trying to paint Riis' clicky-clackity little toe talons. He kept giggling, though, Riis whistling out instructions and speaking seriously about the situation. At first, it was possibly unintentionally funny, though Drew was pretty sure when Riis said, "Please be more dutiful while applying acrylic, honestly Drew," he meant for Drew to fall over laughing, which he did.

Sooner than seemed possible, birds were chirping. The sun was moments from rising, spilling dusty golden shadow across the city, and Drew and Riis sat like he and Amy did on the little fire escape balcony. Exactly like he and Amy did, really. Just… apart.

Always, even now, at least a little apart.

"This has been the most enjoyable night I have had since my arrival," Riis said softly. He was wrapped up tightly in the blanket, but still shivering slightly, squinting out of the folds of it.

Drew grinned at him, head lent back against the rail. He was so tired. Tired and happy. "Same," he said.

Riis stared. "The most enjoyable night you've had since my arrival? Or yours?" he asked, and Drew snorted and Riis squinted and it seemed rather coy.

"Don't be a dick. I dunno. It's just… been fun. The most fun I've had in a while. Even with… all that other stuff."

"Indeed."

They looked at each other for a long time. Riis, for once, looked away first, eyes widening slightly. Drew continued to look, though. The clouds were moving lazy and hazy through the sky, now. They moved through Riis' eyes too, reflected in the dark liquid surface of them.

****

It felt strange, being alone with Riis for two weeks. Strange, but kind of empowering in a bizarre way. They discovered rather quickly that it was only them and a scarce few other students who had decided to stay for winter break, and these other students by and large lived off campus. There was no one to pay attention to them. No one to try and touch Riis' horns, or comment on Drew's proximity to him, which—he could feel it—changed like a magnetic shift in the ground below them, tilting him forward. They walked the grounds together for the first time, ate openly together right there in the library, and, quicker than he would've guessed it would, the last of the fear trickled away.

It was nice. Really, really nice.

Intimate, his fucked up brain supplied when he wondered what made it so nice, and he immediately put that word in a box, locked it in with the biggest imaginary padlock possible, and moved on with life, heart beating slightly quicker than usual.

Now it was the night before the first day of classes and students had already started coming back. Amy technically already was back, but had opted to sleep over Jas' for the night. Evidently her parents hadn't exactly relished the notion of them having any kind of time alone.

So Riis was back at his place. They were eating a spicy curry Drew had made—curry being one of the few foods they'd discovered they whole-heartedly agreed on—and Drew offhand mentioned doing something like this again, maybe next weekend, and Riis went abruptly quiet and still.

"What?" Drew asked, not liking the way Riis was staring unblinking at him.

"Will you still socialize with me?"

"What? Yeah, of course!"

Riis blinked. Slow blink. Then, as if coming out of a trance, he shook his head, looked away, and blinked fast. "Perhaps not in the same way, though," he said tightly.

Drew flinched. "Well… I mean—"

"I understand."

"No, Riis, you *don't*, I just mean—"

"I am a social pariah. You have thus far managed to avoid that status."

Drew breathed. Shook his head, and then quickly said, "I mean, even before you, just *barely*. Just cuz of—"

"Your inherent status," Riis said softly. "Another reason it would, perhaps, be unwise to associate publicly with me."

Drew chewed on his lip.

He had a point. Like, he did. He had a point.

"Can I still go up to your room sometimes? We got a lot more TV to catch up on."

Riis was very quiet for a moment. Then, very softly, "I would like that, yes."

They ended up falling asleep with no wine to use as an excuse that night, curled on opposite sides of Drew's couch.

He woke up the next morning to a clean apartment.

"Jeezus *christ*, Riis!" Drew shouted, leaping forward and attempting to grab the broom out of Riis' hands. Riis being, like, freakishly fast, dodged, and for longer than made sense they continued this before Drew—exhausted—collapsed on the floor and flung his head back dramatically.

"Consider it a thank-you." Riis said primly, carefully tipping his last tiny pile into Drew's freshly bag-inlaid trash can.

Drew swore, heartily, in ways that could've made a sailor blush.

"You're quite welcome," Riis said, and Drew couldn't help it, he cackled.

The trip back to school was discussed next.

They decided to do it separately. Riis left first, in the wee hours of the morning still, leaving Drew to sit for a planned twenty minutes by himself on the balcony, feeling like an absolute tool.

Just. Would it be so bad? To *know* Riis, publicly?

His mom would be upset if she found out.

When wasn't she upset, though. Really.

Making a decision, he bolted down the steps, across the parking lot to the trolley just as it was pulling up, nearly colliding with Riis as he did, and Riis startled and turned. They stared at each other.

Drew, not knowing quite what to do, shrugged.

More than usual, Riis was hard to read. The giant sunglasses were seriously not helping their nonverbal interactions. But he did his short nod, and they boarded together, and Drew sat down next to him in the back.

They rode in silence.

Got to campus and walked through the gate and across the green together.

Then up to Riis' room for him to deposit his disguise. Riis seemed oddly anxious. Didn't quite look at him, but followed him wordlessly back out the room and down the stairs.

For the first time, they walked to class together.

It was frankly less dramatic than Drew had hoped/feared it would be.

No one stopped and pointed. No one screamed. No one questioned the sanctity of Drew's Knighthood and no one spat on them.

He'd kinda been prepared for all of that. A little pumped for it, truth be told. Terrified, but *ready*.

As it was, they were slightly late. No one was even really roving the hallways to notice them.

The first class passed smoothly. History. They sat next to each other. Drew glared at his classmates, daring them to comment. No one so much as glanced at them. Of course, though. They kind of… already sat together in history.

Then physics, with nothing to prove. Nothing new, anyway. Amy was abysmally absent, probably having overslept with Jas, as he was also nowhere to be seen. Drew frantically attempted to do the experiment on his own and failed—just really extremely thoroughly. There was even a small fire.

It was the fire that folks were teasing him about in the hallways after, when he made a beeline for Riis and walked beside him—not too close, because he didn't wanna get crazy here, but very pointedly beside him—down to P.E. They'd be doing the Wargame today. It was frankly all he'd been able to think about before winter break, but now it seemed so small, so inconsequential. Winter break felt like it had truly been a break in reality, a distinct shift, altering all that came after it.

He missed it, he realized.

He missed winter break.

Riis glanced down at him, and then quickly away. Drew shifted slightly closer.

Upon opening the door to the gymnasium, immediately, they were greeted by teeth. White teeth, clean straight lines of them.

Prince Sebastian of the house of the King Admiral grinned too large for his face, spinning around and raising his arms. "Drew!" he bellowed. "Can't run from me now, can you?"

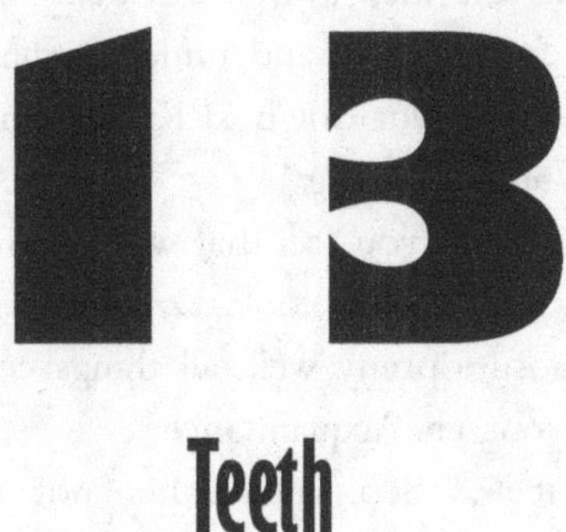

Teeth

The floor fell away. The lights faded. There was only Seb, and his teeth.

Teeth in a face all-too-familiar, though he wore it more confidently than Drew did—no sign of a scowl or anxious glare—bursting with careless pride, everything except Drew's mole shared between them, from the bugging eyes to the flat dark hair.

And the teeth. The teeth were insane.

Distantly, Drew registered people talking around him. Seb *embraced him* like they were good old friends, so while for a second it was like he was almost back in his body, he quickly faded again.

"I mean seriously," Seb was saying, and he ruffled Drew's hair, hard, "I've been trying to find this one for *like a month*, on and off, and where is he? I was *trying* to not interrupt your scheduled classes, but this is frankly *ridiculous*, so here I am! In the flesh!" He laughed in a way that seemed to titter and bellow in the same moment, and Drew was possibly hyperventilating.

"*Candle,*" Riis hissed quietly.

Drew turned to him. Riis was staring at him intensely. "Huh?"

Riis' eyes widened.

"And here's our *exchange student!* Abso-tively beautiful to meet you," Seb grabbed Riis' hand and shook it, hard, with both of his. Riis went totally ramrod straight, but did not jerk away, as he seemed to really want to. As Drew felt abruptly impulsed to do, in a strange twist: just jerk Riis the fuck away from Seb. "It was my idea, you know! Trying to foster peace and understanding every way I can. That's my motto. That's what the next King Admiral will bring, folks. Peace! Peace, and understanding."

"I, eh… I am happy you feel that way," Riis said, and his words were *very* clipped, and a little shook. Drew honestly thought he was holding his composure pretty well, all things considered. "It is my pleasure to make your, eh. Acquaintance."

"Absolutely, it is," Seb said, either not understanding how language worked or just disastrously self-assured, "I hear you're one of the team Captains. I hope you won't hold the game against us, ahaha!"

Riis flinched.

Drew stared. "Huh?" he said, finally speaking. The lone dumb syllable still came out shaky.

"Well," Seb said, "I'll be playing today, too! Couldn't stand to interrupt your game. So! In order to make it fair, I'll be on the opposite side. Wouldn't want to give one side *too much* of an advantage, with a Prince and a Knight on the same field, ahahaha!" and he slapped Drew's back. Hard.

There were scattered snickers at the notion of Drew contributing to any kind of advantage. Riis, however, jerked forward slightly. Only slightly. No one else seemed to notice it, but Drew did, and met Riis' wide eyes as he grinned, forcibly. Did not look at Seb and his teeth as he said flatly, "Sure. Right. Okay, great."

Great.

****

"Are you injured? He hit you…"

"What? No, Riis, I'm fine—"

"Hey uh Drew long time no see how was your holiday uh do you wanna hang out later tonight?"

"…Duncan, can we please just focus on the game?"

"Right. Right, sure. Okay."

"…Yup."

"Okay!" Teach Sir bellowed. Drew was having heart palpitations, truly he must be. He was probably going to die, right here. At least Duncan would mourn him.

Amy was staring at him with wide eyes across the gymnasium, but had made no move to help him. Hadn't even said jack shit to him. Had not messaged him about this. She wouldn't grieve for him. Probably she hated him. Fine. He hated her, too. She was dead to him.

Beside her Seb was all teeth, grinning, baring the laser gun like he'd held one all his life.

"The rules," Teach Sir continued, "No melee. We're not trying to *actually hurt one another*. No sneaky tricks unless they work. When you get shot, you're not to move at all. No leaving the field. You *stop* and you *drop*. 'Cause in a real war, you better believe the bodies don't clean themselves up." Teach Sir grinned, rather manically. He was truly having way too much fun with this. "Okay. Positions!" The lights went dim, dimmer, dark, until it was only the indicator lights on their guns and the steady glow of their vests.

They all scattered. Riis' team had already planned their positions at their last meet before winter break and fell into them easily. If Drew wasn't too busy being a numb walking dead man full of fear and hate, he would've felt sorry for Jas' team. With their incredibly forward-facing new addition, it seemed none of them knew what to do or where to go.

A mad scurry. Seb chose front and center. Like a douche. Waved off Amy like he was doing her a favor. She paused fretfully by him, clearly having already planned to take cover behind that pillar. After a moment of just staring, she turned and crouched awkwardly behind a crate.

Drew's blood was rushing in his ears.

"On your mark… get set… aaaaand go!"

They all moved at once.

The pillars provided little cover. Teach Sir had placed smaller hovels—some made from crates, one made just from a pile of old armor—as both barriers and cover around the gym, and Drew quickly tried to fall into the plan. Tried to ignore this new development and just *move*.

He dove back with Lara as Riis dove forward, as Fay and Duncan rained laser fire down upon the enemy, hitting Jas immediately square in the chest. Amy dove behind Jas as he sank haughtily to the ground, Amy now crawling forward to a new pillar, and Drew fired hard as he could push a plastic trigger back at her, missing every goddamn time, *fuck*.

He saw a weapon rise out of the corner of his eye, spun to face it and—

Seb. Seb, raising a gun at him.

Seb, the notorious King Admiral grin spreading across his face, and Drew. Couldn't. Move.

Drew couldn't—

Thwack.

It was with no small amount of shock he suddenly found himself on the other side of the room—thick, strong, warm arms wrapped around his middle and a hard chest against his back.

He felt Riis' exhale, softly, against his ear. The warmth of the air from his lungs as he spoke in a quick, whistling hiss.

"Stay here if you're going to freeze."

Drew couldn't move anyway. He stayed there. Frozen.

Immediately Drew was shot. Out. He slowly, shakily, sank to the ground.

Riis barrelled forward, moving quicker than was, quite literally, humanly possible. He fired on Amy first, immediately sending her out of commission. Dodged Seb's shot and spun, aiming his weapon high at Seb's chest, something in his face contorting, and then… he stopped. Froze, face still contorted.

Seb shot him, letting out a delighted crow.

The lights came back on.

Dimly, Drew registered Duncan had been sprawled right at the front. Fay had fallen first, and she rose looking distinctly miffed, to say the very least. Lara came out from behind a crate shaking, her vest also a blinking indicator that she'd been hit.

They'd lost.

"What the hell!" Fay bellowed.

"Oh, don't be sore! It's hard to beat me at my own game," Seb crowed.

"You *let* him win." Fay snapped at Riis. Riis blinked.

Hesitated. Then, in a way that clearly felt *incredibly* unnatural to him, Riis lied. "I did… *not* let him win."

"Feel no pain about it. Even beyond my skill and training, there's a certain… biological advantage, don't you think?" Seb crooned. "No offense meant, of course."

Drew stared at Riis.

Riis, for once, did not stare back.

****

"Considering his arrival, I intended to throw the game, yes. Admittedly, ideally, in a less obvious fashion," Riis said softly that night, back at his dorm.

Drew stared at him. He was not the only one. They'd planned a final Wargame Meet to either celebrate or commensurate what would happen today. Win or lose, they'd all begun to enjoy their meets, so. Win: party. Lose: also party.

None of them had considered 'question why Riis threw the match' as another potential theme. Fay looked shakingly, jaw-clenchingly furious. Lara looked confused. Duncan was just staring nervously and intensely at Drew, raising his eyebrows high whenever Drew met his gaze.

Drew wasn't doing much of that, though. Mostly he was staring at Riis. Riis, who seemed tense and small for the first time in a *long* time.

"Traitor," Fay snarled, and pushed up from the couch, stomping around them and practically barreling a shoulder against Riis by the window before storming out of the room. They all flinched as the door slammed.

"She takes her games *seriously*," Duncan said after a minute. And then nudged Drew, like it was their personal joke.

"Are you alright?" Drew asked Riis quietly.

Riis glanced up at him, and then quickly away, eyes wide. "I—"

"Why did you throw it, though?" Lara asked hesitantly. "I mean. I don't mind that you did. It doesn't affect our grades. But… why?"

A loaded silence. Drew knew why he'd thrown it.

If anything, he just didn't know why it'd taken Riis so long.

He somehow knew not to ask that right now, though.

"I am here to foster peace and understanding. Not to beat the future King Admiral at, as he put it, his own game," Riis finally said, very quietly.

"Right…" Lara said haltingly. "Well. Okay, then."

Quiet. Then Duncan spoke, "I guess we should be, eh. Going, then? Drew? Eh?"

"You go ahead," Drew said quickly. Duncan looked at him like he'd been stabbed. Jeezus. This was going to be a *conversation*. He and Lara left, though, and then it was just Drew and Riis.

Riis didn't look at him as Drew rose and walked cautiously up beside him at the window. Riis was picking at the base of one of his horns, staring hard out across the dark trees outside, eyes still wide and a tenseness all over him.

"Why did you save me?" is what Drew meant to ask. *"It's not like I was in any real danger…"*

Riis was clearly tired, though. Exhaustion seemed to dwell in every gentle arch of him. So instead, what came out of Drew's mouth was, "Wanna watch another chick flick?"

Riis blinked, slowly. Stared at him. Hesitated. Then started, "What's a—"

"Movie. Wanna watch another *movie?*"

"Ah... I, eh... alright, then. Yes."

They sat down. Riis put on what did turn out to be, indeed, another chick flick, based solely on the roaring music and the first shot—strange bright flowers in a sloping and wildly untamed field, rich with foreign dark foliage. This movie—it was clear from the get-go—much, much lower budget than basically anything they had watched thus far. And then, also pretty clear all of sudden, not about humans. Drew felt himself startle as an Emni—a real Emni, not the CGI beast from that dumb *other* movie—stepped onto a strange kitchen set. They washed their feet briskly at the door before clacking delicate claws inside and beginning to cook, muttering something in small groans and whistles under their breath.

"I hope you don't mind," Riis said haltingly. "At this time I'd rather not... I mean, I can tell you what they're saying if you—"

"Sure. Like, don't feel fussed about it. But sure."

"...Okay. So they are discussing their sibling's rivalry with their 'father,' I suppose..."

Drew watched. Listened to Riis' synopsis of their speech and sometimes direct translations, which got gradually more animated as the movie went on. It became clear it was a romance of some sort, of course, and also became clear Riis was deeply into it, sometimes spinning off into speculation—either his own or that of this movie's other fans (with whom he seemed to communicate with via online forum, jeez) during slow scenes.

Drew found himself getting heavy on the squat, plush couch. Riis hadn't adjusted the environmental controls in his room, so it was very toasty. Eventually he leaned back. He could still technically see the movie, but it became easier to focus more on how Riis' eyes reflected the screen, the black mirroring back the images of Emni in varying stages of lovesick lorn lamenting something or other.

Simple light, too, seemed to dance there. Like a black pool in the dark, his eyes reflected all the light outside them.

Drew shut his own eyes, the padlocked thing within him quivering, shaking, desperate to get out. Nope.

Nope.

Drew blinked, slowly, and then popped his eyes open with a start.

It was dark.

He was very, very warm.

There was a hand in his hair. Moving delicately over the strands. Just oh-so-slightly brushing them back from his temple.

He stilled. Riis was above him. He was literally half on Riis' lap, Riis now silent, distracted by the movie, the tight line of focus back between his eyes, but his hand was in Drew's hair, and Drew didn't know what to do.

"Eh," he stuttered out, eventually.

The hand jerked back.

They stared at each other. Drew was still very much half on Riis' lap.

He felt a swoop.

Riis shut his eyes, then, and turned his head away. Something clenched in his jaw, and he said, rather briskly, "It's getting late. I didn't want to wake you. But... you should, perhaps, try and get home before it gets too dark."

"Right," Drew squeaked. He leapt to his feet, wobbling dizzily for a moment, and Riis barely flinched forward but seemed to pointedly stop himself. Drew's head tingled where Riis' warm hand had been, mere moments before. "Right. Okay. Uh, bye."

He bolted.

****

"I will not dream."

He said it out loud that night. Blew out the biggest metaphorical candle he could imagine. Everything in him felt alive and awake, but he was also *exhausted*, and he squeezed his eyes shut, said it out loud again through gritted teeth. "I will not dream."

He dreamed.

In the dream, the switch was live and real and protruding from his chest. It glowed like the small fire in the center of Riis' table, burned against his heart, and Drew held his shaking arms around it, cradling it. Just don't go out. Don't go out.

Warm, gentle hands suddenly found his own.

Riis was dark in the dream. He was a dark gray in reality too, but here, he was all horned shadow, and he moved Drew's arms slowly, carefully.

Drew's hands shook. He didn't stop him.

"Let me help," Riis breathed, and his breath was very warm against Drew's mouth.

He stepped forward. A hard chest against his, warm arms around his middle, a soft face against his neck, and the flame sparked, swelled within him and—

Drew woke up tangled in his sheets again, shaking, breathing hard.

Hard.

Honestly just.

Right on the edge.

He flopped back down in bed. Breathed great, gasping breaths, pleasure pulsing deliciously through him like a second heartbeat. Pressed his palm down against himself and barely contained a whimper. Tried to. To calm down.

He was so close.

Riis had been so *warm*.

Eyes shut, he shuddered. Very, very hesitantly, curled his hand around the offending part of himself instead.

It didn't take long. Three solid strokes and he bit his pillow to keep from shouting, the orgasm pooling through his hips like liquid sun, like the warmth of Riis' room when he wasn't expecting company, like *his arms around Drew's middle, fuck, fuck!*

Fuck!

Avoidance

Drew was seriously going to break.

Seriously.

Riis moved with a swift elegance through every task, be it walking down the hall or leaping around the gym during some team sport, and Drew watched him hungrily, helplessly, desperately trying to not think —

Not think about—

He was honestly pretty human-shaped, at the end of the day. Wasn't much taller than Drew. Was taller, though, and wasn't that just. Just fascinating. He had two legs. Two *strong* arms, thick shoulders, a broad chest, sweated like a human did when he exerted himself, a sheen to his dark gray skin, making his muscles stand out in sharp contrast, jeezus—

But it wasn't just that, at the end of the day, that sent Drew bolting to Duncan after class, yanking him into some closet to *handle this.*

The alien shit was nice, too. The horns, growing thicker now, larger. The two on the sides curling down around foldy pointed ears, the two on the top thick and sloping down against his skull. The eyes Drew'd found downright freakish could now make him freeze, flush like a freaking teenager, all dark night and reflective surface. The strange twist of his limbs—legs breaking into long, tapered feet, most of which didn't touch the ground, just the clawed, calloused pad of the end.

Drew remembered, vividly, drunkenly painting Riis's fucking talons that one time during The Notorious Winter Break (a two week period of far too delicious isolation he was absolutely blaming this development for), but tragically couldn't remember what the pad of that foot felt like.

So he'd fuck Duncan, or Duncan would fuck him, or they'd fuck each other, and he'd gasp out quivering breaths, helplessly wondering what this would be like with—

"You always close your eyes near the end," Duncan whispered to him, snickering into his neck.

Drew glared at his ceiling, lips tight.

He also (shocking though it was, considering the sheer *amount* of sex Duncan required) spent a lot of time engaging in his self-love ritual.

It was almost easier that way. He could shut his eyes the whole time. Touch himself and whimper out a swear as Riis came so very easily into his mind. Riis' wry look of amusement. Riis' hands, moving so delicately over any and every task. Riis wrapped in the blanket on his balcony, squinting coyly at him.

Riis shirtless, like he had been yesterday in the locker room after gym, and Drew'd only seen his back before he'd fled, only half dressed, out into the hall, throwing on his shirt with shaking hands as he went. Riis' broad shoulders, christ, he could probably move Drew like a doll, how would those claws feel on him bare, and he knew now what that chest felt like against his back, knew that Riis smelled like salt and was inhumanly warm and god, god, *yes*…

He was never satisfied, though. There was an unquenchable

thirst within him, a hunger that made him ache, maybe even especially after he'd 'gotten that out of his system.'

****

"You've been avoiding me again."

Drew flinched with his whole body. Finished chewing his bite of sandwich slowly and swallowed. Looked up at Riis for a moment, and immediately was transported to his bed, to a waking dream he'd had that very morning, feverish, desperate, Riis' head tilted against his, soft dark eyes boring into him as he… and Drew looked away quickly.

Not, at least, being 'smellable' was a very, *very* real goal.

"Yes," he said after a moment.

"Oh… well. I am grateful you did not try to lie. Wh—"

"I, eh, can't tell you why, though…"

"…Okay?"

A long silence. Riis let out a whistling huff, looked away, and then said stiffly, "I understand you have begun to engage more frequently with Duncan. A period of social isolation is perhaps… normal, at the start of a relationship. It happens in your movies. I would like to tell you, though, that I very much value… what I have come to see, at least, as a *friendship*, and you more than anyone else have contributed greatly to making this place… tolerable."

Drew snapped his head around, but Riis had already turned and started walking away.

He sat there for a long time. Missed P. E.

Duncan found him after, concerned. Started asking, "What's wr —"

Drew dragged him into an unused classroom and sucked him off, teasing him until he was literally begging for it.

****

"Today," Teach said, and Drew knew—even before the

slideshow loaded, based solely on the tenseness in her face—what was about to come out of her mouth, "we are going to discuss… first contact."

She looked expectantly at Riis. She wasn't the only one, truth be told.

Riis blinked quickly. Stared at Teach with the utmost focus.

The slideshow was loaded up. The famous picture of King Admiral and the Emni leader shaking hands, and Drew barely contained a full-body flinch, looking hard at his desk. Teach had scarcely opened her mouth and Riis' hand had shot up into the air.

She visibly grimaced. "Yes, Riis."

"Are we going to discuss the 'Portrait of Interplanetary Peace' as well?"

"Yes."

"Ah. I shall hold my commentary until then."

"You do that. Now, first contact occurred a while after our arrival, when we began to explore. We knew there was a class M moon in the same solar system, but had dismissed it as too small to harbor… yes, Riis?"

"No."

Drew's breath hitched.

"No?" Teach snapped.

"No. Emni were already here when you landed. We sent a delegation to greet you, approximately six days after your arrival."

Still, dead silence.

Riis seemed to take this as permission to continue, "The party members of that first act of welcome were captured. Interrogated. Two died. The remaining four were held for years in the name of 'scientific research.'"

"There are… of course, alternate versions of every historical event," Teach said through her teeth. "What's in our history books —"

"When it comes to war," Riis continued breezily, "recorded history is dictated by the victors. While I concede there must be truth in both our versions, it is important to consider the bias present, regardless of whether or not the 'facts' are published."

Still, dead silence.

"Riis," she said tersely. "What you're saying could get you in a lot of trouble."

"Pardon me," Riis said, and he squinted, very slightly. Just a twitch of the eye. "I am merely attempting to share my own knowledge and experience. Emni classes work... differently than classes here."

"Well. We are not in an Emni class," Teach snapped. "So. I'm going to make this rule now: questions may be voiced at the end of the class. Write your questions and comments down, if you must. But until the bell rings," she snapped, pointing up at the clock above the door, "this is my classroom. I am the teacher. And whoever wishes to doubtlessly *miss their next class* may remain here and listen to... *your* bias."

Riis didn't even flinch.

He did shut up, though.

Drew's fingers gripped his knees, hard. Pinched down. Breathed. Blow out the candle. Blow. Out. The. *Fucking*. Candle.

The lesson wore on. The bell rang. Drew felt like he could feel Riis' internal monologue crowding the air between their heads. He hadn't taken a single note. Drew knew he had his whole speech planned, though.

Everyone rose rather quickly. Amy even burst out after Jas, who had bolted ahead to get out of the room first. Everyone left.

Everyone except Drew.

Riis hesitated. Teach let out a hefty sigh. Sat down at her desk. "Fine," she snapped.

Riis blinked very slowly at him. Squinted, very slightly.

(Swoooooooop.)

A pause. Teach was glaring. Riis spoke softly, then, "Since it's just you... perhaps, later? I do not wish for you to miss your physics class."

Drew let out a huff. Rose and collected his books. "Alright. See you tonight, Riis," he said, cool as he could manage.

Riis squinted tightly at him then, and all of Drew's stupid dumb bullshit reasoning ran out of him in a rush. Riis looked so strained and sad and jeezus. It didn't matter, did it?

It didn't matter.

He went to Riis' room later that night and listened to his passionate lecture. Felt a solid thrumming ache in his chest for more reasons than the usual ones as his view of the universe shifted yet again.

They watched a movie after, sitting close, and Drew was hyper-aware of Riis' leg inches from his.

Found Duncan after. Absolutely buried his face in Duncan's neck, everything in him one solid ache.

Whatever. Worth it.

15

Break Your Own Heart

Seb went home a few days later with much fanfare. Slapped Drew's back again before he did. Made some clipped comment Drew could barely hear over the blood roaring in his ears, but it boiled down to, 'say hi to my father. You see him more often than me, after all.'

Drew continued his 'sexual relationship' with Duncan for another week. And then another.

…and then another.

It was almost agonizing. The clinginess made something in him positively shrink with disgust, but in the midst of the act itself, there was relief. Here he was, a human boy, and for once that was more normal than a certain… alternative.

A rather impossible alternative.

Drew also—though he seriously sometimes still wondered if he was crazy for doing so—continued to visit Riis.

He brought him various pickled things from the corner store, sometimes. Sometimes he just showed up. More than once Drew brought his tablet with his own movie loaded up on it: nothing too risque, in any direction. No war movies. No human-made movies depicting Emni at all. Jeezus christ no movies with sex scenes. Just… movies. Shows, too. Especially if said shows had aliens. He confirmed rather quickly Riis preferred two things in all his television: romance, and a distinct limit on the number of humans.

So long as the non-humans weren't CGI Emni.

They absolutely binged a positively ancient Earth show called *Star Trek: Deep Space Nine.*

"This is very deeply disheartening," Riis said on day six of *Deep Space Nine* all-the-time, and Drew glared.

"Well, why didn't you say so? We seriously do not *have* to watch *Star Trek.*"

"No, no. I am enjoying it *immensely.*" Riis deadpanned, and Drew smirked before Riis continued, "Just, before human arrival in our solar system, there seemed to be a rather popular notion amongst you that humans would come in peace. That we—we being yourselves and extraterrestrial life—would form an alliance rather than find enemies in one another. It's disheartening."

"Yeah," Drew sighed, rather softly. "Yeah, it is. Could've gone so much better."

"Indeed."

Silence for a moment. Quark was planning some scheme; Odo was trying to interrupt it. Then Riis spoke, rather haltingly, "It could have been rather lovely, is my point."

Drew shut his eyes. Something deep in him seemed to burn at the delicate way Riis said it. "Yeah," he said rather roughly after a moment.

Yeah.

That night he absolutely destroyed Duncan. First in, like, a really sexy way.

Then, lying in bed together, Drew scrunched up on the very very edge of his bed and Duncan curled determinedly against his side, Duncan muttered, "I think I'm in love with you," and Drew basically had no choice but to destroy him another way, too.

"You broke that poor boy's heart," Amy cackled at him when

she'd finally gotten home. Drew glared up through his fingers. He'd been absolutely sobbing since Duncan had tearfully left. It wasn't fair. This was what *he* had wanted. Why did *he* have to feel like his soul had been gouged? They'd barely been together two months. Well, maybe three. Maybe even more, jeez. He'd planned to break it off before winter break, anyway, and that had already passed...

"Hey, now," Amy said, softening immediately. She sat down beside him, wrapping an arm around his middle and dropping her head to his shoulder. "It was inevitable. Don't feel bad. Folks who wear that shit on their sleeve basically break their own hearts."

They watched a very anti-romantic movie about some middle aged women living single and free and they ate ice cream and drank so much wine Drew fell asleep on their lumpy little couch, puddled against Amy, immensely grateful for her bright warm existence in his life.

****

Riis didn't comment on his sudden lack of hickies.

Drew didn't know why this bothered him.

(Or, like, at the very least, he didn't dare think about why it bothered him.)

****

"Wait," Amy snapped out, a quarter of the way through spring semester. "You've been... *visiting him?*"

Drew flinched. The physics lab buzzed with chatter, their classmates gratefully distracted.

Amy stared at him.

He hadn't meant to keep it from her. Hadn't meant to tell her, either, had just offhand mentioned something Riis had said last night about Jas, and it had all kind of snowballed from there. "Well, yeah. He's good company. I dunno."

Amy stared harder.

"He was the only one still here during winter break, so... anyway, he teaches me a lot about, like. Drune, and Emni cultures and shit. I should know about that stuff, right?"

"Why."

129

"I dunno! It's not like it's! Like! *Irrelevant.*" His blood was positively rushing in his ears. Drew cackled, slightly manically. Glanced at her, and then away. Her eyes narrowed; confusion shot through with a dawning suspicion.

"Are you… I mean, do you…"

"No." he sneered, and she immediately seemed to calm down. Something in him clenched, though.

It felt like a lie. It definitely wasn't a lie. It felt like it, though.

He did not lie to Amy.

"Okay, cool. Well. It's a weird friendship, but whatever. Glad you're making friends. You should tell your mom; she texts me all the time asking if you've made any friends."

"Oh my god, *what,*" Drew groaned, dropping his head into his hands.

Amy snorted. Finished their experiment quickly, and then leaned back from the slate desk and into the stiff lab chair. Stared at him, brow slightly furrowed still. "Well, I mean. She's worried, what can I say? I kinda even get it. You don't really… make friends easily."

"I make plenty of friends!" Drew snapped. "I'm friends with you."

"I, like, super don't count," Amy said, snickering.

"Okay, fine. I'm friends with Riis, then." The words came out natural and he felt something in him brighten at them.

Amy rolled her eyes. "Duh," she snapped, and the bright thing got even brighter. "Tell her that, then. Make her stop texting me, god."

"I can't *tell her* I'm friends with an Emni. She doesn't even know he's *here,* far as I can tell."

"Just don't say he's an Emni."

Drew blinked. "Huh," he said after a minute.

****

He got his Mom's voicemail. This was an intense relief. He left a hurried message, not looking at his own gawky image on the screen, rambling on about this and that, and then finally adding, "And I made friends with a, uh, boy from school. We're buds. Good buds. Friends! Uh. Amy told me to tell you. Bye," and then hung up.

****

Riis whipped out something purple that night and rolled it into a cigarette.

"It's a Seer day," Riis said bluntly at his questioning stare. "Traditionally, I would smoke with my pack. You'll fit that role, for now."

"Oh," Drew said. He felt a dull, aching glow. Thoroughly liked the idea of fitting any kind of personal role at all in Riis' eyes. Felt very weird and sad about that. About liking it, though. Definitely not about fitting a role. "Sure, yeah."

Riis lit the cigarette—which was thin, and he'd capped it with an engraved metal filter—on the fire in the center of the table. Took a long drag. Purplish gray smoke swirled around him, breaking into smaller swirls at his horns. He passed the cig to Drew.

Drew very determinedly did not think about how his mouth was touching a place Riis' mouth had just touched as he inhaled. Did not swipe his tongue out to taste. Jeezus christ he was *so fucked*.

Riis sat cross-legged beside him on the couch. He shut his eyes.

Drew mimicked him.

They passed the cigarette back and forth. Slowly, Drew realized this shit was not, like, the Emni version of tobacco, or even weed.

It was the Emni version of *something else*.

A fact which probably should've been obvious from the get-go.

The room began to swim before him. Colors bled into each other. He let out a strangled gasp, and then Riis' face swam into focus, eyes soft and squinted, heady with the smoke, and Riis said, the words like lush physical things pressed against his brain, "Don't get upset. Don't fight it. Just let the truesight in when it knocks."

131

****

Drew was on Drune.

He had never been to Drune before. He knew it was Drune, though, because of Riis' rug, which rested orange and red against the horizon, all the fibers of it swirling now; a great woven gas giant dominating the sky.

Riis stood beside him.

He was *tall* in the dream. Taller than Drew, for sure, but also just taller than anyone Drew had ever met, and he seemed to move out of shadow itself into the light of the planet and the sky. The grass whispered, dark as his skin.

The switch burned a hole in Drew's chest.

"I won't flip it," he said immediately as Riis glanced down at it, a soft wrinkle between his eyes.

Riis tilted his head, blinked slowly, and looked back up at his face. "I know. Oh, I know."

Drew sighed. Calm.

Until Riis continued, voice soft, almost gravely, "It's not your role to flip the switch. It is only your role to carry it."

Drew flinched. "I'd tell you, though, if they were ever gonna flip it. Give you time to… to run."

Something in Riis' face darkened. "Don't."

"Don't? What?"

"Don't think of me as an exception to my people. If the switch is flipped I intend to die as well."

Drew's mouth was dry. "What?"

"It's why your role exists. The devastation the last use of the weapon caused… we will never recover, as a species. At least half of Drune is still all but uninhabitable. If we were to be struck again, we would all surely perish. Myself included. I think, whether or not I were to try and 'run.'"

Something in Drew clenched. "But why," he hissed out.

"Because I am Emni. I have never wished to be anything else."

"Oh… I get that, I guess." Drew'd always wished to be something else.

Riis' eyes were hard, staring him down. He could see himself in them, small and desperate and the switch burned in his chest like a contained sun. "Do you?"

****

Drew awoke with a jerk and a start, sweating.

"What the *fuck!*" he snapped, sitting up, and Riis blinked at him —gentle, languid, slow.

Drew was shaking.

"It's alright," Riis said softly. "It is… intense. The first glimpse at truesight."

"That wasn't… I mean, was that a psychedelic?"

Riis blinked a tad faster. "'Psychedelic?' I have never heard this word."

Drew gritted his teeth. He was hyper-aware of Riis' leg pressed against his, and he brought his knees up to his face, hugging his legs tightly. "You can't just *give someone drugs* and not tell them what they do."

"I was not aware—"

"I mean *seriously* that was *insane.*"

Riis' eyes narrowed. "I found our conversation quite productive."

Drew's breath stuttered. "What conversation?"

"About the switch."

Drew stood up. Swayed, dangerously. Riis quickly rose and grabbed him gently at the shoulders, and Drew realized suddenly Riis' hands were warm as his arms had been, that Riis was really the ideal height, and Drew felt an inconvenient swoop of something very much edging towards smellable, and jerked back. Riis stared at him blankly.

"That… that was real? We were really… really on Drune?"

"You experienced our discussion on Drune?" Riis asked shortly, staring at him curiously, and Drew's face felt numb.

"I..." he started. Swallowed, thickly. Looked away. "Where... where were we to you?"

"Earth."

"Earth? You mean—"

"Not Earth II. Earth."

They stared at each other. Riis blinked, very slowly, something almost pained coming across his face. An electric jolt seemed to jump between them and Drew felt himself let out a sound—low, animal—and turned away quickly as Riis' eyes widened.

He let out a shaky, explosive breath. "Okay," he said. His blood rushed in his ears. He turned back to Riis, who had approached him cautiously, and he backed away slightly. Riis froze. "Okay. So. This is... This is getting, like, waaaay too loaded. Way, way too complicated."

Riis' eyes widened. Though he didn't have eyebrows, it had all the aura of raised eyebrows. "Was it not already quite complicated? From the very start?" he said softly.

Drew laughed, frantically. Began gathering his things, hands shaking. "Yes! Yes, you see. That. That is my point. It was already complicated. It got almost simple for a moment, but it's barreling back up the graph to *even more complicated,* and frankly, I can't deal. I can't deal! I don't... don't have the emotional capacity for this." He was babbling.

Riis was silent. Staring at him. The line was back between his big dark eyes.

"Bye. I will, uh, see you around," Drew blabbed out, and then bolted out the room, down the stairs, and slammed out an emergency exit that failed to scream, though the sign above it sincerely promised him it would.

The air was abrasively cold when he hit the outside, and the stinging burn of it felt like relief. Summer was limping in, fading quickly each and every night. Spring had been a short, sweet gasp; a supposition that maybe warmth would happen someday. But the impending summer seemed determined to stay cold, and soon enough it would be Fall, and he would get the switch and turn into what he'd always been told he would. And then it would be winter again, with all its endless harshness. *Good.*

Drew whipped out his tablet, hands shaking. Meant to call Amy. Commiserate on this, or perhaps just talk about nothing, nothing at all. She would know which option to go with. She knew him so well; better than he knew himself. Especially in this moment, when his own body felt foreign.

As he unlocked his tablet, though, a bulletin jumped to the front of the screen.

FRIEND OR FOE? EMNI PRESENCE AT ENSEEO ACADEMY AND THE CREATURE'S CLOSE BOND WITH THE SQUIRE OF SOL II

Fuck.

16

The Article

FRIEND OR FOE? EMNI PRESENCE AT ENSEEO
ACADEMY
& THE CREATURE'S CLOSE BOND WITH THE SQUIRE
OF SOL II

Recently, this reporter got an exclusive interview with one Prince Sebastian of the House of the King Admiral. It was meant to be a short discussion on his recent visit to Americas University of Enseeos. Now, while Prince Sebastian can make a catch-free fishing trip fascinating, I wasn't really anticipating much from this interview, barring perhaps a few zingers and quips.

Ever full of surprises, Prince Admiral Sebastian (perhaps a little loosened by the setting, a bar he had insisted on meeting me at) dished a certain secret about his visit—which was apparently not just to recognize the efforts of the school and officially commiserate with the future Knight of Sol II. It was to check up on a certain—turns out, related—situation.

Since the beginning of this calendar year, there has been an Emni in attendance at the Americas University of Enseeos.

"It's been going to classes and everything," Prince Seb said between sips of top shelf wine. "I'm not supposed to really tell folks yet. I mean, my dad might get mad, but, well, it is relevant, you know! Drew's, like, hanging out with it all the time. They sit together in all their *censored* classes. I know, I basically shadowed the little *censored* the whole time I was there. Some little *censored* even said Drew volunteered to be on the Emni's team for Wargames. Wargames!" Seb then dissolved into laughter and went on to regale me with a highly detailed play-by-play retelling of his involvement with the Wargame, ending with his decided defeat of the Emni on the field. "It was sad, really," he said—by this point he was more than a tad sloshed. "It tried its best. Like, it really honestly looked as if it wanted to rip me apart, by the end. I was too quick for it, though." He then proceeded to do finger guns, shouting pew pew pew pew and 'shooting' at the other customers.

After the interview, I did some digging and sought confirmation. The short and homely guidance counselor of the school crassly avoided commenting, and in fact was rather insulting. One student, name omitted, did agree to give a statement, however. "He's always interrupting our history class, spewing all this bull about how Emni are perfect and humans are basically an invasive species," this student said. "Drew can't get enough of it, though. Even stayed behind after class once to hear more of his lies."

While peace has been considered a standard, sought-after goal since the devastating use of the weapon that thus marked the end of the war over one hundred and eighty years ago now, this reporter must question if we have truly reached the point where an Emni should walk free amongst the young adults of our most elite. *The youngest student at Americas University of Enseeos is barely eighteen. Squire Drew—who seems to have fallen prey to the propaganda of this creature—only just turned twenty this past summer. These are, essentially, our children that we have exposed to—at best—the bias of the opposing side.*

At worst, these are dangers we haven't seen on Earth II for nearly two decades. The history of the Emni presence here being, at this point, a horror story that might be thrown around campfires by our precious youth; children who would never dream that the reality we face here is indeed just that: reality. There is an Emni on Earth II, walking amongst us, eating our food, and learning our secrets.

While we have acknowledged our mistakes in the war, the Emni have never offered so much as an apology for their actions. Even today, radical terrorist groups spring up on Drune and must be stamped out. Our most conscious efforts to bring education and privilege to our lesser-evolved alien counterparts are often met with scorn and even violence.

The peace we claim is tenuous at best.

Why, then, have we allowed the enemy—not only on our planet, not only in our schools, but also, I must wonder—barely six blocks from Capital Hull?

The fallout of this 'exchange program' has yet to be revealed. If it is true that this alien invader has polluted the mind of the Squire of Sol II, however, truly—what kind of a future awaits us?

17

Red

Y ou can call me Red," the woman said, bluntly. Drew glared up at her. Up. High up. Very, very tall, that one. Her doughy face cut a round shadow across the sky. Her shoulders were all bulky paleness in the dim morning light. She was decked out in the traditional grunt fatigues, complete with dirty gray tank top and camo vest. Dog tags glittered at her thick neck, framed by surprisingly soft waves of steel gray hair.

"Great," he snapped. Amy was snickering. "Wonderful. And why, exactly, are you called Red?"

She shrugged one of those enormous pasty shoulders. "It's a nickname. I think it's probably 'cause I had red hair as a kid."

"Ah. Makes sense. Makes. Sense," he said through his teeth.

Amy was silently hysterical.

Red had shown up as they were waiting for the trolley. He had managed to avoid all his mom's calls for the past twelve hours, but she had apparently decided to act anyway. A Grunt. She had sent a Grunt to protect him.

Great. There went his dwindling social life.

There went Riis, too.

He'd decided last night he'd been wrong. Very, very wrong. He *could* deal. In fact, he absolutely *wanted* to 'deal.' He wanted to say this to Riis, wanted to fucking kill that xenophobic newsie as well as everyone who had talked to him, and had planned to gather as many varieties of pickles as he could and bring them to Riis and tell him all of this. But now here was Red, and somehow he doubted that was still an option.

His tablet rang again. His mom, again. Great.

He swiped the end-call.

Then, Red's tablet rang.

Drew flinched as she immediately answered it—serenely, as if she wasn't doing just the worst thing she could in this moment do.

"Put him on." His mom's voice was *hard.*

Red nodded sagely and handed Drew the tablet.

"Eh… hey, Mom," he said haltingly.

She stared.

He grimaced back.

"You are not to attempt to evade the Grunt. You are not to *interact with* your new 'friend' again. You are to let the Grunt *do her job* and you *shall* be giving an interview clearing the air about the… *situation* this weekend."

The door slammed, heartily, on his freedom. He groaned. "Mom, an interview? In the middle of the school year? Really? Do you seriously think that's—"

"It's absolutely necessary. I mean, for goodness sake, kid, we have a very important interplanetary peace talk coming up, Seb's coronation, your knighting… just take it easy on me for once? Now. No evading the Grunt. No further interactions with the Emni. Go to school. Goodbye." She hung up.

The trolley chugged up beside them. They got on. Red hopped up after them with a Gruntly "hup!"

He gritted his teeth.

The ride to school went relatively quickly; very few people

pulling the cord to stop. Upon their arrival, however, it became clear actually getting into the school would not go so easily.

The green in front was swarming with newsies.

As they pushed off the trolley and were noticed, Drew saw the excitement pop across the faces of a few with cameras, a few with tablets at the ready, microphones poised, and he grimaced before they moved swarm-like towards him.

"Aw fuck," Amy said.

Drew was surely, at this point, flat-out dying.

Abruptly, though, Red was before him. She caught his arm and led him forward. "No comment. Move aside. No comment," she said, with all her sage yet forceful neutrality, and he was suddenly, fiercely grateful for her obtrusive presence.

The gratitude didn't last.

Red was not, apparently, the kind of Grunt that waited poised outside of his classroom, ready to act only if something were to go down. Instead, she followed him in. He absolutely cringed, glancing quickly around for Riis, ready to shoot him an apologetic stare at least, but… nothing.

No sign of him.

Riis had never—truly, never—missed a single class.

Perhaps *especially* not history, where he was essentially teaching it, much to the official Teach's disdain.

Drew sat down on his customary cushion, which had of course become the cushion next to Riis, though they still never really acknowledged each other publicly. Their friendship existed in the space between other social interactions. Protected, in that way.

Or possibly it was just that Riis had always been willing to help him save face.

The question Riis had asked over winter break, about whether or not they'd still socialize—as well as Drew's response—burned and churned in his gut.

Drew felt a very real twinge in his chest as Red plopped down on Riis' cushion. Whipped out her tablet and started playing some banal game involving farming or something. There were scattered stares and snickers, and a few truly *infuriating* looks of sympathy from the class, but little attention was by and large paid to his new giant Grunt. Selene of the house of the Secretary, he noticed, was also being trailed by a hulking ex-soldier. She looked about as happy about it as he was sure he did. The grunts nodded at each other as Selene and her new beast walked in, but otherwise did not acknowledge one another.

"Alright, then," Teach started, seeming frankly relieved to not have her co-teach. "I know there's a lot of excitement today, but let's get started…"

Drew tried to pay attention, he did. She started talking about the first use of the weapon, though, and his mind wandered. Surprisingly not to the imminent presence of the switch in his chest, but instead to Riis, and what he'd have to say about this. 'A lot' was probably the answer. It seemed like the kind of thing Riis would definitely have a lot to say about.

And then he thought of Riis, standing with him on Drune.

"I won't flip it."

"I know. Oh, I know."

Drew hesitated. Then whipped out his tablet. Tried to look like he was taking notes as he quickly shot out a message to Riis. Short, simple. To the point.

Drew: Hey, are you ok??

Riis didn't respond for a long time. When he did, it was also rather short, and stuttered the breath in Drew's lungs.

Riis: No.

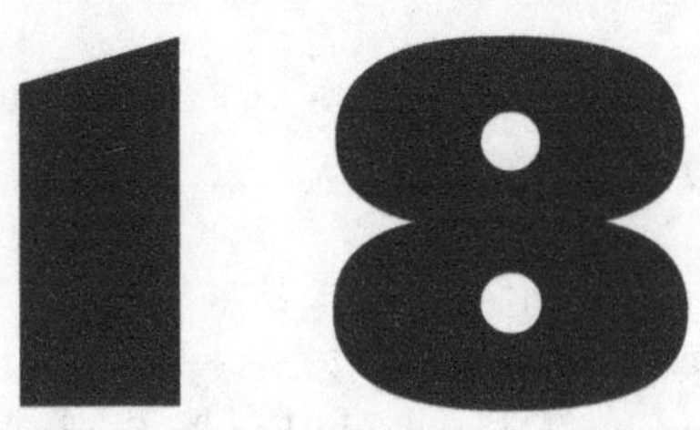

Fabulous

Drew: No?? What does no mean what can I do
Riis: Nothing. It's too late, Drew.
Drew: It's not. Don't fucking say that
Riis: It is, though. We were intending to release an interview with me at the end of the year. I was going to introduce myself, reveal myself as a student. It was all going to be rather controlled. This was not part of the plan.
Drew: so? That's not good enough, it's not good enough to just be like 'oh well'
Drew: no giving up!
Drew: I mean so what, it wasn't part of the plan. Change the plan.
Riis: I have changed it.
Drew: ok, cool, what next then? How can I help?
Riis: I am going back to Drune.

All the air came out of Drew's lungs in a rush.

He stared at it. The last message. When he wrote back, his hands shook.


```
Drew: NO.
```


Riis didn't respond to that.

The day wore on. Drew could hardly focus, hardly think. He felt gouged out, empty in the soul, positively barren. It couldn't end like this.

Riis was finally connecting, doing good work. He talked semi-regularly to Lara now, for instance. Had made amends to Fay. Even Duncan sometimes joked with him, provided Drew was nowhere near.

And Drew. Drew was his friend. Even if he wasn't brave enough to eat with him in public… he was Riis' friend.

It couldn't end like this.

It was during lunch he started trying to evade Red.

For someone so huge and hulking, she moved quickly as a whip. More than once he found himself cornered. She made no comment on it, but started following him into the bathroom, too. Which was, you know. Fucking rude.

He didn't stop trying, though, could not stop trying, had to get to Riis, shout at him for giving up so easily, maybe. Apologize for his own petty freak-out, even though Riis had definitely messed up, too —the drug thing, that had been bad. Not great, anyway. Arguably more of a cultural misunderstanding. Not *malicious*, at any rate.

That didn't *matter* anymore, was the point. The idea that their last interaction would be their last interaction felt like a stab through the heart.

He finally achieved not at least seeing Red when he burst around a corner and out onto the green. Forgetting—because of course he did—the danger of that.

Immediately he was swarmed.

Drew shrank as they all burst forward, as microphones were shoved in his face, as questions were shot out, rapid-fire, *"Squire! Is it true you spent time alone with the Emni?"*

"You played a Wargame together, correct?"

"Has the Emni ever acted violently?"

"No!" he shouted, and for a moment there was silence. Then a further barrage of questions, and he felt the door open behind him, felt Red's hand start to come down solid on his shoulder, and he knew, suddenly, what he had to do.

Drew shoved her off; ducked away. Grabbed one of the microphones being waved in his face.

Silence and stillness again. He saw the bright spark of flashing cameras. Video cameras trained on him. Jeezus.

He spoke, and his voice shook, but he still spoke, "The Emni has been nothing but civil, and a fabulous addition to the class. Y'all are ruining what's actually a pretty good thing, so kindly *fuck off*. I mean," and he felt absolutely insane—crazy, really, "if we're gonna learn to live together, we should really learn to live together!"

Then Red yanked him back through the doors and into the school. He dropped the microphone. The doors slammed shut to a positive explosion of chaos and questions, newsies bursting forth in a wave.

Amy gaped at him, just inside. She wasn't the only one. On the TV over the fireplace in the grand foyer, he saw it: the doors to the school, and then a newsie stepping onto the screen, holding her own microphone, speaking quickly. "You heard it here, folks, from the lips of the Squire of Sol II himself, the Emni is *fabulous* and we need to 'kindly' *bleep off*, wow, I mean—"

Drew bolted for the atrium.

Red was still at the door, trying to hold it closed against the onslaught with one beefy arm and struggling to lock it with her other hand, and he heard her let out a shout, but he didn't stop. Ran through the atrium, into the hallway in the back.

Up the winding stairs, feet positively stampeding, his black chainmail shaking with each step like a thousand tiny ringing bells.

Knocked frantically, hammering on Riis' door, and Riis opened it almost immediately and he burst inside, grabbed Riis by the shoulders, and shouted at top volume, "You're not leaving! I don't care what I have to do, I don't care how much social suicide I have to commit, you've *barely gotten started* and you're doing *fantastic* work, and you are *fabulous* and you are *not leaving!*"

Riis blinked.

Drew felt suddenly ridiculous. He let go of Riis' shoulders.

"Drew…" Riis started, hesitantly.

Drew let out a groan, pushing past him into the room, pacing. Pacing over the orange and red rug, past the lush low sofas and the darkly stained wooden cabinet and the beads, pacing and taking it all in like a drug, god, he just… it couldn't happen. "You're not leaving," he said again.

"…Alright."

"Huh?" he reared on Riis, who was looking at him, squinting slightly, the line between his eyes again.

Riis blinked his absolute most slow blink. Didn't nod this time, just clicked twice. "I'm not leaving."

Drew breathed.

They stared at each other.

"I shall, at the very least, do my best not to leave," Riis continued, rather cautiously. "No one has insisted on it yet, at any rate. They still might, though."

Drew nodded, dumbly.

They stared at one another.

He felt it. A charge that seemed to leap between them, and Riis looked away first, picking at his horns, eyes suddenly wide, Drew heard his breath *hitch*, so very slightly, and Drew wanted—

Drew wanted—

Knock knock knock!

"Fucking hell," Drew swore.

Riis moved to open the door. Seemed shaky—almost relieved, to be honest—for the interruption, and Drew flushed, looking away.

He expected Red. Instead, Amy flounced past Riis into the room, grinning. "Hey boys!" she crowed. "Drew, you totally *lost her*, she's frantic, running all around the school, shouting about not getting paid enough. Good one, kid!" She patted his head, scritching once, and then reared on Riis and Drew flinched. "So, Riis. Nice to meet you."

"I…" Riis seemed distinctly startled. "We've met."

"Not really, though. Not the way we should've. That's on me, and I'm, like, sincerely very sorry about that. Can we start over?"

"…Ah. Alright. Thank you. Quite nice to meet you." Riis held out his hand cautiously.

Amy shook it enthusiastically. Something in Drew clenched.

He hadn't realized it.

He'd wanted this.

He burst out laughing and they both stared at him. He rolled his eyes skyward, though, and said, still smiling, "Alright, great. Now we all know each other. What do we do now?"

Redder

It was at that point that Red barged in and grabbed Drew by the ear. Riis lost all his diligent politeness and burst forward, hissing like a feral cat. Amy started shouting about Drew's rights like he was being arrested; Red barked at Riis that he had to *"stand back I am authorized to—"* and Drew shouted—squeaking, shrieking—"Oh my god! I'm going, I'm going! I'm going! Just please *calm the fuck down, jeezus!"*

He walked out with his hands shaking in the air. Also like he was being arrested. Amy let out a huff, making like she was going to follow him, but he shot out quickly, "No, no, stay here. Just... come up with a plan? Please? You're the two smartest people I know. I'm sure you can think of *something...*" At which point Red shoved him forward and he tripped out the door.

The last thing he saw was Riis' wide eyes. He stood frozen, one arm still slightly outstretched, watching Drew go.

Fuck.

Okay, fuck.

****

"Hey, Shrink Kanak. Uh, do you have time right now?"

"For you, Drew? Sometimes, yes."

"Great. Great, uh," he shut the door behind himself, moved to sit down, and immediately, Red slammed the door back open.

He gaped as Red then turned, gently shut it again, and sank down on the floor by the door, whipping out her tablet and opening up what must've been her favorite beep booping farming game.

"Eh… *pardon me…*" a positively frigid voice behind him. Drew turned.

Shrink Kanak had risen to her full, less than impressive height. Her round face tightened into a bundle of absolute offense-based defense and Drew instinctively flinched. "My sessions are *private*. Always. Who are you?"

Red looked up. "Huh?"

Shrink Kanak positively glowered. "Who. Are. You?"

Red blinked. Shrugged. "You can call me Red."

"She, eh. Had red hair as a kid," Drew supplied helpfully.

"Okay. Red. And you are here because…?"

"Hired by the Knight of Sol II," Red said, dropping her eyes easily back on her game. "I'm here to protect the young Squire from a potential threat."

"Potential threat?" Drew snapped. "Seriously, if he wanted to kill me, he would've already. Hell, it's my life, and I say Riis has *permission to kill me,* if he so wishes, so if you would please—"

"No can do, Mr. Drew, your mother was very clear about my job. I'm here to protect you."

"Okay, but he's not even here right now, sooooo I can only assume you're trying to protect me from Shrink Kanak?" Drew shrieked out. "'Cause she's the only other one here right now, and I'm pretty sure I could take her!"

"No, you couldn't. But shut up for a second, Drew," Shrink Kanak snapped, and Drew flinched. Kanak stared Red down for a moment, and then let out a huff. Walked primly around her desk and squatted delicately before Red like Red was a sulking child.

Red glanced up for barely a second, clearly distracted by her game, and then her eyes widened slightly and she looked up again, meeting Shrink Kanak's gaze.

"Red, right?" Shrink Kanak started sweetly, and without waiting for Red to answer continued, "So. It's my job to speak to the students. Guide them. Counsel them. Help them with their troubles and their woes. Be a *listening ear.* Notably—a listening ear far removed from any and all *prying ears.* I consider this space sacred. This office can transform into a den of intense, emotionally raw therapy and revival, when I am able to do my job."

Drew actually snorted at this point; he couldn't quite help himself. He certainly could help himself to cut that shit out, though, as soon as Shrink Kanak sniffed hard and continued: "Your presence here invades this sacred space. Prevents me from *doing my job.* So please, would you kindly *wait the fuck outside?*"

Drew held his breath.

Red blinked, eyes slightly wide.

Then dropped her gaze back to her game, "No can do. Sorry, lady. The terms of my job were very clear. Protect Drew."

Shrink Kanak literally looked like she might explode in the head.

Red glanced up at her again, and then down. Then, to Drew's immense surprise, flushed slightly and reached into her pocket and whipped out a pair of earbuds. "I, eh... can do this, though. I guess," she said hesitantly, pushing them into her ears. She shifted a bit before going back to her farming game, now only a faint doot doot emanating from the earbuds.

Drew let out an explosive, positively exhausted sigh. "Well. That's like a full fucking mile further than I ever got with her."

Shrink Kanak reared on him, eyes made of *fire* and he flinched. "What the fuck is this, Drew?" she snapped.

"My, eh. My mom hired her. 'Cause of—"

"The article," she let out a huff. Came around and plopped forcefully down on her cushion. "I swear to god, that fucking dogshit article. I think I made that newsie crap his pants, you know. Pity he didn't put that part in there."

Drew gaped at her. Then burst out laughing.

She shot him a pointed look that *almost* looked affectionate. Let out a huff and leaned forward, pushing her little bowl of nuts forward as well. "Well. If this is as good as we're gonna get for now, might as well take advantage of it. What can I help you with today, Drew?"

Drew snorted. "Um, well. *This*, for starters. But also, *that*. And then, *the other thing.*"

Shrink Kanak laughed. "This being Red."

"Yeah."

"That being… the article?"

"Uh huh."

"The other thing… Riis."

Swoop. "You guessed it."

Her eyes narrowed.

Drew found himself immediately babbling, "I mean, Riis could also be 'that.' 'That' or 'the other thing.' But, eh. 'This' is Red. Yeah."

She stared at him. He laughed, weakly. "Okay," she said after a moment, taking pity on him thank *god*, "so I have a solution."

"Oh thank fuck—"

"I don't normally like to give advice."

"Okay, bullshit, but okay—"

"But I'm going to say right now, Drew, if you don't *stand up to your mother*, no plan will work."

Drew breathed. She looked pointedly at him, and he looked away.

"I do stand up to her."

"Drew," she said. "Do you want Riis to fail? Do you want him to go home? Do you want to just *never see him again?*"

"Hey!" Drew said, shrinking.

"You don't," she finished. "So, it's time to cut the bullshit, don't you think? I don't mean making snarky comments now and then. I mean *standing up to her*. And I have a plan. A plan that could at least help in the short term. But it only works if you can *stand up to her*."

****

—AMY created the group BADASS ALIEN BUDDIESSS—
Amy: HEY HEY HEY BUDDIIIIIEEEESSSS
Drew: Amy. Amy oh my god
Riis: Hello, Drew.
Drew: This is so NOT what I meant by 'a plan'
Riis: This is but a piece of the plan. We worked together on it, along with Shrink Kanak. I believe it might even work out well.
Drew: ok great. And I mean it's great to be able to talk to you guys but Riis I doubt you came up with the GROUP NAME
Riis: No, that was admittedly Amy's idea.
Amy: BADASS ALIEN BITCHESSSSS
Amy: I mean BUDDIIIIIIESSS
Drew: jeezus
Amy: he made me name it buddies instead of bitches :3 i sometimes still forget
Riis: Yes. I have seen enough of your movies to know the other term is rather crude.
Drew: uh yeah
Drew: i mean sometimes it can be like affectionate but yeah
Amy: kinda a complicated word
Drew: for sure
Riis: …Anyway.
Drew: yeah let's get back on topic
Amy: so i still think we do it like this~ we stage a fight and Riis saves Drew in front of everyone <3 :-O <3
Drew: uum no
Riis: I think maybe no.
Riis: The plan we are currently formulating with Shrink Kanak does have merit.

Riis: Essential information is that Shrink Kanak wishes for you to come into her office tomorrow at 1000 hours.

Drew: will you be there??

Riis: Well, yes. I am a key player in our plan.

Drew: ok cool. Cool.

****

The next day, in History, Drew watched the clock. As the shorter hand neared the 10, he started to feel something like an electric charge shivering over his skin. He stayed chill about it, didn't start madly giggling, as was his first instinct. But he did start rapping his fingers rhythmically on the desk, shifting awkwardly on his cushion, feeling the absence of Riis beside him—and the rather striking presence of Red—like the stars were misaligned. Amy was also absent. Because of the plan? He still didn't quite know what the plan was.

He was up out of his seat, things already gathered, even before the bell rang. 0958. Just enough time to run up there and be *right on time*. Teach shot a look his way as he ducked past her, but whatever. He was the freaking Squire of Sol II, whatever, whatever.

Whatever.

Red followed him wordlessly.

Drew was kind of nervous, truth be told. Kind of doubting what was about to happen. Riis had described the scheme as 'an educational lesson focused on the goal of bringing certain truths to light within this "Red" rather than attempting to sway your mother.'

Amy had said, 'we r gonna SHOW RED WUTS WUT >:-D .'

So, possibly, they were going to kill her.

That'd be kinda crazy. Possibly impossible, too, she really was *very large*.

Either way, he'd decided to trust them, so he knocked fast on Shrink Kanak's door just as the bell rang and students started spilling out of classrooms. He heard a nearby shuffle and realized with a start Red was already pulling her earbuds out in preparation, and Drew felt a very unexpected twinge of affection for her. He really did hope they weren't planning on trying to kill her.

Shrink Kanak opened the door. Orange robes today. "Hello!" she all but sang, and Drew opened his mouth but she was focused on Red, who, upon realizing this, visibly *flushed*, seeming a tad floored.

"Eh... hello."

"I'd like to apologize in advance for this. This is... most unusual. I try not to get too involved, but there's something that concerns me, with regards to Drew, that I thought you ought to know about." Shrink Kanak's head was tilted delicately up; she was not breaking eye contact with Red.

Red's face still matched her name. She reached a slightly fumbling fist into her pocket, producing her tablet and saying quickly, "Okay, I'll get his Mom on a call, let me just—"

"No! Eh, no. You misunderstand." Shrink Kanak dropped a light hand on Red's beefy arm. The tablet lowered, oh so slightly. "It's you I'd like to talk to."

"...oh?"

"Yes."

"Oh! Okay. Eh. Why?"

"Just promise you'll hear me out?"

"...Um..."

"Please?"

"Well... well *sure*, I guess, I mean—"

"Wonderful! Please step inside," Shrink Kanak said, standing back with a flourish of creamsicle robes, and Drew walked in floating on air, utterly dazed by this point. He caught a glimpse of Amy and Riis on the other side of the door and tried very hard to communicate with his eyes how utterly gay and fabulous that *whole goshdarn interaction* had been, but at that moment Red stepped fully inside the office, still more than a little frazzled, saw Riis, and immediately snapped out of it and went to grab at Drew again.

Drew shrieked like a small child and ducked. Amy raised her own hands, like *she* was being arrested, yelling "Woah woah woah woah!" Riis stiffened and his eyes widened but he didn't pull any angry cat moves this time, perhaps now understanding the situation a little better.

Shrink Kanak immediately bellowed out through all the excitement, though, "You agreed to hear me out!"

Pause.

Red looked ready to blow a gasket. "The terms of my job are just, like, *super* clear. I protect Drew. I protect him from the threat of the Emni. I—"

"He's not a *threat!*" Amy bellowed.

"I do indeed come in peace," Riis said.

There was a weighted silence. Drew couldn't help it; he giggled.

Riis shot him a look that told Drew he clearly understood what he had just said and why Drew found it funny, and Drew started laughing harder. He raised his hands, taking a breath, trying to calm down. "Okay," he said. "Okay okay okay. So. Can you just... just hear them out, Red? Please? And if you do, I swear I won't try and run away anymore today at all. Okay?"

Red stared at him. A bit of her cheek twitched. She seemed, however, to be seriously weighing the pros and cons of this.

"Fine," she finally said, "but I won't be keeping any secrets. I report back to the Knight of Sol II at the end of each shift, and there are *very* specific questions, and I *will* be answering them. But. I guess I did, eh. Promise the nice lady..."

Shrink Kanak positively *beamed.* Red went redder.

"Please, sit down," Shrink Kanak said, gesturing at a cushion. Red awkwardly sat. Her fingers twitched, almost like she was fighting a baser instinct to take out the game, but she remained focused on Kanak, who... turned out the lights.

Pulled down the wide white blind over her window.

Drew turned to Riis in the dark, tried to mouth, *"what the fuck?"*

Riis blinked. Tilted his head, clearly confused. Amy stuck out her tongue.

"This is just a little educational slide show we made for you," Shrink Kanak said lightly, and pushed a button on a positively ancient looking remote aimed at the equally elderly looking projector on her ceiling, and the small room was suddenly full of music that sounded like it could've been the intro for one of Riis' movies.

The slideshow immediately started, and Drew felt the ground open up under him as the first slide came up, words in bold courier new formatting, the letters stamped it seemed across the blind: WHO ARE WE TO INTERRUPT FRIENDSHIP?

Ok. Okay, they were fucked.

"Who are we to interrupt friendship?" Amy bellowed. She had, he realized, notes. Her tablet out, her face scrunched and joyous, she was reading off the tablet, nodding slightly. Riis looked just totally calm and chill beside her, like this wasn't fucking insane.

"Riis and Drew didn't hit it off right away," Amy spoke, and then a freaking video came up of him falling in the mud, he hadn't even known that *existed*— "For obvious reasons, both felt a little weird about the other. However, that weirdness soon turned to affection…"

A shot of the school covered in snow. Winter Break implications, he guessed.

Drew was absolutely going to die.

"While it is an unorthodox friendship," Riis cut in, speaking lilting and bold, fuck, "I admit I have grown to… to care rather deeply for Drew," Drew blinked. Riis continued, pointedly, "and would never at all wish to harm him."

"The misconceptions from the general public are just that— misconceptions." Shrink Kanak now, oh lord, and the slide shifted to several angry human faces, the words 'stock image' watermarked all over it, *christ*. "To claim that this Emni is a threat just based on what he is suggests that all Emni are a threat. Is this what *you* believe?"

The slideshow ended.

They all looked so *proud*.

Red actually hesitated.

Drew gaped at her. He felt like he'd just seen some kind of shit propaganda commercial to elect friendship. But, if it had worked…

"No," Red said thoughtfully. "No, I don't believe that about Emni. I'm sure Emni are just as diverse as humans."

Ho shit.

"I'm just doing my job, though. So, yeah. We're gonna go," Red said, rising and flicking her neck to the side and stretching her thick arms, cracking some joints so loudly that Drew flinched. "C'mon, Drew. You're not running away from me anymore today, remember?"

Drew shut his eyes. Jeezus, maybe he needed smarter friends.

"Wait," Riis said softly.

Drew stopped. Riis glanced quickly at him, but then focused his attention on Red. He bowed his head very slightly, just dipping it before raising his chin high. "You are a warrior."

Red blinked dumbly. "Uh-huh."

"I come from a line of warriors myself."

"Okay…"

"We follow a certain code. There are… ones we vow to protect. Much like you have vowed to protect Drew." And then, like a fucking madman Riis abruptly slammed the heel of his palm against the point of one of his centermost horns. The hand came away with a drop of blood. "I vow to protect him as well," Riis said, and his voice was quiet, yet sure.

Silence.

Drew breathed. Stared at Riis, who was just… not looking at him at all, was cutting his curious shadow in the still-dark room, was staring earnestly up at Red with his big dark eyes, was—

"Oh… okay. I guess you can do that when I'm not here. I'm here now, though. No need," Red said bluntly, and grabbed Drew by the arm.

Drew jerked back.

"Drew," Red snapped, rearing on him, "You promised—"

"What's it matter! I'm going to anyway!" Drew found himself shouting. He felt alive in his skin, he felt like he could feel Riis' heartbeat in the air emanating from the tiny wound, which he'd gently pressed the sleeve of his stupid lovely button-down shirt to, each motion so small, so delicate, even a fucking *blood oath* to protect him performed with precision and loveliness, oh fuck—

"What? Huh?" Red snapped.

Drew was a live wire, thrumming with electricity, "I'm! Going! To! Anyway! You literally can't stop me, alright! No one can! If it's the last thing I fucking do I'll *still* visit him, *still* spend time with him, so yeah, fuck you and your 'keeping me safe' BS, you're only making it so I have to lie and sneak around!"

Dead silence. Red blinked rather quickly, staring blankly at him.

"So," Drew snapped, and his ears were *burning*, but he pressed on, albeit shakily, "I *will* sneak out. I *will* get away from you again. I *will* go see him," and Riis was staring at him wide-eyed and absolutely still, and Drew pointedly ignored this as hard as he could as he kept talking, "so it's really, like, in your best interest to just… just let me see him," he finished lamely.

"He could get into all sorts of danger if he's sneaking around," Amy quickly supplied, finally being helpful.

Quiet.

Red chewed on this.

"Well," she said hesitantly. "I do want to make sure you're *safe*, first and foremost."

"I would even argue," Shrink Kanak chimed in, "that in my professional opinion, you will be causing Drew *emotional damage* by keeping him from one of his only two real friends."

Oh lawrd Drew was literally going to *burn up alive through sheer embarrassment.*

He gritted his teeth though, whole face static and hot, and said, "Yup. Eh, damage. Wanna… avoid that, right?"

"Emotional."

Drew snapped his head around. Riis was squinting at him, the line crinkled up between his eyes again, all of him soft and gentle and just *thoroughly amused*. "She said emotional damage, Drew. Don't forget the 'emotional.' It *is* relevant."

Drew shut his eyes. "Right," he said.

"Well," Red said, looking legitimately concerned, oh god bless her, "I wouldn't want that. 'Emotional damage' sounds tough. I'm sure your mother wouldn't want that, either."

Quiet. They all were poised and still.

"Well. Alright then," Red said.

Drew let out a breath like a popped balloon. Amy whooped. Shrink Kanak grinned. And Riis... Riis seemed to relax; exhale in such a miniscule way it was hardly noticeable, but Drew saw it.

Something warm fluttered softly in his gut, gentle amidst the wreckage of what had contained it.

Jeezus. Blood oath. What right did he *have*, seriously, how dare he—

"But. I'm not about to start lying to my employer. She *will* know they are interacting. I guess I might just tell her that I'm not comfortable harming Drew by forcing him to do things he doesn't want to," Red said thoughtfully. "I suppose she never said 'forcefully drag him away from the Emni,' technically. So, yeah! I won't lie, but I won't stop them anymore. But I won't lie."

Everyone quickly looked at Drew, who shut his eyes. "Eh," he said hesitantly. "That's fine. Um. I'll deal with... that fallout." Shrink Kanak was smiling small and wry when he opened his eyes.

"Okay," she said softly, "Okay. The team is back together. Fabulous. Now, team... time to work outwards. What do we do then about *everybody else?*"

20

Pickled Eggs

R iis walked hesitantly into history class the next day, face blank.

Silence.

Drew, as they'd planned, raised a hand and spoke. "Welcome back, Riis," he said delicately, hyper-aware that this was their first real and honest most public interaction. "I saved a seat for you."

"Thank you very much, Drew," Riis said, sounding just really fucking practiced about it, but luckily no one seemed to notice this. Instead, they merely stared as Drew scooted over, patting the seat between him and Red.

Riis sat down. The eyes of the class still on them, Drew reached into his backpack and produced a jar. "I brought you your pickled eggs," he said.

Riis blinked.

Drew flushed.

This had not been part of the plan. This was pure improvisation, inspired by the fact that Drew had seen them this morning in the corner store while he was getting his on-the-go coffee and thought, *This is exactly the kinda gross shit Riis likes*, and then been utterly powerless to do anything but buy them.

He felt bad that 'being openly nice' was the plan, when it came to their classmates. Bad that it hadn't just been reality already. Bad that he'd had to have someone point out to him hey, you hold social sway, shitty little royalty. Maybe use that to help Riis, rather than worrying you're gonna lose it by doing so.

Riis took the jar, delicately. "Thank you," he said after a moment. Softly.

Drew gritted his teeth, feeling a by-now-familiar swoop. "Don't mention it."

****

"You put on a lovely show this morning."
"Ha."
"The eggs were a sweet touch."
"Seriously, how do you know, like, *everything?*"
"Hmm. I'm actually not a Med Caste, I'm an advisor to our lord President. All hail."
"Oh my god. That is *blasphemy.*"
"And what we're all doing isn't?"
"No." Drew's voice was a hard line drawn in the metaphorical sand.

Shrink Kanak raised a single haughty eyebrow at him, clearly biting back a grin.

****

"Shrink Kanak definitely approves of how this is playing out," Drew said gleefully to Riis and Amy the next day at lunch. They'd decided that today they would meet in a small courtyard near the back of the school to eat together, as it was largely less populated. Yesterday they'd tried eating in the Caf, making a big show of eating with Riis. Lara, her friend, and even Fay at one point had rather cautiously joined them. Well, Fay hadn't been very cautious about it. Drew still wasn't sure she'd realized she was sitting at their table at the end of the day, but it still counted.

Duncan had sat nearby and stared big sad eyes at them.

They'd decided rather quickly, for mental health reasons, lunch could remain private.

"She does," Riis said shortly. He was sucking pickled eggs into his mouth. Literally sucking them down one at a time. It was utterly disgusting, yet also… doing funny things to Drew. He was trying not to pay attention.

"She does? Huh?"

Riis shrugged. Glanced at him, and then away. Paused with an egg against his lips and said, "I speak with her regularly as well," before sucking it down.

Drew shifted uncomfortably. "Really."

"Well, yes. We're required to."

"Once a quarter."

"Oh? Is it only that much? In my culture it is suggested we seek guidance daily," Riis said shortly.

Amy cackled. "You're a therapy ho just like Drew," she said, with no small amount of glee. "No wonder you two kids connected."

"Ho? What is a ho?" Riis asked seriously, and Drew and Amy both exploded with laughter.

Against the tree on the edge of the courtyard, Red let out a huff as she clearly lost some part of the game beep booping on her tablet.

****

"The Grunt I hired tells me you're not listening to me, Drew."

Drew stared solidly back at his mom on the tablet. He felt a twinge, still, of frantic shame.

Not a powerful enough twinge. But it stuck around, even in the face of a fierce wave of pride, pride for what he was doing.

What Riis was doing, really.

"I'm not."

"No, you're not."

"It wasn't a question. It was a statement of fact. I'm *not* listening to you, when it comes to this. To him."

"...Ah."

Quiet. Then a sharp, "It's an Emni, Drew. An alien. A member of a species that all but made our survival impossible, here, on our own—"

"On a planet in their solar system," he said flatly. In his peripheral vision, Riis shifted slightly. He was staring at Drew, and Drew pointedly did not look up. He rather desperately wanted to, though.

His mom's breathing hitched. Quiet. And then a very hard, "I hope you'll keep these new delusions to yourself during the interview. There's only so much damage control we can handle. Our resources are already run raggedly thin, just from your *explosion* outside of the school. 'Fabulous.' Jeezus, Drew, really."

Drew shut his eyes. Opened them, and smiled, strained and quick. "I'll behave," he said shortly. Her face relaxed at this.

After she'd hung up a few minutes later, he chucked his tablet across the room. Hoped fiercely, in that insane moment, it would break, maybe even explode or burst into flame or something else *decisive* and *chaotic*, but it just flopped to a halt on Riis' plush carpet.

Riis startled, letting out that swear-shaped whistling grunt he made, sometimes. Amy just laughed, though. "Don't worry about it," she said to Riis. "Drew is nothing if not dramatic."

"I am not!" Drew snapped out.

"He cried dramatically!" Amy was cackling, feet up on Riis' stone table, slumped comfortably into his low couch.

"Hey!" Drew shot back. "I resent that."

"Drew said with a dramatic flair!"

"Oh my god!"

"Drew dramatically lamented," Riis deadpanned, and they both jumped, Amy immediately dissolving into hysterics, Drew gaping, Riis just squinting, rather coyly.

"Traitor!"

****

They watched more Star Trek—this time, as a trio. At night when Red was off-duty, by and large, but sometimes in the middle of the day, too: the three of them curled up on the squat couch, Red sitting hunched by the door with her game. Riis had eventually offered her a pillow, and she had accepted, thanking him. That was really as far as their acknowledgement of her had gone, and she in turn seemed to politely ignore them, as well.

There were a few episodes of *Deep Space Nine* that appeared to be mysteriously absent on Flix, so they pirated those, and Drew felt himself freezing when two women embraced and began kissing on screen.

Silence. He could feel Amy sneaking stares at him. He didn't move so much as a muscle, though.

"Are they enacting some kind of secret Starfleet plan involving the exchanging of biological material?" Riis asked quietly, totally deadpan, and Amy choked on her watery tea.

"Riis," Drew said, head in his hands. "No, what? Oh my *god*, Riis…"

Riis, though, whistled harshly and then let out his belting bellow of a laugh, making Amy jump and Drew dissolve into a fit of mad cackling. "You motherfucker," he got out eventually, breathless.

"It amazes me what you will believe I do not know," Riis said smartly, squinting softly at him. Drew grinned, feeling bashful.

Amy shifted between them, then, and they broke eye-contact. Continued to watch the women kiss, and then break apart. The characters then decided it was too tumultuous a destiny, whatever. Parted ways for a heavily implied lifetime, staring longingly at one another before one boarded her vessel, appearing to leave for all eternity in the final shot.

Fuck that, honestly.

****

"Am I cock-blocking you?"

Drew choked on his toothbrush.

Amy stood behind him in their little yellow bathroom in her nightshirt, a twisted look on her face, and he shivered, spat, and looked away from her reflection in the mirror, staring instead at his frothy spit in the sink. "No," he snapped. Not immediately. Not soon enough at all.

In his peripheral vision he saw her nod, slowly. She hesitated. And then added, very gently, "if I am, if you… you want me to leave you and Riis alone…"

"Stop," he snapped, much quicker this time, and she stopped.

He went to bed with his heart in his throat. Shut his eyes and imagined warm arms, warm hands.

Touched himself with his own shaking hands, and desperately hoped for a nice, solid dream as he fell into a shivering sleep.

He barely had to hope anymore. He had them almost nightly, at this point.

****

Riis lay next to him in a field. Strange flowers swayed in the breeze. The sun rested on Drew's skin like hot chainmail, warm and heavy light pressed against every part of him. It was summer again.

He rolled over onto Riis, whose eyes widened and he laughed his belting bellow, the sound reverberating up through Drew's chest. He ducked his head down into Riis' warm neck and *breathed*. He smelled almost briny, like the sea. Clean and good.

Then—as he always was—he was pushed back. Pushed off Riis and onto the ground, but immediately Riis rolled over him, his mouth on Drew's, on his chin, his neck, his ears. He unraveled Drew slowly, whistling out soft language now and then, language Drew couldn't understand, could barely hear.

Riis' knee up between his legs. Riis' hands roving over his chest. Clothing shed slowly, bodies exposed reverently. Hips pressed down against his in a slow grind and he groaned, ached, felt it swelling inside him as their heads tipped together, as Riis whispered his name so softly, and he fell apart.

He woke up aching, fiercely as he had been before falling asleep.

Probably more. Let's be real. As always: much, much more.

News

Are you nervous?"

Drew actually snorted at that and looked quickly away. "About what?" he asked, and his voice was high. There were just a lot of shiny shivering options there.

Shrink Kanak snorted her own small snort, rolling her eyes. "The interview tomorrow."

"Oh. Right. Um… nope."

"Nope?"

"That's honestly about the only thing I'm *not* nervous about."

"…Interesting."

"How is that 'interesting?'"

"What *are* you nervous about?"

Drew froze.

Her eyes narrowed. The slightest, quizzical smile lifted the corner of her lips.

He cackled madly, looking away, pulling at a floppy bit of hair over his eyes, "You know, the switch. My impending Knighthood.

Interplanetary War. The usual. You know?"

She snorted. "I don't think you have to worry about interplanetary war, Drew."

He let out a mad, startled laugh. "Why?"

"It's literally been generations since the one instance where the weapon was used. We're moving forward. Moving into a good place. A peaceful place. This interview, for instance? Big news. A big deal. I'm *assuming*, anyway."

He chewed his lip. "You're assuming right," he said after a moment. It would be a big deal. Especially once the cameras caught his special guest walking onto the stage with him.

Her eyes were light, her mouth still pursed in that small smile. "I want you to know," she suddenly said, very quietly, "I'm very… very *proud* of you, Drew."

Drew actively flinched. She laughed.

Later, walking slowly to his last class of the day, he considered it, though.

His chest was tight. It felt odd. Odd and good, to have someone be proud of him for something he was proud of, too.

****

"Are you nervous?" Drew asked quietly.

"I am unspeakably terrified," Riis deadpanned immediately, and Drew glanced quickly at him, knowing by now this was not a joke. This was just Riis, being blunt and honest as ever.

"Don't be terrified. It'll be great."

"Hm."

"I'll cut in if they start being an asshole to you."

"…thank you."

"Don't mention it."

Riis blinked softly at him. Ugh. *Swoop.* Drew looked away quickly, back at the stage, the positively blinding lights poised and focused on the low table with three cushions around it.

Newsie Steven was speaking. "So, it is my incredible pleasure to welcome not just Drew—Squire of Sol II, haha! But a special guest he *personally* requested to bring along. Let's call him... Riis."

Scattered applause from the live audience. Riis seemed frozen.

Without thinking about it, Drew reached forward. Squeezed his hand, short and fast, and Riis jumped, turned to him.

They stared at each other.

"You're on! Go! Go!" a woman was hissing at them, then, beckoning fast out at the stage, and Drew dropped his hand and stepped forward quickly, used to this by now—he basically had to do three interviews every summer at least—and Riis followed, haltingly.

The applause died almost immediately as they stepped out on stage. There were even scattered gasps. Newsie Steven laughed, nervously. "Well. Come in, eh, gentlemen. Sit down!"

Drew sat. His Mother wasn't in the audience. She'd had to stay with King Admiral as he was doing some kind of peace talk on Drune. He felt like he could *feel* her stare through time and space itself, though, and knew he'd be getting an absolute earful as soon as this particular act of rebellion reached her.

"So," newsie Steven was talking, hands steepled before him on the table. "You two are classmates, eh?"

"Yup." Drew spoke when it became clear Riis wasn't about to.

"Interesting. And how has that... been?"

Drew glanced at Riis. Riis was staring, eyes wide, still looking stunned. Great.

He turned back around, flashing a practiced grin at the cameras, flipping his hair back conveniently in the same motion, and then looked back at Steven, heart hammering. "It's been great! Been really learning a lot. It's nice to get... um, lots of perspectives, you know."

"Lots of *perspectives?* My. Can you tell me more about that, please?"

Drew barely contained a full-body flinch.

At that moment, however, Riis cut in quickly, and his words seemed to spill out like he couldn't contain them, "Perspectives on the war, and the colonization of my people, is what I'm assuming Drew is talking about."

Utter silence.

Okay, wow.

Drew's heart was beating out of his chest.

He laughed, nervously. "Yup. About… all kinds of things…"

"Colonization of your people?" Steven asked, grinning, still grinning like a loon. "What do you mean by that?"

"Do you not know the definition of colonialism?" Riis asked softly. "I learned it on Drune. Standard is not my first language, and I made an assumption it was yours. My apologies, I assumed you would know the word as well."

Drew dropped his head into his hands.

Okay.

Okay, fuck.

Maybe he should've been more nervous about this.

"Excuse me," Steven started, clearly on the hysterical edge of offended, "I—"

"He's not trying to insult you!" Drew shot out quickly. He was shaking, he realized, and quickly lowered his hands, fisting at the hem of his nice chainmail. "He legitimately doesn't think you know the definition…"

"Indeed," Riis said shortly. He blinked, rather quickly. "I make it a practice of mine to not judge ignorance unless it appears to be willful. Obviously, I suppose." And then he gestured at Drew, who absolutely immediately burst out into rather hysterical laughter.

Riis jumped. Squinted fast at him. Looked back at Steven, who was practically gaping.

"I'm sorry, did you just call the Knight of Sol II ignorant?"

"No! He was making a joke *that time*, jeez…" Drew stumbled over the words in the rush to get them out.

"He is a bit, yes. Nothing he can help. Also—he is not *yet* Knight of Sol II."

Drew groaned. Oh lawrd. This. This was crashing.

"I'm sorry, I have to just question the *gall* of that, the—"

Suddenly Steven held a hand to his earpiece, though. His manicured eyebrows shot up. He looked at them with a mad gleam in his eyes before turning and saying quickly into the cameras, "Excuse me, but we've just received an important news update, airing it now. We will be back shortly."

"Cut!" someone bellowed.

Then, there was chaos. Several people, Drew realized, squinting through the light, were whipping out tablets. There was a mad dash and chatter, the sudden noise of several voices overlapping as different news videos started playing at once at various volumes, and Steven stared at him and Riis, looking poised, excited as a cat that knew it had cornered its mouse.

"What's happened?" Drew asked quickly.

He felt static in his bones.

He looked at Riis, who had frozen, the hard line deep between his wide eyes. Riis turned to him, and he saw himself reflected in those eyes, pale and stricken. Saw his own eyes widen as one loud tablet blared the news out, and there were scattered gasps.

"The peace talks have not gone according to plan, repeat, an attempt was made against the King Admiral's life, he is being moved to a safe location, a safe distance from Drune, along with the Knight of Sol II. It is being debated whether or not we have lost our tenuous peace, whether or not the switch will have to be flipped..."

Drew shut his eyes.

The world around him slowly faded.

One voice cut through the thick of the dark, though. One soft, terrified voice.

"Drew..."

22

Try Harder

Red interceded, because it was her job, and despite how annoying she could be, she did her job well. Steven and his manager practically threw a tantrum, wanting to interview them post-news, wanting it *bad*, but Red swept Drew away with a jolt and he reached out and grabbed Riis, too. Riis, who had gone very still, eyes wide.

They were rushed out the back and packed into a car. Red in the front seat clicked the fob and slammed her foot down on the ignition and it drove off with a roar and a screech and—

And they might flip the switch.

They might flip the switch.

Drew couldn't breathe.

He felt, suddenly, a hand in his. Claws shaking, and he gripped them hard. Stared at Riis, who stared back, terror clamoring behind his dark eyes, and Drew felt a wave come over him—of dread, of panic, and of something far more sharp and sweet and yet now just bone-achingly *painful*. Finding his voice in this, he spoke quickly. "They probably won't. They… they probably won't. Why would they? A single attempt… probably by just, like, a, just a fringe radical group…"

"No," Riis said. His voice was gravelly, slipping back into a thick whistle in his fear. "Why would they? Wasn't even successful… such a small thing."

They stared at each other.

Drew's tablet suddenly buzzed and blared, and they both jumped. He answered it quickly, hands shaking.

"Mom!"

"Honey, my darling boy," she said, and there were tears in her eyes, but her face was hard, determined, *ready*, no, "Listen to me: despite it all, I love you, just remember, I *love you*, I only wanted what was best. Just remember. We have a role. A destiny and a cause. Let this strengthen that in you, not chase it away. Be brave, my darling," and she was crying, and he let out a hollow noise and crouched over the tablet, shaking.

"Mom, no, just—"

"Be brave," she said, and then hung up.

He shook. Tried to call her back.

No answer.

Looked up, frantic, amazed his body could contain such a swirling depth of fear and dread. He could barely breathe. *He could barely breathe.*

Riis had curled his legs up under himself, like he was sitting on one of his squat sofas. His eyes were squeezed shut. His arms wrapped around himself. He shook.

Drew didn't think about it.

He fell into him, and Riis jumped, but then they were holding one another, both shaking in the backseat, and Riis was so *very* warm and life was terrible and terrifying and so sharp in this moment he knew, suddenly, he would live here forever.

In some small way, he would always be here.

For a long time, silence. Their breathing. He pushed his nose into Riis' neck and Riis *shuddered.* Clutched him closer.

The radio of the car blipped to life, all of a sudden, in a burst of static.

Report came on.

King Admiral was on his way back.

Knight of Sol II was as well.

For now, the switch had not been flipped.

Peace talks resuming over video.

It was safe.

It was fine. For now, it was fine.

They remained clinging to each other in the back of the car.

****

Amy greeted them back at school. Red, being strangely clever and considerate for a Grunt, had pulled around to the Caf loading dock instead of the main entrance. They'd avoided the by-now-rabid newsies on the green out front. Amy glanced watery eyes up as they came in through the kitchen and out into the caf, and then those eyes widened and she rose shaking from where she'd been slumped in a corner seat and made a beeline for them.

Drew was prepared for her to hug him; he squeezed her hard, inhaling her familiar perfume and letting out a choked sob against her neck. Riis, on the other hand, seemed utterly floored to be grabbed into the embrace as well.

"I'm so sorry," she sobbed out. She was crying. Jeezus.

Drew shut his eyes. His heart hadn't stopped pounding. "It's fine, nothing happened. It's fine."

"Nothing happened. For now, nothing happened," Riis said softly.

Drew shuddered. Felt suddenly like—

"I think I'm gonna go throw up," he said numbly, and then started towards the bathroom, moving with increasing speed as it became more and more urgent.

He didn't realize Riis had followed him until he felt a gentle claw touch his shoulder while he was hunched in an open stall over a toilet, retching.

Drew jumped, jolting out of his skin, and let out a harsh,

shaking laugh. "Oh jeez. I just. Super don't want you to see me like this," he said. And then it seemed to break out of his throat, a strangled sob rather than puke, fuck, fuck, and he was sobbing on the floor of the bathroom and Riis crouched down and held him with quivering claws.

He pushed his face against Riis' warm chest and squeezed his eyes shut. God.

"You can't get the switch," Riis said, then. Very quietly.

Drew laughed.

"I am not attempting a joke," Riis said softly.

Drew cringed. "I know," he said.

"So."

"So?"

"What do we do now?"

Drew stared at Riis. "Nothing," he said, and it came out in a bursting breath of panicked air. He laughed again, holding his hands to his head, over his eyes. Riis gently took his hands away and held them and he shuddered.

"Nothing? I seem to remember you stating that 'nothing' was not an option, when it was myself facing… a difficult situation," Riis said calmly.

Drew laughed again.

It actually hurt sometimes. Knowing Riis.

"Listen, there's nothing to do about it, okay? It's destiny. It's caste. It's… me with the switch. There's no escaping it. I *know that*, I would've already if I could—" and he stuttered to a halt in his words. Shook. Dropped his head to his knees. "I would've already if I could," he said again, very softly.

He'd never told anyone that. Not a soul.

"You haven't tried hard enough."

Drew blinked, sitting up slightly, shaking still. Riis was staring at him, hard, unblinking. "What?"

"You have not. Tried. Hard enough," Riis said through his teeth, and Drew suddenly realized something—Riis was *angry*.

He'd never quite seen Riis angry before. Not really. Definitely not at him.

It tasted bad. A distinct sour twinge that leapt from his gut to his throat.

"What do you mean I haven't tried hard enough, I mean—"

"Consider someone other than yourself," Riis snapped. "I will lose a great many—if not *all* of my loved ones, should the weapon be used again. If you believe you have no choice but to count yourself amongst them, then you *have not tried hard enough.*"

Riis stood, then. Walked shortly out of the bathroom—shoulders hunched, head down, horns pointed forward, and left Drew sitting on the floor and gaping at where he'd been.

23

A Great Deal

S o."

Drew flinched. "So…"

"Exciting weekend," Kanak said.

Drew immediately began to rise, heart hammering. "Okay, I'm just gonna—"

"Hold your horses there, Drew. I value all your visits, truly I do, but this time more than possibly ever before, you actually *need* to be here. Don't just bury this. That'll just hurt you more, in the long run."

Drew stood, silent and still. Didn't look at her.

"Your mother almost died."

He breathed. Blow out the candle.

"Your mother was almost murdered," and he flinched, hard.

"Okay, you could get in a lot of trouble for—"

"Your mother was almost *sacrificed*, whatever, doesn't it all mean the same thing in the end?" she snapped out, and he finally did meet her eyes then, which were held steady on him, and he sat back down, slowly.

When he spoke, the words hurt coming out, as if each was a small stone he had to actively regurgitate. "It's… it's important. It's being the Knight of Sol II. If anything, I think it's… more important now."

Kanak blinked twice, quickly. "...Oh?"

Drew let out a faltering, inappropriate laugh. His heart—as well as a few other vital organs—were trying to climb out of his body. He understood where they were coming from, more than ever before. "I mean god, you're saying, like, my mom almost died. And yeah, yeah, that fucks me up. That fucks me up a *lot*. But so many more people than just my mom almost died. A whole intelligent species, maybe even, almost died. Riis… Riis was almost the last of his kind. Jeezus christ, I mean..."

She didn't say anything. Looked at him with utmost focus. Didn't move.

Drew dropped his head into his hands. It felt like someone else's head, someone else's hands, and he flinched. "Like. I'm not discounting my fear and my grief. I'm not discounting what I *almost* went through. What my mom almost went through, 'cause yeah, it would've been like… like a murdering. I'm not saying it wouldn't be. But Riis. Fuck. Fuck! Riis almost lost *everything*, and—"

"You were with him when it all went down. What was that like?"

Blow out. The candle.

"Was it difficult? You two have kind of lucked out. Been able to kind of skate over the opposing sides of this. I'm guessing it was rather more difficult to do that, with all the—"

"We had each other." Drew swallowed, looked away. Ached with it, but continued speaking, "I wouldn't have been able to get through it if he hadn't been there."

"...Ah. So you found comfort in each other."

Drew flinched. "Jeez, don't say it like that, it's not like… I mean, yeah."

Kanak tilted her head to the side and regarded him carefully. "Yeah?"

"Yeah. I mean. To everyone else, everyone around us, it was like it didn't *matter*. Like it was just 'politics.' Just 'news.' Exciting, maybe even. Like it was the finale of some great TV show. To us it *mattered*."

"That makes a lot of sense to me."

"So you get it, then."

"Get what?"

He snorted, staring over her shoulder at the tops of the trees, brushing soft against one another in the breeze, little buds of leaves now unfurling, slowly. "Why the Knighthood of Sol II is important. I never realized it before. That it's like... like we're the last line of moral defense. The last thing to prevent them from just *flipping the switch on a whim*."

"Hm." Shrink Kanak nodded, shortly, like she'd already known that. Well, fuck her. He continued, haltingly, shakily.

"My mom called, later. She said she was worried 'cause the King Admiral couldn't do it. Isn't that fucking awful? She said he hesitated, couldn't just kill her right away when it looked like that's how it 'had to go,' and that was a *concern*. Fuck! Like... at least he hesitated. He might not see the Emni as people, but he knows my mom's people, so he didn't just *do it*."

"You see the Emni as people."

"Well, yeah!" he said, voice getting very high at this point, "Of course! They are people! Riis, Riis is the most *people* of all the people I've ever met, *jeez*, I mean..."

"Ooh. Now I'm getting all the juicy deets," she said.

He couldn't quite meet her eyes. "Oh my *god*, shut *up*."

"You care a great deal about him," she added softly.

Drew breathed. Shut his eyes. Dropped his head down on top of his hands, and considered just... saying it.

"Well? Do you?"

"Yes." The word was very small. Too small. He said it anyway. It shivered brightly in the air between them, and he felt a careful hand come to his. It held his fingers tightly. After a moment, he squeezed it back.

24

Utterly Fucked

Riis didn't mention their 'fight' or whatever, so Drew didn't either. At night, though, lying in his bed, it positively swelled in his mind, obscuring all else: was he someone Riis would count as a loss? A 'loved one?'

The thought seemed to feed some feverish beast in his gut that positively purred as the idea entered it. The notion of Riis grieving him hurt and felt just really, abysmally good at the same time.

He knew, at this point, he was utterly and completely well and truly fucked. Was pointedly not naming it, but *knew*. It was hard to deny the obvious fact that he dreamed about Riis almost nightly, that he touched himself, aching with it, just the barest glance feeding his feverish imagination for days.

That it was the glances. The words. The laughter and the gentle touches, when they came, that always sent his head spinning in more ways than just the one. He wasn't delving into that, though. Nope. So long as it was just him being a weird pervert who (desperately) wanted to fuck an alien, that was all dandy. He could live with that.

"You're like, head over heels gaga crazy in love with him," Amy said flatly over coffee on the balcony one day.

He could not live with that, though.

"Shut. Up," he said through his teeth, glaring down at his own coffee. Faced with this, he decided hesitantly to concede to the more tolerable truth. "He's… muscly, that's all. You know I like 'em 'athletic,' as you put it. I dunno. He's…"

"He's *fabulous*, right?"

Drew glared off at the sky. It'd been a while now of them poised on their little fire escape, wrapped in the same blanket, and pretty much the whole time he'd been skimming a news article on his tablet that had covered his and Riis' aborted interview. Or like. More accurately, he'd been staring at the picture that had been snapped for the article. Early in the interview, before the news break, Drew hysterically laughing and Riis squinting slyly at him out of the corner of his eyes. Reluctantly, he shut off his tablet. Looked away, out at the sea, glinting almost too brightly to look at at the end of the street.

"You should tell him."

He actually burst out laughing. It hurt. But it was funny all the same.

Amy didn't laugh, though. She frowned at him. "Really," she said.

"I *can't*," he said, rather frantic at this point. "I mean. Even if, if it was *true*—"

She rolled her eyes, heartilly.

"It's not… I mean, it's just… *insane on thousands upon thousands of levels.*"

"So?"

"What do you mean, *so!*"

"So, name some of the levels. Actually, first, name just the really *silly* ones."

He stared at her. "What?"

"I mean," she crowed, delighted, "if there's *thousands* some must be just *hilariously ridiculous*, so I wanna hear those first. C'mon. Silliness to the front, Drew!"

Drew stared at her. Felt an insane smile tugging at the corner of his mouth before he could bite it back. Said, straight-faced as he could, "He uses *perfect capitalization and grammar* in chats. Punctuation, too! We're simply too different. It just wouldn't work out."

She howled with laughter.

****

The end of the year loomed larger and larger on the horizon, as the weeks wore on. Amy and Jas fought, and then made the decision to 'just be friends,' which seemed to only fuel their need for each other more, spending more and more time locked away in Jas' dorm room. More than once Drew was banished from their little apartment for the night, and he basically as a rule found solace in Riis' room.

They finished Deep Space Nine. Decided they didn't like Voyager. Moved on to a cartoon about rock-based alien lifeforms which was beautifully animated, but also easy to talk over, get distracted during.

So they did that a lot, and Riis told him about Drune.

"The planet you call Jupiter II has a starring role in virtually all Emni faiths and practices."

"Really?"

"Yes. You must understand—it takes up most of our horizon. It would be putting it mildly to say it is enormous. An integral piece of the sky. Seers of old theorized it was the heart of flame, which is a sacred thing on Drune."

"Fire is?"

"Yes. At least in my culture, my faith. We all keep an ever-burning hearth. Without it, if we were to die, our soul would have nothing to tether it. Nothing that could guide us to our heavenly home at the heart of Jupiter II."

"Jupiter II…"

"…Yes?"

"What's it really called?"

"…"

"You always use the Standard names for things. What's it really called? Teach me."

Riis let out a sharp, shrill whistle, followed by a click.

Drew attempted to imitate, letting out a less sharp, much less shrill whistle.

"... close."

"You're sweet. It definitely wasn't."

"Try this." Riss growled, followed by a whistle.

Drew did the same.

"That was much better."

"What did I just say?"

"My name."

Drew sat up. They'd been leaning back on the low sofa, the show playing softly in the background. Barely a hair from touching. He felt a chime in his chest as he looked at Riis, whose eyes remained closed.

He said it again. It tasted good in his mouth.

The line formed between those eyes. They didn't open, though. "Yes," Riis said, very quietly. "Very good."

****

Drew woke up the morning of Riis' departure with a weight in his chest. Breakfast turned to dust in his mouth. Coffee was just battery acid made edible.

The sky itself seemed meaningless.

"You'll write to me, right?" he'd asked yesterday, already aching deep inside at what tomorrow would bring.

"...If you would like that, yes. I would... also like that."

They'd exchanged email addresses. Easier that way.

Though—Riis had warned him—Drune was a long way off. Very, very far. Signals would not always be leaping between their worlds. Every now and then it would trip across space stations and their letters would reach each other, but by and large, they would not get each other's messages for days at a time unless one of them paid for a hyperspace call. Which, when Drew looked it up, he learned was *insanely expensive.*

Drew sat on his balcony and drank his stupid battery acid coffee. Stared at the gorgeous summer sunrise, pink and purple and hazy bright, twin moons pale on the edge, and he flat out wanted to die.

It wasn't fair.

It wasn't *fair*.

"Do you think he's coming back? Next year, I mean?" Amy asked him quietly.

Drew shut his eyes.

No. No, he didn't.

He hadn't asked. The question positively clawed at his throat sometimes, but he had never, ever asked.

They took the trolley in silence, for which he was grateful. Arrived at school just as parents had started pulling up, families and friends, childhood boyfriends and girlfriends from back home, too, all greeting their students and helping to lug bags and backpacks and clumsily collected boxes and bins into cars, all of them laughing brightly, joking, hugging and kissing one another.

Riis stood silent by a tree. There was a space around him, bare of other people, as there always was. He looked tense.

Drew walked directly up to him. Riis looked somewhere over his shoulder, face tense. Drew paused, a few steps away, and then—heart in his throat—hugged him hard.

Riis jumped.

Gently, after a moment, placed a trembling hand on his back. Drew pulled away slightly. Riis still wasn't looking at him, though; was looking tensely at a car that had just pulled up before the gate, some kind of government vehicle, dark windows. A woman stepped out, dressed all in formal command blue.

She waved at Riis shortly. Hesitantly, he waved back.

"We'll miss you, Riis!" Amy cried out, and flung her arms around him. He startled, but held her back, honestly far more tenderly than he'd held Drew, and Drew wanted the ground to open up and swallow him. He knew people were staring. He well and truly didn't care. He wanted so many things, in that moment, he could barely contain it: all the want he felt. But he stood, and looked, and ached, instead.

Riis finally met his eyes. Blinked slow at him over Amy's shoulder. She backed up.

He opened his mouth for a moment. Looked hard at Drew, and then said, very quietly, "Try harder."

Drew shut his eyes. Shook.

Then, just barely, a single claw on his jaw and his eyes snapped open, he gasped, and the hand was back by Riis' side before he could really even react, and definitely before he could say jack-shit Riis had grabbed his meager belongings and fled to the car, moving his usual speed of *far too fast to be normal,* and flung himself into the backseat.

The woman got back in the car, much more human and calmer.

Drew gaped as they drove away. Breathed.

"I wonder if that's like kissing for them," Amy said coyly.

Drew burst into tears.

"Oh shit," she said, and grabbed him, held him tightly.

He couldn't stop crying.

25

The Stone

Summer break was a thick soup of isolated evenings and the relieving lack of interviews. What had been normally an ordinary summer shitfest was now something Drew no longer had to participate in, having more than proven he ought not to be allowed in front of cameras—according to his mother. Add the ingredients of boredom and a general, aching despair, and you had summer break. Served lukewarm. With stale crackers. No spoon. Just a funnell, and a near endless supply.

Day after day stretched on, long and languidly uninteresting, uneventful, and he was alone beyond the house staff and the looming end-of-summer Event of the switch going in his chest. An Event his brain rejected focus on in a shit defensive move that winded him. The grunts followed him over the clear green grounds of King Admiral's estate during his morning walk, Red even counting herself amongst them on Tuesdays, now. He looked forward to Tuesdays. They rarely spoke, but still: she was someone from the year before, where everything had become bright and sharp and lovely, lovely, lovely.

Lovely.

He didn't write to Riis first. Riis didn't write to him first either, though. So.

It hurt. It hurt to think of writing, but it definitely also hurt not to write, too, and wasn't that just *not fucking fair.* In the long-run, by week two, he half-heartedly figured maybe it would hurt less if he just stopped. Cut this down at the quick, if he was anywhere near the quick anymore. It felt far too late, but he hoped—

"Maybe Amy can come over," his mom said softly one morning, over breakfast.

King Admiral adjusted his tablet, letting out a, "hmm." Drew blinked up from his eggs.

"Yeah… I mean, yeah. That'd be cool. Wait, but isn't she like, not *allowed* to—"

"Before the wedding, technically yes," his mom said primly, and he flinched, "though really, that's happening *when?* We need to plan sometime! It shouldn't be too big a deal, having her here for a few days. I know her parents are quite busy this summer, she must be lonely. Especially without you, Drew. And it's not like you two don't live together, anyway. We'll put her in the cottage."

King Admiral looked up then, briefly. Caught his mother's eyes and she looked away first, lips tight.

'The cottage' was really supposed to be where Drew and his mom lived.

They'd moved into the main house two months after King Admiral's wife's death, though. A year after Drew was born.

His mother slept in the King Admiral's room. Drew slept in Prince Seb's old playroom. Prince Seb slept at school, far away.

"Sure," Drew said quickly, not liking how thin either of their lips looked, both of them tight in the cheeks, holding words in their mouths that probably shouldn't come out in front of him.

It wasn't official, that he 'knew.' That anyone 'knew.' It wasn't spoken of: the King Admiral, the Knight of Sol II, and their bastard Squire son. Drew preferred it that way. It was utterly ridiculous, but he preferred the feigned ignorance to what he imagined acknowledgement to be like by, like, a lot.

"Wonderful!" his mother said. "You should start thinking, Drew, about any details you might want for the wedding. Though," and she let out a soft chuckle, "I must insist you be a gentleman and let Amy get her way most of the time. A wedding really is the *bride's* day, when it comes down to it."

He gritted his teeth. Put on a smile. "Yeah, sure, Mom." he said quietly.

Sure, Mom.

****

Amy got off the train and it was like reality suddenly cut—crisp, fresh, and bright—into a swampy bullshit lies sandwich and he was bolting across the station and leaping into her arms before she'd even put down her bag. She shrieked, laughing raucously, and distantly he heard a camera app clicking—not newsies, thank god; but his mom though, jeezus christ— and he tried hard to not care. Buried his face in her neck, flung his full weight into her arms, and breathed.

"Drew! Sweetie, *she's* supposed to do that, you cad!" his mom called out, chortling. Amy spun him around gleefully before slapping a wet kiss on his mouth, much to his mom's delight.

"I missed you," was all he could get out. She blinked, and her eyes softened. They both knew she wasn't the only one he missed, and he knew from her soft eyes that she understood immediately, and suddenly he wanted to cry.

So he did, just a little. In the car on the ride back, Amy curled against him in the backseat, he buried his face in her dark hair and *cried*. Very, very little. Very, very softly.

"You lovebirds are so cute," his mom tittered. Amy snorted. Continued to rub a small circle on his hand. Drew ground his teeth.

Sucked in a breath.

Blew out the candle.

****

"I think she's just *so* elated at the notion I *might* be fucking a girl right now she doesn't even *care*." Drew lamented, passing the spliff back to Amy, who giggled manically into it, sending a wasted puff of smoke up between them. "Seriously!" Drew hissed out, "Like, I literally just walked *right past her* out the door to the cottage. She was in the living room! I walked *right past her.* I really wouldn't have been surprised if she'd offered me a condom."

"Ooh. Think you can get her to give you a flavored one? I *am* kinda peckish."

Drew choked on the smoke, coughing so hard his eyes started streaming and she exploded into giggling, shrieking laughter yet again. She'd always been an easily amused high, and a frankly clever drunk. Drew wished he could lean into substances as inherently successfully as she did. Instead, each inebriation was like the flip of a coin: would today's exploration into the world of drugs be mad acidic panic sweats, or a giggling good time?

He remembered that night getting drunk with Riis, painting his talons and watching movies, and had to shut his eyes, cut off the memory with a snap. That. That had been something closer to the second, though it seemed so far transcended past it, too. A whole other realm, barely touching the drunkenness aspect.

There was also fear, there, when it came to getting fucked up. Nestled uncomfortably against the truth of his mother's careful rationing of white wine sips, claiming that full inebriation 'did funny things' to her, in the long run. King Admiral's near continuous flow of scotch, though he functioned on it like a fish on water. And Seb, who probably should—just frankly—say goodbye to the stuff forever. He didn't handle it well. Didn't handle any of it well. What's more, didn't seem capable of stopping once he started. And he was always starting.

"Hey, hey," Amy said softly, scritching the back of his head lightly, "What are you thinking about? You alright?"

Drew shut his eyes tightly. Forced himself to smile—it came out more grimace—and shrug. "I dunno."

"Hmm. Is that your pet name for him? 'Idunno?' Weird."

Drew flinched. "I really wasn't—" he started, but she cut him off with a mad hooting cackle. He looked away, and she quieted pretty quickly, though.

The two of them were on the squat porch of the cottage, drinking coffee in the middle of the night like maniacs and chain smoking all the weed and tobacco Amy had brought with her, like they did. The stars up ahead burned so brightly, the frothy milk of universes stirred up between them and *him*, and Drew looked, again, for Jupiter II. It could be spotted, here out in the countryside, away from the intruding blaze of city lights. Distantly, it could be spotted. It looked like a red star, almost, very faint.

Very, very faint.

Drune, of course, was too far and small to see at all.

"You two keeping in touch?"

Drew dropped his head into his hands.

"What!" she said, and he flinched. "Drew! Just *write to him*. Maybe it'll make you even feel better, I dunno, like—"

"So here's where the party's at," a growly, only slightly slurring voice, and Amy jerked forward in surprise as Drew froze.

Froze.

Slowly willed himself to look up and face the teeth.

Seb stepped out of the shadow. His teeth seemed to move into the light before he did himself, his smile a jagged edge on a knife-sharp face, eyes gleaming, relishing it as he spoke, "Who's this you're talking about, Drew? Who, exactly, is this 'him' you should be writing to? Is it who I think it is?"

Fuck.

The bugs trilled.

They breathed.

Seb grinned.

Silence, for a moment. Then Amy snapped with stunning bravery right in the face of the future King Admiral, "Oh, fuck off, Seb."

Drew could have kissed her. If he wasn't slowly dying inside his face.

Seb laughed like she was joking with him. Poking fun. Like they were old friends, and then he stepped shortly forward onto the porch, holding out his hand and twitching his fingers slightly. Amy hesitated before handing him the spliff.

Seb took a long drag. Held it in as he spoke; the words coming out stiff with full lungs, "Well, I mean, it's a *valid question*, isn't it? The whole world's asking, Drew, even if your—" he exhaled, hard, "—*mother* isn't putting you in a position to answer it."

Drew shut his eyes. His heart seemed to beat behind them, pulsing against the lids. "Yes," he said softly. Determined, at least, to not lie anymore. "Yes, it's who you think it is."

Amy stiffened beside him.

Silence. Seb took another drag, not bothering to pass it back to them. "Well," he said. *"Do* you have a pet name for it, then?"

Drew's eyes snapped open. Amy's breath hitched, and her hand tightened on his arm.

Seb smirked in the dark. Another long drag, and the smoke curled around his nostrils as he spoke next. "I always wondered about you, Drew. Never quite managed to wonder as far as you ended up going, though. Huh. That's a lack of creativity on my part, I guess. Or perhaps I'm just too thoroughly *not* into… what would you even call that, anyway?"

Drew's heart was hammering in his ears. His teeth hurt from grinding tight in his mouth, he—

"Beastiality, maybe? Do they count as animals?"

Amy lurched sideways towards him, letting out a squeak as he burst to his feet and jerked forward on mad instinct. She grabbed him, hard, and he was yanked back down on the bench with a thunk, his head was *hammering*, he saw red, he saw *red*, Seb was *laughing*, and Drew saw—

"Who's that, then?!"

Red.

Red stood stocky and still and *far* more noticeable than Seb had been in the dark. She squinted, slightly. Her face was hard, though, an ice to her normal stoicism as she spoke shortly, "Prince Seb. Your father, the King Admiral, sent me to find you and escort you to bed. Says, and this is a quote, 'You've had enough fun. If you're going to visit, ask first, and don't just break into the liquor cabinet and wander off. At least say hi.' Eh, end quote."

Seb glared petulantly back at Red. Seemed to consider for a moment if he could evade her, and Drew *sorely* hoped he'd try, but Seb sucked in a breath through his nose, composed himself like he was pulling something up from a bog, and shot a grin back at them instead. Sucked down the rest of the half-smoked spliff in one go before flicking the burning butt of it into the woods, and said, smoke billowing around his mouth, "Well, I'll see you around. Good luck with... *whatever* you would call your situation, Drew."

He followed Red shortly up the hill, back to the main house.

Amy swore, heartily. Shakily, she began to roll another spliff, though Drew passed on it when she held it out to him. He knew it wouldn't do him any kind of good, right now.

****

"Knock knock!" his mom said, with her mouth rather than her fist, hovering by his open door, and Drew glared.

She grinned at him, stepping lightly into his room and sitting prim and golden on the edge of his bed. He put his tablet down. Stared at her. "Yeah?" he said, eventually.

She let out a huff. "Drew, honey, you used to tell me *everything*, when did this—"

He flinched, and found himself apologizing before she could even get the words all the way out, "Sorry. Sorry, mom, I'm just... just tired."

"Oh, I know, sweetie. It's been a tough year."

He nodded. Looked away. She reached forward and took his hand then, squeezing it lightly, and he shut his eyes.

Would it be so bad? To trust her, yet again, to not break him down?

He almost laughed. Squeezed her hand back gently, though.

"Seb said something... something rather rude."

He absolutely went rigid. Breathed.

She continued, lilting words coming out rather quickly, "which is fine. I mean, it's all… it's all Seb being Seb. I wanted to talk to you though, about, eh. The Emni."

"Riis."

"Eh?"

Drew looked away, out at the stars. "His name is Riis."

"…Okay. Riis." she said, and they both let out a breath, then, and he almost wanted to cry. "I know… Riis must've said and done quite a bit that confused you."

He'd been feeling rather somber, but at this point he literally had to bite his tongue to keep from cackling—*Mom, you don't know the half of it…*

"I just wanted you to know something. Something your ol' mama has learned through the years, being what you'll be, someday. Someday soon! I mean, wow, it's almost halfway through the summer already… anyway. I just wanted you to know something."

"What?" he asked. He could see them both in his mirror by the door, and it was easier to look at her, there. She looked so soft and gentle in the light. So delicate, compared to her harsh gremlin son, crouched forward on his bed. Even their reflections made him flinch.

She turned, looked him dead in the eyes, and spoke softly, "It's not our job to think about it."

Drew stared.

She stared back. Did not break eye contact.

Drew shook his head. "What?" he asked, finally, sure he must've misheard. This was his mother. His golden mother who was constantly telling him to think about this, consider that, really just dwell on *why* and *what* and *where*—

"We don't think. We don't change. We carry the instrument of change. Ready, for all who must wield it," she said quietly, and Drew felt a chill run right through him. The dull light glowed in her chest, making her almost ethereal, and she continued, softly, reverently,

"We're not the sword. We're not King Arthur. We're the stone. Do you understand?"

Drew breathed, shallowly. She looked pleadingly at him, though, so he nodded once, dumbly. Fuck.

Fuck.

"I knew you would, baby," she said, and leaned forward then and kissed his forehead. He felt her lips stick as they pulled away, and knew he had soft pink lipstick there, now.

She moved to go then, shoulders still tense, and he found himself calling out, "Mom?"

She turned, peering over her shoulder at him. He flinched. "Eh," he said. "Goodnight. I love you."

She blinked, and then beamed in a way that could've convinced a flower to bloom in the dead of winter. "Oh, I love you too, honey. Goodnight."

She left. Left him alone in his room, in the dark, frantic energy welling up in every pore of him.

It's not our job to think about it.

Easier—*far* easier—said, than done.

With shaking hands, Drew did what he'd wanted to do all along. What he hadn't done, hadn't done at all, all along, and it had nearly killed him.

Why hadn't he done this from the start?!

Fuck that. Fuck that so, so hard.

He opened his email and began to write.

26

Letters All Start With Dear

Dear Riis,

How do you write your real name? I'll draw it and attach it to the top, after the 'dear.' By the way, letters all start with a 'dear'. It's not weird.

Anyway. Nothing much is happening here. I'm spending time with my mom, which is nice, I guess. She's normally really busy. She has to go wherever the King Admiral goes, so we ordinarily follow him around and there's lots of people all around us all the time, but this break it's been decided we should all maybe lay low for a while. Seb unfortunately visited this summer for a couple days. Bad news. Good news, though—Amy visited, too!

How is your break going?

Drew

Dear Drew,

I am aware that letters traditionally start with the word 'dear.'
It is less a break and more a debriefing. Those involved in

bringing me to Americas University of Enseeos wish to learn what I have learned, and understand what I have accomplished, if anything. I have also returned to my school here. School does not have breaks here if you choose to attend after you have left childhood.

Is it normal to send a human child away to school for most of their life? We are required to do so, but I was under the impression that most human children studied primarily at home before University age, considering your caste system which requires they go into their lineage profession.

╟┤╤╨

(it's written like this)

Dear ╟┤╤╨,

Wait, you're full on 'required' to send your kids away to school? HUMAN school? Isn't that kind of immensely fucked?

Yeah it's kinda weird, but less weird the higher up in caste you get, and Prince Admiral Seb is kind of, like, the highest caste you can be. King Admiral actually wanted to send me away, too; pay for my schooling and everything. My mom put her foot down, though. She wanted to keep me close till I reached University age, train me herself since there's really no one else with our same role. Or 'lineage profession' or whatever.

They have a really weird relationship, King Admiral and my mom. Especially since his wife died. It's something I always kind of wanted to talk to you about, but didn't. I dunno.

I miss you.

Drew

Dear Drew,

It is indeed fucked.

Also, I wish you had talked to me about it. I can guess a little. I have heard the rumors, but I wish I had heard more from you.

About many things, new and old, not just that.

There are things I wanted to tell you, too. Teach you about Drune, but also just say. Things I picked up while away from you, jokes or questions I formed. Upon seeing you again, I'd forget most of them, and we would move forward without me voicing them. They crowd my mind these days and make focusing on my studies difficult, to say the least.

All this to say, I miss you as well.

⧻⧻

Dear ⧻⧻,

Jeezus. You can't just say shit like that.

Drew

Dear Drew,

Why? You said it first.

We are honest with our feelings here. You know this. I personally respect that you tend to be honest and open with yours as well.

It is, perhaps, my favorite thing about you.

⧻⧻

Dear ⧻⧻,

The things I didn't say to you make me breathless and dizzy. I miss you. I miss you so much it hurts like I've lost a limb, but nope, I have both legs, both arms, and isn't that just crazy. It feels like a part of me has been taken, gouged out, and I'm trying to live while bleeding from its lack. Everyone's like 'oh, how's your summer break going?' and I have to smile, nod, not cry, not tell them what it's really like, to live without being able to run up the stairs to your too-warm room and watch some shitty chick flick and sit near you, just feel you being there beside me.

No one has ever spoken to me like you, expected more from me than to just be a willing sacrifice. So they've expected absolutely everything and absolutely nothing in the same breath, and you've always just expected respect and an open mind. Which you're owed, ten thousand times over.

I miss you so much it hurts. I dream about you every night.
Love,
Drew

Dear ⊩⊣⊤⊥,
Hey, sorry about the last letter, I get it, that got weird.
Just forget it, okay?
Drew

Dear ⊩⊣⊤⊥,
Please don't be mad. I'm sorry.
Drew

⊩⊣⊤⊥,
I know you aren't writing to me anymore and this'll be my last letter.

I just want to tell you my mom died. I don't know why I want to tell you, but I do.

She didn't die 'cause of the switch, she didn't get killed, she just died, like a person does. Just died. I was there. She fell over and I couldn't wake her up. I didn't know what to do. What I could do, without—

She just died.

Aneurysm, they're saying.

I don't know what to do. I don't know what to do.

They're going to put the switch in me next week. It was supposed to be at the end of the summer, but now it's happening next week.

What do I do?

Drew

Dear Drew,

Run.

Love,

27

Run

Amy picked him up in her new car.

'New' here meaning, new to her. It was totally beaten up, looked distinctly like it ought to be broken-down but mysteriously continued to chug along. It was painted with non-car-paint—a lurid green—so it looked both neon and dull at the same moment. He had to stifle a fairly manic laugh when he saw it.

He got in and she immediately reached over, pulled him into a tight hug and held him.

Drew shook in her arms.

Then she pulled back, glanced nervously around the dark servant's exit of the estate. Then, headlights off, she crept down the drive and onto the main road. Flicked the headlights on and they were off.

They were off.

He was running.

Fuck you, Riis, he thought to himself, seething. Freaking out internally more than he ever had before. *Fuck. You. In. All. The. Ways.*

"So I hit up my cousin," Amy said haltingly, flinching at the volume of her own words, as if volume meant anything at this point.

Drew opened his eyes. Lifted his head from where he'd smooshed it against the cool glass of the window. It left an oily shine.

He hadn't really had a shower since—

"The one who went casteless and now he's kind of just a spacer. He drives a freighter between worlds, moving materials," she said. "He said he can give you a ride if you can work."

Drew stared at her.

She flinched.

"Work? On a freighter?"

"Well, yeah."

"I've never worked a day in my life."

"Well, you're the one who's trying to run away! Be casteless! You kinda have to, now, don't you think!" she snapped, and he swallowed his tongue. She breathed slow, forceful breaths, staring straight ahead. It still took him a moment to realize it, though. She was crying.

"Amy..."

"Shut up. No. I get it, I do. I've always kind of... wanted this for you, even," she said tearfully. "But it's my life, too. I was gonna marry you, I was gonna be Lady Knight of Sol II or whatever. Whatever! It was gonna be great. A little heartbreaking, but great. We were gonna have fun with it."

"I'm sorry," he said quietly. Shut his eyes, dropped his head into his hands. "I'm sorry..."

She let out a warbling sob shaped laugh and he hated himself.

"Listen," he said, panicking, "if it's really important to you—"

"Abso-fucking-lutely not, no-siree-bob, you are *not* chickening out at this point!" she shouted, and he burst out laughing.

It felt weird in his throat, the laugh.

Turned pretty quickly into a sob.

She reached out and grabbed his hand. Held it tightly, all the way to the spaceport.

****

The spaceport was not a kind he'd ever been to before.

He'd never really *left* Earth II. So he'd never even been to a real one, for tourists who actively sought out visitations to other planets and moons, including Drune. He'd left the atmosphere once or twice for a fancy party. Eaten caviar and lobster with a star-struck view, schmoozed with the elite with Earth II's hazy horizon as a backdrop. He'd never been further than that. When his mom went off-world with the King Admiral, he'd always been left behind.

This was a different kind of spaceport, though, that was for sure. Different than any he'd ever seen in movies, too.

It was, essentially, a barren field with a cavernous garage that looked like a converted barn on the edge of it. Tiny ships crowded the garage-barn, bigger ones in varying stages of disrepair resting just outside it. Amy's cousin's cargo freight was the biggest docked ship, and it loomed over the barn like some kind of enormous grub, solar wings folded in on all sides.

He ground his teeth.

Amy took his hand, hard, soon as they got out of the car. They walked towards it together, bugs trilling around them in the dark. The freight only got bigger the closer they got. Jeezus.

Amy's cousin looked exactly like Amy. He had her same narrow face and bright dark eyes, but he was a man with a scraggly black beard and so much straight energy he literally kind of disgusted Drew on instinct. He called Drew 'bro' and slapped him hard on the back, and Drew glared at Amy and she rolled her eyes. Then it was time to say goodbye, and all his annoyance fled like a startled bird.

She grabbed him first. He shivered in her arms, pushing his face hard into her neck, trying not to let it hurt him, but it did. Her perfume, her arms, her bony shoulder were all so familiar they broke his heart.

"I'll come visit you guys," she whispered. The whisper had weight. "Soon as I figure out how the fuck to get away with that, I will."

"I love you," Drew said, eyes squeezed shut.

"Oh jeez, Drew, I love you *so* much," she hissed, and kissed him on each cheek.

He kissed her nose, her forehead, and then a solid smack on the mouth with her face squished between his hands. "Whoa, get a room!" the cousin said in his straight bro voice, and Drew didn't even care.

"Message me," she said. Her eyes were bright.

"Course."

He followed the straight cousin onto the freighter. Felt the loss of her at his side, but also something else, something electric and feverishly exciting, like he was suddenly conducting a charge.

There were so many memories at this point, banked up, stored up. Acidic moments of fear, grief. Holding his mother on the floor, shaking her. *"I don't know what to do! I don't know what to do!"*

It seemed like he never knew what to do.

He did now, though. He knew it in the depths of his soul.

Go to Riis.

Go to Drune.

Run.

28

Straight Cousin

I t's only for another week," Drew muttered quietly through his teeth as he squeezed in-between two shafts of something-or-other, trying to reach the whatsit he was supposed to twist three times, maybe, probably counter-clockwise. Hopefully, anyway. That was what he was planning on doing, so that had better be what he was supposed to do. Straight Cousin had said a lot of words he didn't understand. It seemed to boil down to 'you see that doo-dad? Do a twisty on that doo-dad, in this way.'

Straight Cousin gave him the 'easy jobs' because he was 'a terrible employee' and Drew was *immensely* grateful for that.

Now if only he could remember Straight Cousin's real name.

Amy was offensively unhelpful.

In her last email she'd taken up his whole tablet's screen and then some with just HAHAHAHAHA over and over again in response to him asking, pleading with her, please just tell me his name.

Everyone here called him 'cap' or 'bro.' This was too weird for Drew to fit his mouth around. Definitely too strange for him to fit his *brain* around, far too sporty and military and ick, so in his head he just called him Straight Cousin.

Which bit him in the ass almost *immediately*.

"What did you just call me?" Straight Cousin snapped.

Drew absolutely froze at the crowded mess table, arm still outstretched, the pepper Straight Cousin had asked for clutched in his sweating hand.

"Eh…" he said.

The crew was dead silent around them.

Oh, fuck.

"Straight Cousin," Smalls (who, in the way of Smallses, was very large) said, eyes wide. "He called you 'Straight Cousin.'"

Straight Cousin stared at Drew.

Drew very awkwardly laughed, scratching his head. Spilling pepper on his face in the process. Fuck. Helplessly, he dissolved into a sneezing fit.

Then Straight Cousin burst out with a positive explosion of rough laughter, slapping him once on the back, hard. Drew descended into frantic giggling, and the crew started laughing, too, thank god.

"So," Drew said finally, eyes watering, voice shaking slightly, still feeling like he had narrowly dodged death, "What's your real name again, then?"

"Straight Cousin will do," Straight Cousin snarked, rolling his eyes, and then he was Straight Cousin, official. Whoa. Cool.

****

Dear Amy,
He told me to call him Straight Cousin! I'm saved.
Luuuuurve,
Drew

Dear Drew,
You absolute tool did you call him that to his face??
You are so not saved.
Kisses,

Amy

Dear Amy,
I've never felt so saved in my life. That's a fact.
Smooches,
Drew

Dear Drew,
Well, that's for sure I guess <3
Love,
Amy

****

"You're always sending out those emails. You got a boyfriend stationed on Drune?"

Drew froze. Straight Cousin was helping him (aka: doing the whole thing) fix a tube thing that had disconnected from a computer-ish thing. It was apparently 'easy' but Drew was, again, 'a terrible employee.'

"Uh…"

"I mean, I'm just assuming you're gay or bisexual or generally queer or something, correct me if I'm wrong. Not many straight people go around calling other people 'Straight Cousin.' Unless—is it *Amy* who's—"

"No, no," Drew actually laughed at that. "Amy is just… straight Amy, as far as I can tell."

"Well. It's tough out there. For queer kids higher in caste especially. I'm definitely not judging. I mean, it's really not something that matters so much, outside the military industrial complex that is Earth II."

Drew laughed a tad frantically at that. Did not correct him

though, jeez. "Uh," he said, "yeah."

"So—is it a boyfriend? You don't have to tell me; just trying to get to know you better."

The casual honesty here touched Drew, and he hesitated, but then spoke, "Nah. I'm kind of, like. Hopelessly in love with him… but nah."

"Oof."

"…Yeah."

"He a soldier?"

Drew actually snorted. "Definitely not. More an academic, I guess."

"Cool. He casteless too?"

"…yeah…"

"Well. Chances are a bit better, then, for a happy ending between you two."

Drew laughed. It hurt a little, but he laughed anyway.

It was then that there was a jolt that rocked the entire ship, and a dull glow suddenly shot across the small port window beside them.

They'd been halted. They were now being towed.

****

"This is all you're moving?"

"Yeah," Straight Cousin said, calm as anything. Their legal cargo lay sprawled now in the cargo bay. Crammed above them in the vent, Drew tried not to breathe too loud.

The officer had sent lackeys searching the ship. They had, shockingly, come up with exactly *zero* contraband. Which Drew knew was flat-out bullshit, but it seemed the crew had been prepared.

"No one else on board?"

Through the vent, Drew could see Straight Cousin's face tighten. Drew clamped a hand over his mouth. "No? We don't take passengers. We're a freaking freighter."

"Sir, I am an officer of the law. Be respectful while speaking to me."

"…Of course. No, though, *officer*. No one else."

"Well…" the officer was still in Straight Cousin's face.

She didn't buy it.

They were *fucked.*

"You're headed to Drune?"

"Yeah, that's right." Straight Cousin was somehow still calm, Drew didn't know how, he would've been hyperventilating, "I mean, yes, officer. Headed there to drop off these medical supplies. Then heading right back. Got a job with a mining company out there. Just bringing some resources back to Earth II."

"Ah. That's nice."

"Yeah, I mean. Anything to help, eh… serve the cause."

"Make some money, too, I take it."

Straight Cousin laughed. "Well," he said. "It's certainly a plus."

The officer nodded. Spoke shortly then into her earpiece, "Moving out. Nothing here."

Drew exhaled very, very slowly against his hand.

Blew.

Out.

The candle.

Quietly.

The officer and her lackeys left. The hull closed. Everyone was very still, though, until about a minute after the sway and the whirr of the patrol ship undocking and pulling away.

Then, Straight Cousin exploded with nervous laughter.

The others immediately followed suit, and soon it was just a bunch of straight boy laughter and no one *getting Drew the fuck out of this vent* and he bellowed down at them, "I am *dying* can we laugh later, *please!"*

They ragged on him, mercilessly, over dinner that night. To be fair, he was still shaking. Straight Cousin slapped him on the back, making him jump in his skin, and said proudly, "Our very first hiding-a-fugitive escape. We should get a badge for that."

"Maybe we could become pirates!" Smalls said excitedly.

"Word. That'd be pretty cool," Straight Cousin said, nodding.

"*Ugh.* Uh. I mean. Thank you… Straight Cousin…" Drew said

finally, still pretty much vibrating with anxiety.

Straight Cousin grinned. Then, to Drew's chargain, ruffled his hair. "No worries, Gay Friend."

Drew seriously should not have liked this comment as much as he did.

Later that night, in his bunk, he got out his tablet. Smalls, his roommate, was snoring so loudly he couldn't sleep. Not that it would've been easy to do otherwise, adrenaline still coursing through his limbs. Because of the whole almost-getting-captured thing. But also because he'd finally decided today to say something. To write back.

He kind of had to. Drew'd realized today—halfway there already—he had *no idea* where to go after landing.

So he took a breath, heart hammering. Reminded himself Riis had *told him to run*.

Had signed his letter 'love.'

Drew opened their email chain, hit reply, and started to type.

29

Flustered

Dear ⊩⊣干⫫,
I took your advice! I'm running.
Where should I go once I get there? I have no idea where you even live. Strange.
Drew

Dear Drew,
What?!
Love,
⊩⊣干⫫

Dear ⊩⊣干⫫,
Listen, I'm sorry but I'm tired of you yanking my dick around.
You told me to run. I'm running. You ended it 'love' I dunno! God, I'm not gonna send this. I'm gonna send this. Ok. don't hate me.
Love love love love,

Drew

Dear ╠┤┳╝,

Sorry about that last email. If you haven't opened it, please god delete it without doing so.

Drew

Dear Drew,

You are honestly the most confusing person I have ever met. Human, Emni, or otherwise.

Love,

╠┤┳╝

Dear ╠┤┳╝,

Well, I do like to feel special.

Where should I go once I get there?

Love,

Drew

Dear Drew,

Where are you landing? I'll meet you there.

Love,

╠┤┳╝

Dear ╠┤┳╝,

Really? Can we slow-mo run into each other's arms like in your freaking chick flicks? Jeezus I missed you so much.

Love,

Drew

Dear Drew,

No. What? No.

You still haven't told me what a 'chick flick' is, but I am beginning to suspect it is an offensive term for the movies I enjoy.

Where are you landing?

Love,

⊫╡╤⫪

Dear ⊫╡╤⫪,

Some place called St. Memphis. Six days from now, probably around sunset.

Can I at least hug you?

Love,

Drew

Dear Drew,

You fluster me beyond comparison.

No, you cannot 'hug' me. Not in front of people. Touch is… different here, outside of one's home.

St. Memphis is a farming island off the coast of Washington Village, where I live. There is only one spaceport. I will be there.

Love,

⊫╡╤⫪

Dear ⊫╡╤⫪,

Ditto.

See you soon.

Love,

Drew

Hugs

Drew was standing anxiously in the middle of the cargo bay during the landing. Which turned out to be stupid; he fell flat on his face as they clunked to the ground—Straight Cousin and the crew raucously laughing at him from their positions, professionally clutching various pieces of the ship. Drew's nose started gushing blood like a faucet.

It was not how he wanted to greet Riis.

He found he wanted to greet Riis much, much more than he wanted to be impressive doing so, however, and ran off the ship as soon as the hull opened, shouting a goodbye to Straight Cousin and the crew on the way down and out, and clutching a rag to his thankfully-not-broken nose. It was very golden and dark here, the sun setting, Jupiter II enormous, taking up most of the sky, and he found himself gaping at it as he faltered in his steps.

He'd barely made it off the ship and to the tarmac when a clawed hand grabbed him and he let out a breath that hurt, spinning to face him, and they stared at each other.

Riis.

Riis, head tipped down to see him, eyes tight, a line of focus between them, and he could see himself reflected back. Sloping horns and black eyes with strange lids and all of it was so familiar and good it made his teeth hurt, and one clawed hand gripped Drew's arm, hard.

"Hey," Drew said. He could barely feel his face.

"What happened?" Riis practically shouted. He seemed tense, alive behind his eyes, and his hand gripped Drew's arm *harder*, shaking slightly, and Drew had totally forgotten about his nose until the other hand rose and touched it lightly.

"Oh," he laughed, dazed. "Oh, I fell."

Riis glared at him, like he found this personally offensive.

"You really are tall, you know that, right?" Drew finally said dumbly, throat dry.

Riis squinted, looked away. Touched one of the horns, which seemed to have actually gotten a bit longer than before even, wow. "I am relatively short, by our standards."

"You're tall to me," Drew said brazenly.

"Yes. Well. We should… eh, come with me."

The hand on his arm tightened. "Yeah," he got out. Followed.

Riis seemed to move faster and faster the further they got from the spacedock. Pulled him by the arm until he was basically decking it next to Riis, gasping for breath, and Riis spun him around the side of the building and Drew had just enough space to say "Riis, *what —*"

Before Riis grabbed him, hard, in an embrace that literally lifted him off his feet for a minute.

Drew breathed. His hands came to Riis' back and he clutched. Tried not to groan as he buried his face in Riis' neck. Let out a shaking breath nonetheless.

Riis stiffened, shuddered. Jerked backwards and stared at him.

He had blood on his neck, Drew realized. He'd forgotten *again*, his *nose*, shit—

"You have no idea what you're doing, do you?" Riis asked

haltingly, looking oddly dazed.

Drew let out an explosive breath. Grinned up at him, through the blood. Wanted to cry with relief. "Nope," he said. "Not even slightly."

Riis laughed, softly. Looked away, and then back. "Well. You wanted 'a hug,' so… anyway. My pack is eager to meet you," he said then.

Drew shrugged, grinning. He had never felt so light. "Great, cool. Let's go. Uh, you have some blood there…" He reached up to Riis' neck to wipe it away and Riis shivered, stepping back then. Wiped it away himself, hand shaking slightly.

"Let's go," he said softly, and took Drew's hand like he was a child. Led him—far slower and calmer this time — around the spaceport and out to where a lone, strange looking car sat waiting.

They got in the car. Riis immediately took his hand again. Held it tightly as he pressed a series of buttons with one swift claw and the car turned on, and then automatically started driving off in some direction that Riis didn't seem to be directing it to go, at least in real time, considering Riis was now staring at him, quiet, eyes wide.

Drew looked back. Honestly just drank in the sight of him like he was water, and Drew had definitely been dying of thirst.

"I missed you so much," he found himself saying, hoarse.

Riis' eyes widened. Shut. "Hm. I, as well."

"Oh? You missed you?"

"What?" Riis looked just so, so flustered. Drew wanted to *tackle him*.

"What you said. It means you missed yourself."

"Ah. Well, perhaps…"

Quiet, for a moment. Riis looked at him, and something painful flickered in his eyes for a moment. "I missed myself when I was at school. I missed you when I was away. It seemed I couldn't win. Despite the very real fact that it didn't seem wise, I have been… I've wanted you to come here for a long time."

Drew let out a shuddering exhale.

Would it be so crazy? If he just—

It didn't seem like Riis would *mind at all* and wasn't that insane, wasn't that—

"We're here," Riis said quickly, as the car pulled up to a dock, and Drew was confused at first before remembering Riis lived on the mainland.

They were the only ones waiting for the ferry at this late hour. They sat with their feet hanging over the edge of the dock, hands clasped tightly between them like a secret, and Drew felt strange, almost *young*. Raw and thrilled in the same moment, awake with wonder. They were just two kids, dangling feet over the dock. Holding hands in secret.

"Here we are," Riis said softly. The ferry chugged almost silently up to them. Riis handed over his car keys to a bored looking Emni who had leapt off the ferry even before it reached dock and they went in the passenger entrance. Empty. They had their own boat.

It was stiflingly hot, so Drew walked through the inside passenger holding out to the nose of the boat, laughing in a burst as the clear sea breeze hit his face again, the sky darker now, but bright at the same time, Jupiter II huge and rolling. The car was loaded up and they were off, and the sea raced below them, the great gas giant making each ripple spike red as flame. He peered down into the sea, locking his legs between the slats of the rail so he wouldn't fall in. Drew wondered insanely if there were lobsters here, like there were on Earth II, a relic of ancient Earth that had invaded and taken over the planet's local crustaceans. That seemed like a crazy question, though. So he just peered over the edge and looked, the wind cool as a palm pushing back his hair.

Riis stood away from him. Drew felt the charge between them like a chime, and couldn't stop turning back to him, grinning. Always, always: Riis met his gaze.

He was positively giddy by the time they reached the mainland.

Washington was a sleepy little city, though Drew remembered Riis had called it a 'village' in his letter. It reminded him vaguely of the outskirts of the city surrounding Capital Hull proper, where folks lived in great stacked shipping-container-made apartment buildings like the one he and Amy rented a unit in. While quite a few of these existed here—little lights in the cut windows showing glimpses into whole other lives—there were also squat, sloping, square buildings; built smooth out of dark, red clay; swirling designs delicately thumbed (clawed?) all over the surface. Most folk seemed to be sleeping, but a few Emnni sat out on stoops and wandered between houses, calling out to each other in whistling grunts.

No one really paid them much mind, down on the dark dock peering up at them.

It was thrilling.

The car was unloaded and they got back in. Instantly, Riis' hand was in his again. His thumb rubbed a small circle on Drew's palm. God.

They rode for a little while longer, until they reached the outskirts of the small city—squat dark trees getting thicker and thicker—and then, "We're here," Riis said softly.

Well, wow.

"You *live* here?!"

"...Yes."

"Riis this is a *fucking mansion.*"

"...Yes."

Drew cackled, madly.

Riis glared. "As you enjoy saying in such instances, I believe I will utilize 'shut up,'" he said, tersely.

Drew honestly couldn't stop laughing, now.

He didn't know what he'd been expecting.

Probably, like. A cave, maybe.

Jeez.

He squeezed Riis hand quickly; an apology for something he hadn't voiced, but frankly shouldn't have thought. Grinned at him. "Let's go meet the fam."

"My pack?"

"Yup."

"...Alright."

The house was *enormous*, probably more an estate than a mansion, though Drew really didn't know the difference at the end of the day. The architecture was a bizarre mix of sloping, adobe red blocks with the swirly designs and what was clearly, Drew realized with a start, human architecture. It looked almost like a craftsman. Just. With a lot of clay-built additions spreading out on all sides. The glass in all the windows, it seemed as a rule, was stained. Bright colors everywhere.

There was a light on inside, and the door on one of those additions opened, and another Emni stepped out.

Drew faltered, fell back for a moment and Riis startled, jerked back by his hand. He turned, "It's alright," he said softly, "my, eh, 'sister,' I suppose, she's kind and calm, she—"

The sister all but tackled Drew.

She was taller than Riis, a lighter gray than Riis, decked out in a strange kind of draping green robe thing that almost resembled something Shrink Kanak might wear, and letting out the belting bellow-laugh even before she reached him. He let out a shocked shriek and Riis snapped something whistling and grunting out, clearly a reprimand of some kind, but she shouted into Drew's ear, "THANK YOU FOR THE TAKING SUCH GOOD CARE OF OUR SMALL BABY!"

Drew burst out into hysterical laughter and Riis hid his face, swearing.

She blinked big dark eyes down at him, barely an inch from his nose. "The name of mine is—" she croaked and hissed with glee.

Drew nodded, feeling a tad insane. "Nice to meet you..." He attempted the same sound in return.

"PERFECTIONISM!"

Riis spoke his sister's name and gave her something that sounded like a sharp warning. To Drew's ear, it was a pair of warbles, a groan, and a whistle.

Drew was led with enthusiasm back inside the house, where he was greeted with further enthusiasm of varying flavors, and it became clear to him that Riis was like, weirdly stoic and proper for an Emni. Or at least for his 'pack.'

Hands were grabbing at Drew's hair, floofing it around and pulling at it. Children who came up to barely his hip, with horns that were just small nubs at their crested foreheads, were asking excited, whistling questions. One Emni poked his *ear* and suddenly Riis barked something out at them all and they backed up, quick as they'd crowded him, hoots and laughter bouncing off the walls.

Drew swayed, utterly dazed, still with blood down his shirt.

"My sincerest apologies," Riis looked humiliated, "we don't often have human guests, and—"

"That was the most enthusiastic welcome I have *ever* received, and I'm basically, like, alien royalty," Drew said flatly.

Riis jumped. Squinted slightly, looked away. "Well," he said. "You are not royalty."

"Ouch."

"You're *not*. Not legally."

"I *am* an alien, though, right?"

The line between Riis' eyes was back, and he was squinting so small his eyes were just the gleam of light reflecting off them, "Undoubtedly."

"MY GOODNESS."

Riis suddenly looked *very* flustered as his sister smacked him upside the head, bellowing something. Drew had no idea what was happening. He laughed, though, utterly delighted.

Relieved beyond measure.

"Get the human a clean shirt," one of the adults snapped out, and Riis jumped, glancing down at Drew's shirt, which was, you know, still kind of like something out of a horror movie.

"Right," Riis said quickly, and pulled Drew back into a hall and up some stairs and into a room, beads clinking behind them.

Drew let out a breath. It looked almost achingly familiar. A squat green couch. The rug, on the floor. The beads in the doorway. The cabinet, even, against the wall beside a neatly made round bed.

All that was missing were the doors propped against the window.

"Eh, here, you can wear..." Riis trailed off.

Drew looked at Riis, and he felt such a brightness in his gut it seemed to overflow, up his body into his eyes, and he took off his bloody shirt, not breaking eye-contact until he had to, and then reached out to grab Riis' offered replacement.

Riis was very still. Staring at him.

He hesitated, before he put the shirt on, heart hammering. Considered—

Riis let out an explosive breath, bursting around him then, out of the dark room. "I... I will see you out there, dinner will be served soon, I should help."

Drew pulled the shirt on slowly, alive with wonder. It was very strange and drapey, but smelled distinctly like Riis.

Food was served rather quickly after that point. Despite the startling heat of this planet, there was a fire roaring in a great stone hearth that rested open to the rest of the room, and they ate around that, shoveling what looked almost like rice but seemed softer and pulpier into their mouths, adding various dressings and vegetables and meats.

Everything was, to some degree, pickled.

Drew couldn't care less.

He ate approximately six different kinds of mystery pickles. Laughed, joked nervously as well as he could with the Emnis, sat with his knee pressed hard against Riis' leg, and Riis didn't move away. There was mead—a sour honey wine that was *dangerous*, and he kept forgetting it was, kept having glass after glass until the world shimmered on a bright knife edge.

Eventually, the children seemed to win some argument and determinedly put on 'a performance,' as Riis called it; a kind of musical lilting play in which they wore all manner of strange costumes that seemed to be assembled from simply what was nearby.

Drew laughed with the rest of them, even though he didn't understand most of what was happening. Eventually just leaned back on a squat plush couch and sighed, grinning, each blink lasting longer than the last.

He woke up to Riis whispering his name, softly. A clawed hand gentle on his jaw.

The room was empty. They were alone. Drew could barely hold his eyes open, but he rose when Riis pulled at him, followed him dumbly, leaning hard against his strong shoulder.

Riis all but carried him up the stairs to a new room with a bed. It was the same squat, low, circular dealio that had been in Riis' room, flush with pillows and blankets. The room was barren besides the bed, though a stained glass window rested tipped open to the sky. He was deposited gently in the center. He felt his boots being pulled off, and the sky through the window was full of Jupiter II, spinning softly towards him. Then Riis, cutting a shadow across. His eyes squinted and gentle, the line between them.

"Goodnight, Drew," Riis said softly.

He cut the loveliest shadow. Pointed, slopey horns up top, thick curling ones on either side. The gentle line of his nose running into his mouth. Drew reached a finger up. Traced it down, slowly, running it back and forth over the mouth, and Riis stilled over him.

His breath hitched.

God. How was it possible to want someone so—

"You don't know what you're doing at all," Riis said again. His voice shook. He did not move away, though.

"I do," Drew said softly.

Riis shivered.

Drew, brave off booze and desperation, leaned forward quickly.

Riis' mouth was sloping, hard lines. His breath came out warm, a sigh against Drew's lips, and Drew shuddered and suddenly he was under Riis on the bed, his hands held tight on either side of his head, Riis over him, eyes startled and wide.

For a moment they just breathed. Stared at each other.

"Try harder," Riis finally got out, voice breaking slightly. Drew blinked. The hands left his wrists, and Riis was gone.

Drew was alone. He lay there, dizzy and confused for a long few moments before he fell asleep.

31

Festival

Drew woke up with a headache that felt like a second heartbeat throbbing in his temple.

He groaned for a minute, squeezing his eyes shut. Dread coiled in his gut.

He opened his eyes, and Jupiter II was half-sunk into the horizon, dusty through a bright morning sky out a high, semi-circle window.

Immediate joy.

He was on Drune.

Riis. He had *hugged* Riis yesterday, rather passionately. Held his hand in the car. Fallen asleep against him during his small pack members' show, and it was all a bit hazy after that, but still.

He had dreamed Riis kissing him softly, leaning over him on the bed.

So, head and heart both pounding, he still walked—whistling—out of the room, squinting at the light. Found the bathroom Riis had shown him last night, made his ablutions, washed his face, felt *significantly* better, and ran down the stairs to the big main room, practically colliding with Riis.

"Oh!" he jumped.

Riis froze. Looked carefully at him. Drew blinked. "Eh… Riis?" he said after a moment. He was like. 99.9 percent sure, but this reaction was *strange*, and—

Riis immediately seemed to close off, shut down, "Yes," he said, rather cool, and Drew flinched. "I was just coming to wake you. Give you this," and he pushed a hot drink into Drew's hands. "It's tea. Tea with an egg… an egg… the part of the egg that's the most good in it."

Drew snorted. "Egg yolk?"

"Yolk. Yes."

Drew shrugged. His mood could absolutely not be kicked. "Sure," he said, and downed it.

Immediately felt like puking.

Actually kind of let out a huff, bowing slightly, clutching his guts and Riis made a very clear step back, eyes widening. He didn't puke though, thank christ, and almost immediately after felt much better. "Nice! Amy would absolutely *kill* for that hangover remedy."

"It's just tea. Strong tea, and egg."

"Oh… well, I'll have to tell her…"

"Better tea than humans drink," Riis clipped out. He seemed so strange, closed off, frankly *chilly*.

Drew laughed, rather nervously. "Well. To be fair, I never got to tell you about the paper bag around the tea."

"I know about that. I never understood it. I can always taste the *ink*, too, I mean…" Riis trailed off.

Drew waggled his eyebrows up at him.

"You're supposed to take the bag off," Riis said flatly.

"Yup."

Riis let rip his favorite swear-shaped whistle, heartily. Drew laughed hard, and Riis seemed to soften reluctantly, as he looked at Drew with a humorous, affectionate spin on contempt. Things seemed a bit better, then.

****

They had breakfast as a group, and it was the first non-pickle-based food he'd gotten in over twenty-four hours and Drew *devoured* it; strange eggs with some kind of incredibly spicy relish. His first bite had him gasping and flapping his hands over his mouth, and Riis' pack laughed heartily, the whole room suddenly overbrimming with bellowing belts. A television was playing some gentle morning show, whistling, clicking voices soft in the room, and suddenly Riis was jerking forward to flip it off. Drew didn't know why until a picture of his own face popped up.

Ah.

Well.

It was, at least, a kind of flattering picture.

Riis pressed a button on the side of the TV—a remote being either not present fast enough or just not a thing here, Drew didn't really know. It blipped off, and there was silence. Riis stepped back, turning and staring out over his pack. Daring them, it seemed, to speak.

Then, a taller Emni let loose a snapping whistle comment at Riis, whose face stayed tight and strained.

Immediately, there was what seemed to be an opposing comment, and then, a kind of mild chaos.

Drew slowly put down the small scoop thing that seemed to be the popular utensil, here.

Riis' 'sister' bellowed something harshly ending with a whistle and then a distinct 'Drew' at the end. Riis grabbed her hand, seemed to nod on instinct, but clicked too, approximately six times. The first speaker harshly bellowed out another comment, and Drew stood shakily, stood beside Riis and his sister, wondering—but also kind of knowing—what was happening.

Riis barely glanced at him. Sister, though, suddenly dropped a heavy claw down on Drew's shoulder and spoke quickly and clearly in a whistling belt. He heard his name more than once.

Then, something odd happened. Riis jumped, shrinking, quickly covering his face with his hands.

An abrupt, stunned silence in the room.

Drew desperately wondered if there was some kind of translation app he could download. Then he felt like an idiot for not doing that, like, at least a week ago in preparation. He felt stupid, and small, and woefully unprepared. Especially when the first tall speaker let out a croaking cry whistle and Riis flinched like he'd been struck.

Riis shook, hiding his face, claws digging into his own forehead. So Drew had to do *something*.

"Listen," Drew spoke haltingly. "Eh…" he had immediately commanded everyone's attention. At least ten pairs of big dark eyes were now blinking in his direction. Most with a cautious curiosity at what he might say, it seemed. Only one or two with a pointed sneer. He swallowed. "I can leave. If it's… too much of a risk, I mean, I thought he *told you*," and he shot a glare in Riis' direction. Riis, he realized with a swoop, hadn't lifted his face from his hands. Behind his hands, though, Drew could see him—eyes wide; the line between those eyes deepening. "I don't want to endanger anyone. I can go. I can—"

"No!" this voice bellowed out harshly, quivering with everything but fear. Drew jumped as he—along with everyone else—turned their attention to the smallest of the adult Emni. They rose slowly from their squat cushion beside the table, and several clawed hands reached out to help, but they waved these offers off. "Squire of Sol II is who has been chosen by the gut. The doctrine is clear. He is now part of our pack. No exceptions. We stand by our pack. We will be standing by Squire Drew."

Silence, at that. Drew blinked. Glanced quickly at Riis, who was peering through his fingers at this speaker, eyes squinting and soft. "What's, eh, chosen by the gut?" he asked, as quietly as possible.

Riis flinched like he'd been downright smacked.

Sister didn't, though, suddenly letting out a mad whistling cackle, and soon the whole room was overflowing with bellowing laughter, even from a few who'd seemed grudging at this smallest Emni's speech. They all began to move back around their business, a few hands coming down gently on Riis' shoulders like he'd just gotten married or something. The speaker approached him, and despite what was clearly just a *deep* embarrassment, Riis bent and pressed his nose against theirs, briefly.

They whistled something out softly, ending distinctly with Riis' real name. Drew recognized it, having practiced saying it rather often at this point.

Riis mumbled something back.

"Riis?"

"I will, eh... explain later," Riis said softly. Sister cackled again. Riis picked at a horn. "Eh. For now, there is... there is a party, of sorts, a celebration today. Festy-val I believe is the word in Standard."

"Festival?"

"Yes, that. Eh. We were all going to go. If you would like to join us."

Drew grinned. "Sure."

Riis squinted at him, but looked away rather quickly.

Preparation for the festival began after breakfast. It seemed to involve a lot of painting one another's faces and horns. Riis was one of the painters, and Drew watched him paint the younger ones with something almost like a sweet pain swelling in his chest. Riis whistled soft language out at them, higher than he normally did, baby talk seeming to be at least slightly universal. They giggled bellowing, whistling laughs back, and he feigned confusion, eyes bright and amused.

Drew sat awkwardly at the edge, not wanting to intrude, until Sister pulled him heartily into the fray and plopped him down decidedly in front of Riis, just as he finished with the last child.

Riis absolutely froze.

Drew flinched. "You don't have to, I mean, I don't wanna, like, be inappropriate, like—"

"What?" Riis ducked, glanced around. There wasn't a *lot* of attention being paid to them, but Drew saw more than one pair of eyes flick in their direction. "No… why would it be inappropriate? No."

He dipped the short, strange brush in the paint, which had been spread container-free over the smooth stone table. Reached out and swiped some slowly down Drew's nose.

Drew shut his eyes.

"Cease moving your head," Riis snapped. Drew opened his eyes and glared. He tried to stop moving his head, but apparently failed, as Riis reached up, faltered for a moment, and then gripped his chin decidedly with one clawed hand, leaning forward with focus.

In a room full of folks who probably weren't eager to smell anything, Drew frantically tried to think of really, really un-sexy things. It kind of worked.

He hoped.

Sister cackled.

Maybe, okay.

Riis gently ran the brush down his cheekbones. Over his eyebrows. Something seemed to soften in him then, and he hesitated before he painted Drew's mouth, very gently, so lightly, his eyes widening as he did, the brush shaking slightly, and wow, Drew was definitely smellable at this point.

Riis seemed to have finished. They stared at each other. Riis hadn't let go of his chin.

Drew let out a breath.

Riis jumped, jerked his hand back, and the spell was broken.

Sister let out what was clearly a catcall. Riis hollered something back, Drew laughed, dazed, and things went back to normal.

He was hyper-aware of the paint on his face, though. It seemed to contain all of Riis' carefulness.

Sister painted Riis' face quickly, and then they were all off, and for the first time Drew saw the outside in the light. Jupiter II had already partially risen again on the opposing horizon. It rolled pale in the bright sky, but still orange and red and enormous, and it truly did look like a whole world of softly swirling flame. Beyond Jupiter II, the sun was small and distant, less bright than he was used to, but it was still almost oppressively hot. Balmy in a way he'd never felt outside of a greenhouse or something. He eventually took off his drapey borrowed overshirt, tying it around his waist, feeling slightly awkward and skinny in his tank, but no one commented. His steps were light, easy for how heavy it felt, gravity being definitely a tad more here.

Riis' pack wore a striking variety of clothing, the only common theme seeming to be 'draping.' Drew had always kind of wondered what Emni wore, amongst themselves. In human movies their CGI versions tended to dress almost like cavemen. At school, Riis had worn approximately four different outfits, cycled through and clearly well-cared-for, and also clearly human in style. Button-downs altered to contain his broad chest. Pants that fell strangely down his legs, the ends of his clawed feet looking small at the bottom. The only thing he'd never worn was shoes, and it seemed shoes were unimportant here. Everyone clacked claws down from the house into the dirt outside. The clothes were rather simple in print—there was none. Complex in the way they fell, draped, and sometimes even ruffled, though.

Riis was walking slightly ahead, diligently focused on the destination, and Drew ran to catch up. Riis glanced at him, squinting slightly. Then, to Drew's thrilled surprise, reached out and grabbed his hand, swinging it between them.

They walked in silence for a bit, Drew just *enjoying this,* so thoroughly it seemed to glow like an ember in his gut.

"So, what's this festival?" he asked at last.

"It's to celebrate love."

"Ooh. Spicy. We have one like that."

"You don't."

"Eh?" Drew blinked, laughing, feeling positively elated. "We do. It's called—"

"Valentine's day, yes. Valentine's day celebrates but one type.

This is a festival to celebrate the whole breadth of the emotion. The love between... mated pairs, yes. But also between siblings. Pack members. Parents and children."

"Oh," Drew said, something in him aching, deeply. "Cool."

Riis abruptly stopped.

Drew almost collided with him.

"I forgot," Riis said softly.

"Huh?"

"We don't have to go. If it... it might be *painful* for you. Your loss is so new, I—"

Drew flinched, glanced away. The other pack members had almost caught up with them. "I wanna go," he said quickly, voice shaking slightly.

Riis looked hard at him.

"Really," he added.

Dark eyes squinted, the line between them deepening, and Riis let out a breath. "Your feelings on the matter are far more complicated than you are implying," Riis said flatly, and kept walking, tugging Drew by the hand along with him, Riis' blunt claws tightening on his palm.

Drew laughed, feeling awkward and a little broken. "Well. I'll tell you if it's too much, then."

"That's all I ask."

"Okay. Fine, I'll tell you if... if it's too much."

They came upon the festival in pieces at first. Various painted folk—mostly Emni, though Drew was surprised to see quite a few humans—trotting towards the stretch of dark sea he saw glittering at the end of the street. He could distantly hear music; warbling strings accompanied by raucous belting vocals. Everyone seemed fresh and bright, hands held all over the place, swung between pairs, trios, children and adults, whatever.

They came to a black-sand beach with a deep green sea. A great paper-mache-clearly-supposed-to-be-an-Emni-but-kinda-just-looked-like-paper-mache art project loomed. Totally naked, Drew couldn't help but notice, with what looked like a giant hole in its belly.

Drew, feverishly curious, skated through his memory bank of shirtless Riis (of which there were but two barely glimpsed examples) wondering if Riis had just a *hole* in his belly.

Because what.

Like, he was far too gone to mind, but what.

"It's supposed to be the hearth that holds the soul. The fire will be lit there," Riis said, as if he could read Drew's mind. "Then the paper Emni will burn."

"Wow," Drew said, a little floored. "You're gonna just… burn it down?"

"It's a tradition."

"I wasn't knocking it. Cool."

"Yes," Riis said, seeming amused. "'Cool.'"

Drew snickered.

It was then that a fiercely painted Emni burst forth from the crowd, crowing. Riis let go of Drew's hand and jumped forward, and with more enthusiasm than Drew had *ever* seen in him, caught the other Emni and pressed his nose against theirs in an instant.

The world stilled.

Riis muttered something soft almost against their mouth. They laughed. Cackled, really.

They turned shining eyes on Drew, then, and Riis took their hand, swinging it slightly. Spoke while looking at them, "Drew, this is my friend, my friend eh—"

"Arnold!" the friend bellowed, seemingly on a whim, and Riis burst out laughing.

Drew reached out his hand. 'Arnold' took it in one, the other hand still clutching Riis'. Their eyes shone as they said in delicate Standard, "I have heard so much about you! 'Riis' spoke of you often, in his letters. It is my most sincere pleasure to meet you, finally."

Drew shut his eyes. Just for a moment. Opened them, and said, "Yes. Wonderful to meet you, too."

32

Perfect

A rnold was perfect.

They had met, apparently, when both had been selected as potentials for the exchange program. It was barely by a hair that Riis had gone instead. Arnold was apparently 'brilliant.' Lived far away, though, and they hadn't seen each other since Riis got back.

They moved with Riis' same surprising grace. They laughed at all his deadpan jokes. Jokes he at first made in Standard, conscious it seemed of Drew, but quickly dissolved into their own language, a secret humor shared between them. Arnold held Riis' hand gently, and while Riis held Drew's hand in the other, he seemed to point towards Arnold like a plant towards an askew grow light.

Not askew, though. It wouldn't be askew. Because another way Arnold was perfect was that they, too, were an Emni.

Drew felt just so, so stupid.

Stupid, and small, and like he wanted to be angry. He truly wished with all his broken heart that this feeling could turn to anger, get hard and sharp rather than the mucky brokenness that it was now, the swamped rubble of something he must've imagined. But he couldn't. He couldn't be mad at all.

Not at Riis, anyway. Not at Arnold, who lit up Riis' face, made him soft in the mouth. Brought that line of focus between those big dark eyes, again and again.

Unable to focus the anger on them, the rage that came with hurt turned on Drew like a ravaging beast, and he wanted to die.

More than ever before, he wanted to sink into the ground and *die*.

He had even begun to think maybe Riis wanted him. Returned his desperate feelings. Signed his letters 'love'; Drew 'flustered him beyond comparison'; he had deluded himself into believing something impossible, and now, in the face of the fallout, wished it would simply obliterate him.

It didn't.

As the day wore on, they separated a bit from the pack, as did many other members, going off as they did with friends and partners. There were booths and kiosks selling various trinkets, games set up by volunteers. Riis tugged Drew along with him and Arnold, and Drew flat-out wondered why. Why.

He went, though. He was utterly powerless to do anything but follow Riis, wherever he led, like a fucking lovesick puppy.

He hated himself.

At one point things calmed and a speaker came to the front before the paper mache Emni, calling out in whistling grunts and bellows. There was laughter and fanfare in the crowd, quieted each time the speaker's voice rose, and Riis let go of Drew's hand to scratch at a horn, turning and laughing about something with Arnold, and Drew quickly fell back.

Fell back, and snuck away, down the beach.

No one followed him.

At least, he thought no one had. As he sank into some reeds around a turn, however, there was a shrill whistle and his head shot up.

Not Riis.

He recognized her by the paint she had applied this morning. Riis' sister.

Sister hovered before him for a moment. Then spoke haltingly. "You are pain."

Drew couldn't help it; he laughed. Wanted to cry, but couldn't gather his tears. Stared out at the whispering green sea, instead.

She trotted up to him though, sat beside him—at a slight distance, and he was surprised when she scooted closer, dropping an arm over his shoulder.

Drew breathed. Stared at the sea. At Jupiter II, rolling on the horizon.

"Your, eh… Mother? ⊢╫ say she die."

Drew shut his eyes. Great. Now broken twice.

"Love is very tough. And death."

He snorted. "Yup," he said quietly. Then a smaller, softer, "Yeah, it is."

"Drew!"

Riis burst frantically before the reeds, relief washing over his face as he saw them. He froze as he realized Sister was with Drew. Hesitated. Then spoke softly, "You told me you'd tell me."

Drew couldn't quite meet his eyes. Even looking at his delicate tapered feet hurt. "Oh, uh…"

Sister rose, then, stretching. "I will leave." she said bluntly, and then clicked twice at Riis, whistling out something rather harsh sounding that made Riis flinch, before padding down to the sand again, trotting slowly back to the festival.

Riis stared at him.

Drew stared at his feet.

"What can I do?"

Drew shut his eyes.

Riis let out a sigh, and came up to him. Crouched and grabbed his chin, then, far more confidently than he had this morning, and said very softly as Drew helplessly raised his eyes to look at him, "What can I do, Drew?"

It was then that the tears came, of course.

Riis let out a breath like he'd been wounded, and suddenly he was on the ground with Drew, holding him tenderly, and he shuddered as Drew immediately pressed his face into Riis' neck but this time he didn't move away.

They held one another, and Drew cried.

Eventually, after a long time, the sobs became further and further apart. His eyes dried, but the pain was like a new presence in his gut, weighty and immovable.

"Would you like to speak on it?" Riis asked softly. He sat beside Drew now, one arm wrapped tight around him, Drew's head on his shoulder. "Your mother's death. You said you were there?"

Drew shut his eyes. Shook.

"You don't have to. It might help, but only you know if you are —"

"She fell down," he said quietly. It had gotten dim, the final long golden shadows before darkness. The day had flown by so quickly. He remembered then that days were shorter here, and felt stupid. "I thought she'd just fallen. I called out to her, came around the table. Her eyes were open."

Riis skated a hand gently through his hair, and he shuddered. Continued, eyes squeezed shut, "I knew right away I think, but I couldn't let myself know, and I shouted. I shook her. It occurred to me then to maybe try CPR, to try compressions, like… it's a thing, where you push on someone's chest and try and get their heart to start again, but… the switch."

Riis went very still.

There was cheering, far off. The smell of smoke, and the sudden burst of flame. They'd lit the Emni.

"The switch. I was terrified. I knew, consciously, that it wasn't just *there*, it was encased in plastic in her chest, but I couldn't… couldn't save her." Drew finished finally, barely a whisper by the end.

"You were afraid you would activate it. If you… tried

compressions," Riis finally spoke, and his words were very soft.

"Yes. I thought of you. I thought of you and I… I couldn't even try. I didn't even try."

Riis let out a hard breath. His hand tightened in Drew's hair.

Then, because it was all lost anyway, Drew spoke softly. "I don't think I've ever loved anyone so much in my life."

Silence.

He could hear Riis' heart beating fast against his ear.

"Your mother?" Riis said.

Drew shut his eyes. In for a penny, whatever. Let out a shaking sigh and pulled his head back, looked up at Riis, whose eyes were wide, the line between them, and Drew reached up and touched that line lightly.

Riis didn't move.

"No," he said finally, and Riis let out a breath in a rush.

Silence.

Drew breathed. Looked. Loved him so much.

"You don't know what you're doing at all," Riis finally spoke, very quietly.

"I know it can't happen. I know it's not… not what you want," and this hurt, and he shut his eyes as the line deepend, as Riis' eyes grew bright, "I just, I need you to at least *know*, it's you, I love *you*, so much it makes me crazy, so much everything, everything I do and think and feel leads back to it, so much that—"

"Chosen by the gut means I've begun to bond with you."

Drew's eyes snapped open.

Riis' eyes were still so wide. He spoke again, and it was barely more than a whisper, and Drew suddenly realized he could feel his breath against his mouth, that they had gotten so close in the sand they were practically nose to nose, and his own breath hitched.

"It's… before forming a lifemate bond, it's the step before—"

And Drew understood in a shocking jolt to the system and let out a strangled sob and surged forward and kissed him, hard.

Riis shuddered, let out a low growl, hands suddenly on his face and for a second it seemed like he was going to lean forward into it, like it would be good, so good, so *utterly perfect* but instead, he pulled Drew's face back, pushed his forehead against Drew's, breathed raggedly against his mouth and Drew pushed back, helplessly breathing against him, eyes wide and light and god, god...

"You do *not know what you are doing at all...*"

"I do! I do, though, God, *Riis*, I—"

"No! We... we mate for *life*, Drew, we do not casually throw ourselves into such things, we do not—"

"I want you for life!"

Riis shuddered. Faltered, in what he was going to say next, and Drew pushed forward helplessly, kissed him again but pushed past, forward, burying his face in Riis' neck.

The growl again—low—seeming to unearth itself from the depths of Riis, and suddenly Drew was on his back in the sand and Riis' face was in his neck, Riis' mouth skating over his shoulder, exhaling hard there and it sent a shock straight through Drew and Riis swore, one hand running over his chest, coming to grip him hard at the hip, the other tangling in his hair. Riis came up and pressed his mouth against Drew's and Drew felt like he would break, and be fine with it, utterly fine.

Riis pulled back, though. Looked down at him. He could see himself reflected in Riis' eyes, lips parted, ragged breath, face flushed, and God, he had never wanted like this, never—

Riis shut his eyes, then. Dropped his forehead against Drew's. "You say that today."

Drew let out a strangled sob. "I'll say it tomorrow, too."

"Maybe. The next day?"

"Absolutely."

"Ten years from now? Twenty?"

"Of course."

Riis pushed off him then. Sat in the sand beside him, and Drew breathed, feeling the loss of Riis over him for a second before rising to sitting. He touched Riis' back. Riis flinched.

"You say that too easily. Words are meaningless to humans.

Declarations are without merit."

"Hey," Drew shot back, "I've never said a single meaningless thing in my life. Especially not to you."

"You don't know—"

"'—What I'm doing at all,' I know, I've heard you say that before," Drew snapped. "And I get it, you're *very* smart, but you're wrong, here. You're wrong." He squeezed his eyes shut. Dropped his mouth to Riis' shoulder, god, he smelled like the sea, smelled clean and good and exactly like Drew'd known he would, "I know exactly what I'm doing."

Riis let out a strangled noise, and it twisted in Drew's gut. A shaky sob. Just a single, shaky sob.

"*Riis*, he whispered softly against his shoulder, "I have loved you for so long. I'll love you for the rest of my life; I know I will."

"And if you are wrong, it will kill me," Riis said harshly, and Drew froze.

Riis stood, then. Shaking slightly, he detangled himself from Drew, and Drew caught himself quickly, but remained sitting, staring up at Riis from the sand. Riis' face was hard, something feverish and bright in his eyes, but a staunch *decision* all over his face.

"There's been others, like us. Humans have been here for generations. It was bound to happen. Always, it ends the same. The human grows tired, or finds someone else, or simply *leaves*. Even beyond that—we are ruled by you. There is ignorance at the heart of this thing. I must prioritize *my people*, must work to free *my people*, who are at your mercy, who—"

"I'll prioritize your people too!" Drew said helplessly. "Even beyond this, I believe I should! I have for a long time! I'll do whatever, anything—"

"It is not an attack against you, merely fact: your words are meaningless. Each instance of 'us' has begun with such a declaration. If we are lucky the human stays on Drune after ending the... entanglement. If we are lucky they do not simply... simply go home, back to stars we are barred from, a planet where I'm the first of my kind to set foot for generations—" and Riis' voice broke "—Killing us through distance. Even if I did not die—and I am quite sure I would—it is torture, to live with a broken bond. Torture. So no, I cannot take you at your word, Drew. If you want this you must, as always, *try harder.*"

"Try harder at what?!"

"Understanding," Riis said through his teeth. "Understanding the sacrifice."

Drew stared. And then, he couldn't help it, he laughed, harshly. It hurt, coming up, and Riis flinched like he'd hit him. "Understand *sacrifice? Me?* I don't understand *sacrifice?!* Riis, I am, quite literally, a *sacrifice!* It's all I was raised to be! The notion has been hammered into my head my whole life, it's my identity, my destiny, my *whole fucking purpose*—"

"Is it still?"

"What? No, of course not, you taught me—"

"Exactly!" Riis shouted. "Exactly! My! Point! Humans are unlikely to legitimately commit to *lunch plans,* much less an Emni lifetime bond, a mate, I cannot, I simply *cannot*—" and his voice broke, and he turned away then, bolting.

"Riis!" Drew shouted, but Riis, inhumanly fast as ever, was already halfway back to the festival, back straight, shoulders hunched.

Broken

The walk back to Riis' house was easy.

Just a straight shot from the beach to his home.

The front door was unlocked.

Quiet. No one was back from the festival yet.

Drew's hands shook as he turned on the television in the kitchen. More for something, anything to distract him than anything else. He could still feel Riis' mouth on his neck. His breath on his shoulder. Riis' hand on his hip.

His pain, emanating in a strike from big, feverishly bright dark eyes.

Drew flipped through until he found a channel in Standard, a haughty human woman he'd never seen before speaking—

"—and is it really necessary, at this point, to have a Knight of Sol II? Sure, it's *tradition*, but with the current Knight missing, with a break in that proud lineage—who would it even be? What purpose would they truly serve, at the end of the day? Why not just keep the switch where we can reach it, in case of emergency, rather than—"

Drew flipped the TV off. Stared at the dark screen.

Breathed, shallowly.

He knew, all at once, what he had to do.

What he *could* do.

Not just to prove himself. Not just to stand by his word. It was simple, really. It was the truth. There *was* a way he could act, protect Riis, his people. Protect Drune.

There always had been.

Riis' tablet was on the table. He thumbed it open. Wrote a quick letter—a simple thing, very simple, not enough space to contain all he wanted to say. Signed it off with a 'love,' because it was all he could do.

Then he looked up public transit back to the spaceport.

****

Drew called home, shoveling all his money into a hyperspace call, creating the paper trail he'd been trying to avoid up till now. The trail that would tell whoever might be looking where he was, soon as he accessed his checking account. It didn't matter anymore.

He called just to hear and see her again; his mother's golden bright face in the answering machine blip before the message. Someone answered, though, and his heart stuttered in his chest.

"Drew?"

Seb glared out at him, haughty and disheveled.

"Yeah," he breathed. "Yeah, yes. It's me."

Seb snorted. Looked away. The video was glitching, grainy. "You realize I could have your ass court-martialed, right?"

"I'm coming back."

"Hm. I guess I can wait till then."

"No, I… didn't intend to leave. I want the switch. I just had to… handle something, first. I want the switch. I want to be Knighted."

Quiet. The train station was largely empty. He'd already taken the first ferry back to St. Memphis, and the tiny farming island was quiet, folks he guessed busy at home. "Okay, so you didn't abandon your post."

"No."

"You… only slightly AWOLed."

"Only slightly, yeah."

Seb let out a huff. "Okay. I suppose I can get behind that. We've all had our wild nights that get out of hand, eh, *brother?*" and then he took a swig of something, coughing slightly into it.

Drew flinched. "Yeah…"

"Dad's not as mad as he should be," Seb said coldly, then. "It'll probably be fine. See you soon." There was a blip as the call ended.

"Drew…"

Drew froze. Turned.

Riis stood in the empty shuttle station behind him, eyes wide and anguished, and Drew shut his own eyes quickly.

Don't

I didn't mean for you to *follow me*, jeez *Riis*, I—"

"No. No, no, you're not… you're not doing this."
"I am."
"No."
"No, you taught me that I have a choice. I have a *choice*. I choose to… to act, or whatever," he finished lamely, voice shaking. "I choose to get the switch."

Riis shuddered. Shut his eyes.

Drew wavered. Reached out towards him, and when he didn't move away, caught his hand. Held it tightly. "I'll do what I can," he breathed out, and Riis' eyes snapped open. "I told you. I told you I'd fight for your people."

The shuttle arrived behind him. Riis' hand tightened in his.

"How is this… how is this what I asked, I didn't, I didn't ask for this, I didn't—"

Drew kissed his hand, shutting him up immediately, though not in the way he would've liked. Riis jerked his hand away, leapt backwards as if burned.

They stood, divided by a few solid feet at this point, staring at one another.

"Drew," Riis said as he turned away, started towards the train, "Drew, no, please, I can't—"

"You can. This is why I have to, *Riis*, jeez…"

"No, don't do this, just don't—"

"Hey Riis," Drew said softly, turning to him from just inside the doors.

Riis stilled, staring at him, eyes shining and hard. "What."

"Blow out the candle," he said, and the doors closed.

Riis stood frozen, staring at him. The train began to move and he seemed to come back to himself in a jolt, running after it, and Drew dropped his head against the glass and shut his eyes as they sped faster, faster away, and Riis slipped off behind them and he couldn't see him anymore.

35

Love

Dear Drew,

I was wrong. I'll be with you. I have wanted it so badly I can sometimes hardly breathe. Come back. Be with me.

Love,

Dear Drew,

It infuriates me that you see this as helpful to me. Harm to you is not helpful to me.

Love,

Dear Drew,

Please. Come back. Don't do this.

The mere fact that they will cut into you makes me shake. So much could go wrong.

What if your mother did die due to a complication with the switch? You cannot do this. I would die. I would die.
Love,
⊞⊞

Dear ⊞⊞,
You really, seriously better not.
Drama queen.
Love,
Drew

Dear Drew,
I better not?? This is MY 'better not?'
You infuriate me.
I love you more than what I can hold within myself.
Come back. Let me share it with you.
Love,
⊞⊞

Dear ⊞⊞,
You know, I never liked the phrase 'being a tease' because it implies, like, blame for sparking something up in someone else. You're doing that, though. You're being a MAJOR tease jeezus christ you make me crazy STOP.
Love,
Drew

Dear Drew,
No. Come back. Let me touch you.
I will touch you every day, for the rest of our days. I want to

touch every part of you. Let me.
Love,
⊩⊣⊤⊥

Dear ⊩⊣⊤⊥,
Jeezus.
Love,
Drew

Dear ⊩⊣⊤⊥,
I love you. I'm doing this. Seriously admittedly hope you'll still want to touch me, after, because wow. Would love that.
Love,
Drew

Dear ⊩⊣⊤⊥,
You ok?
Love,
Drew

Dear ⊩⊣⊤⊥,
I might've pissed you off, I get that, just please let me know you're ok.
Love,
Drew

Dear ⊩⊣⊤⊥,
Please, god, be ok.
Love,
Drew

Dear █┤┤┬█,

If you're fine and just like laughing about this I'm going to be so furious you have no idea. God, please, just be ok. I love you. I love you. I'm doing this for you, and I know that pisses you off, but please be ok.

Love,

Drew

Dear █┤┤┬█,

Please. Please be ok.

I love you.

Love,

Drew

36

The Knight of Sol II

A my was part of the reception when he got back to Earth II.

She held him and he shook in her arms, and then Seb's hand was coming down cold on his shoulder.

Seb embraced him, hard, kissing him once on the head like he was his kid brother, like that was *really* their relationship. His fingernails dug hard into Drew's shoulder.

Drew breathed.

Blow out the candle.

Amy's face was made of fear.

The crowd at the spaceport cheered. Cameras flashed. Newsies clamored. He didn't even bother smiling at them.

Blow out the candle.

It would be tonight. It would be tonight that he got the switch.

Blow out the candle.

The culmination of all that he'd been trained to have and want. His purpose would complete itself neatly tonight, but all he could think about, all that pressed against his mind was Riis. Riis, not writing back.

Blow.

Out.

The.

Candle.

****

Amy held his hand in the hospital. He was lying in a cushy private room. Nothing but the best for him.

He'd had visitors today. Shrink Kanak had visited, face tight, held his hand just as tightly and looked at him with a fierce love and hadn't said much. Just looked hard at him and he'd looked back at her, and then she'd said. "I know why you're doing this."

He'd just blinked.

"It's very brave."

Silence. He was very tired of being brave.

She'd kissed his head before she left. Strange and mom-like and it had broken his heart a little.

The Previous King Admiral had also visited. He had handed the King Admiralship over to Seb, his only true-born son, earlier that day. Apparently hadn't spent much time at the coronation party, though. He'd visited Drew, instead. Spoke stiffly, from a distance.

He had Drew's face, too. The buggy eyes looked tired beneath the previous King Admiral's wizened brow.

"I'm sorry about... about your mother. It was always a possibility... pity, though, that it had to be like that. So pointless."

Drew had nodded. Nodded twice. Two short bobs of the head. Had said, "Yes."

The previous King Admiral had left rather quickly after that.

Now he and Amy were alone, though, and Amy's slender hand shook in his. "Are you *sure?*" she kept asking, even now. As if there was any kind of turning back at this point.

He might not be shackled to the bed. He might be a 'willing' sacrifice. As willing as he'd ever been, quite frankly. He still couldn't leave, though. He knew that much just by the guards stationed

262

outside his room.

"You're sure it's the only way? The only way to launch the weapon?" Drew asked softly. He'd been asking that a lot, too.

Amy's mouth was a tight line. She nodded, shortly. Spoke under her breath, "It was designed that way. That's the *whole point*. They'll have to build a whole new weapon if they want to have a functioning one again, and who knows... who knows if there's even the resources for that, frankly, I mean..."

He nodded. Shut his eyes.

"Drew, are you *sure about this?* I mean... I understand, I get where you're coming from, but this is your *life*. This is your life, your whole *life!* And they will... will never stop hunting you. Never."

"I'm sure."

"You won't be able to stop running. You won't get a moment's peace. You—"

"I'm sure."

"Really? And what do you plan on doing, if they do catch up?"

Drew squeezed his eyes closed, hard. "...Fight them?"

There was a loaded silence.

Amy snorted, and then they were laughing. Then the doctor came in, and excitedly told him it was time, as if he was about to birth a baby or something like that, and Amy's laughter turned thickly to a near hysterical sobbing.

Amy cried—cried *hard*, clung to his hand and kissed his face, and normally this would be enough to sway him no matter what his cause was. Today it wasn't, though.

Today, he would get the switch.

****

Dear [illegible],

It's done.

It hurts.

It's worth it all. You're worth it all.

I'll be back soon.

I love you.

Please be ok.

Love,
Drew

****

The switch glowed dully through his skin. He looked at it in the mirror. Poked so very lightly at it.

There wasn't even a protrusion. They'd slipped it in amongst his organs and the only indicator that he carried death in him was the glow. The glow, and the dull twinge of it, there.

Drew ran his hand down his chest.

Remembered Riis doing the same, in the sand on that beach.

Moved his hand back to his side, shaking.

The switch felt like an alive thing, and he tried to calm down, terrified his heart would be strong enough to flip it.

Seb let out a groan from the other room and Drew buttoned his shirt up quickly, hands shaking, shaking.

"Drew are you *done in there?* Do I have to lug my ass all the way down to a *different bathroom?*" Seb moaned.

"I'm done," Drew snapped, coming back out and flopping down on the cushy chair in the corner of Seb's room. His chest twinged and his breath hitched.

Seb stared at him.

Drew stared back. "What?"

"I didn't hear you flush." Seb muttered, drunkenly, and then laughed at the way Drew's face tightened. "Don't worry, I know, I know. You were just… just *looking at it*, weren't you? Jeez. I would. I would, too, if I were you."

Drew said nothing.

"They say they buried it deep. Deeper even than they buried it in your whore mother," Seb slurred. He was still wearing his coat from being crowned almost two days ago, now. They'd finally made him give back the crown itself a few hours ago to be cleaned and kept for ceremonial purposes. He'd thrown nothing short of a tantrum and shouted that he was King Admiral now, he could do what he wanted, wear the crown forever if he so wished. His father—who Drew'd never seen raise a hand to anyone, and he'd lived with the man his whole life—had slapped his true born son, hard.

Then the previous King Admiral had turned to Drew, and calmly said, "Take him to bed. Stay with him until he falls asleep. I don't want him choking on his own vomit."

Drew shut his eyes and remembered Riis' pack. Their laughter and bright warmth. The way they cared for each other.

It wasn't fair that Seb and King Admiral didn't get that.

"I'll have to really go digging when the time comes," Seb said, and cackled madly, lifting a flask to his lips. "Then we'll see. We'll see."

'When.'

Drew shut his eyes again, hard. Blew out the candle.

Amy would be at the servant's entrance in six hours.

He just had to survive until then.

****

The floor creaked as he crept across the boards and Drew flinched.

Seb didn't stir, though.

Drew opened the door carefully, closed it with even more care. He wouldn't be able to bring anything that wasn't on him, this time. It was too much of a risk—going across the livingroom to his own new room. Gathering things and then walking back with them; too risky.

He had his tablet. He had his clothes.

He had the switch.

This was good enough. Would have to be good enough.

He snuck, sock-footed, down the hall, holding his shoes, avoiding as best he could the floorboards that creaked. Made it to the kitchen, reached for the door…

"What are you doing?" A very soft, gruff voice.

Drew froze. Turned.

Red sat across from the door in the dark, a cup of tea on the counter beside her, her tablet open on a game she hadn't started playing yet.

They stared at one another. Drew let out a shuddering exhale.

"You know," Red spoke softly, "your mother hired me to protect *you.*"

"I know," he said shakily, head spinning. He didn't know what to do.

"I hate it when a job changes. I don't really abide by 'change' well." She glanced down at her tablet. A strange twist in her face. "Go ahead, Drew. Run. There. Job done."

Drew let out a breath like a gunshot. Turned and bolted out the door. Down the steps. Out to Amy's car, which was silent, dark and waiting. Flung himself inside and into her arms and she let out a surprised shriek before covering her mouth quickly with her hand, jerking to attention and maneuvering the car creeping down the drive and onto the main road before flicking on the headlights.

For a while they just breathed, staring out ahead at the road, which rose up to meet them one white dash of divider at a time. A swell of black tarmac, ever flowing.

Eventually, distantly, the lights of the spaceport.

"Did he write you back, yet?"

"No."

"Drew… what if he's—"

"No."

"…Okay, but still. What if."

Drew breathed shallow. Blew out the candle against the glass window, and it made a little cloud of collected condensation that faded in the inhale. Returned, on the exhale. "Then this was still the right thing to do," he said finally.

He knew it was.

She shivered. Kept driving.

****

Straight Cousin fist-bumped him when he arrived. "My worst employee, back again," he said flatly in his Straight Cousin voice.

"Back and worse than ever," Drew deadpanned, distantly.

Amy was already crying. "You're sure you can get him there safe? And soon? He's gotta get there *fast*, and in secret, I mean—"

"Yeah, yeah. I got my speedy ship out just for this occasion. You just gotta work towards getting me back invited to the Xmas party," Straight Cousin said, and Drew felt a sudden ache of affection for him. Just, really, for having a want like that. Straight Cousin turned on Drew. "You remember my name?"

"Straight Cousin," Drew said immediately, and Straight Cousin laughed. Slapped Drew on the back.

Drew rolled his eyes. Hugged Amy goodbye, tight as he could. Promised to write.

It all hurt too much to really feel, right now. He still held her hand hard until he had to move beyond it, until he had to let go, step forward into the small ship. Watched her until the door clanked up behind him.

The ship, dinky in a way that did indeed look speedy—took off with a *whoosh* and *pfeew*, and Drew said goodbye to Earth II.

37

Please

Dear ⵌ,
Please. Please, love. Be ok.
Love,
Drew

Dear ⵌ,
I think a lot about the first time I saw you.

I can't say anything like 'oh, love at first sight!' and I can't say 'oh I didn't think anything of it BUT THEN' because both would be bullshit lies. I didn't love you at first, and I definitely didn't not think anything of you.

I knew when I saw you I was living in one of those moments that'd always hold a piece of me, though. I just didn't know why yet.
Love,
Drew

Dear ⌗⫲⊤,

Remember when we got stuck in the elevator? I think I started falling in love with you then. Weird.

Blow out the candle!

Love,

Drew

Dear ⌗⫲⊤,

I can't stop crying. Please. Please be ok.

Love,

Drew

Dear Drew,

⌗⫲⊤ is experiencing something we call 'distance sickness.' It is difficult; we cannot take him to the hospital, as you would be unable to come to him, then. It is only you who can stop this and save him.

It is confusing. This rarely happens before a true lifemate bond. He claims he has not fully bonded with you, but still. It is distance sickness.

You say you love him. I love him too. I understand this.

Get here quickly.

Love,

Arnold

Risk

Arnold greeted Drew at the spaceport, along with Sister. Both grabbed his hands, and as soon as he was in Sister's car Arnold let out a croaking cry and flung their arms around Drew.

Drew held them back. His arms were shaking.

They'd exchanged a few emails at this point, as Straight Cousin's little ship crept at breakneck speed closer, as Riis worsened, as Drew was powerless to stop it.

After all of it, all of it, it couldn't end here.

"Is he, he's alive, right, is he—" Drew was practically shouting and knew it, but couldn't stop it, all of him seemed awake with panic.

"He's alive-ing, he's alive-ing!" Sister cried out quickly.

"He is very sick," Arnold said shakily.

"Because of *me?*" Drew got out. He was shaking. He didn't get it he didn't get it.

Riis had been right.

He had *no idea what he was doing at all.*

"Yes," Sister said, with real affection but the words cut him to the quick and he held his hands hard over his eyes.

"You will fix him," Arnold said quickly. They grabbed his chin, lifting it harshly so he was facing them. "Your presence alone. It's the cure, to feel the electricity of the missed one's brain. We all survive off this, like we do food. We survive off the presence of others who survive off us. You will fix him."

Drew shuddered. "Yes," he said. It was the only thing he could believe without drowning in it.

They got to Riis' pack's family house and Drew was bolting out of the car before it fully stopped. He ran inside—it was different than before, a somber weight over the home, god, no, and he froze, not knowing where to go.

A child—one of the performers of before—froze too upon seeing him and then gestured wildly behind themself.

He booked it.

Knew, suddenly, where he was going.

His old room. For that one night he'd slept here, half-drunk and a lifetime ago now, and he found Riis lying there where Drew'd lain before, a candle lit beside him.

Smacked the beads out of the way, ran inside the room and fell onto him. Pushed his head against Riis' helplessly, willing his 'electricity' or whatever *there*, go *there*, fix him! Whatever, just *do it!*

Riis breathed shallow. Didn't acknowledge him for a long moment, *no*, but then—

Then—

The gentlest claws in his hair.

Drew let out a sob. Sat up and Riis blinked up at him, surprised, woozy with it, it seemed, and Drew shouted as loudly as he could, "You are SUCH A FUCKING DRAMA QUEEN, RIIS!" and then kissed him like a punch.

Riis laughed, weakly, against his mouth. Reached up and pushed him away, though. His hand stilled on Drew's chest. His breath hitched.

The switch glowed between them like an ember.

"I had to," Drew said, hard.

"Why?" Riis spoke like the word had been broken out of him.

"I needed the ability."

"The ability?"

"To fight for you. To stop it. Somehow, maybe, stop it. Even though, I mean, you're right. I have no idea what I'm doing. Not at *all*. I know what I need to do, though."

Riis breathed. Looked at him. Drew thumbed over the wrinkle between his eyes. Everything in him shook, but he continued, voice as steady as he could make it, "It'll never happen. No one will ever flip it, so much as touch it, not while I live, not while I—"

"That's kind of the point though, isn't it?" Riis said weakly, and Drew burst out laughing.

"I can fight them!"

"No you can't."

"Oh come *on*, I'm scrappy enough, I—"

"I shall fight them. You will… will be safe. As long as I live. I swore it, after all. You will be safe. I know what I'm doing, even if you do not."

For a long time they just looked at each other. Riis' hand tightened on his shirt, then, and Drew let out a breath and pushed closer, past his mouth, burying his face in Riis' neck and fluttering his eyes shut, loving it, all of it, starting with the hitch of breath that elicited and ending with the whole fucking universe.

"I didn't want this, though. Oh, I didn't want this." Riis' voice was very small.

"Well, you're stupid, then."

"No. This… it's too big a risk, Drew, it's—"

"It's always a risk," Drew murmured against his neck. "Always. I know *that much*. I say take it. Nothing's worth nothing if you don't take it."

Riis breathed. His hand trailed up Drew's chest, then. Cupped his face.

The kiss, when it came, was simple. Just a press of lips. Drew realized he didn't know if kissing was even, like, a thing, here. If Riis just did it because he knew Drew liked it, the way Drew had begun to find pushing his face into Riis' warm neck immensely exciting for that same reason. So many things, so many lovely little details to unravel. So much left to discover, here.

"I love you," he said against Riis' mouth.

Riis squinted softly up at him. "Yes," he said, "I know. And I love you. I love you, as well."

39

Not a Wedding

They were in a shitty little motel, as they had been since the day after his return to Drune. The plan had been to 'run,' but running is harder than expected when it involves a giant Emni boyfriend (fiancé? Husband? All good words) recovering slowly from, uh, Drew going home for like, not even a full three weeks.

Someone had come knocking at Riis' pack's house, though. Someone looking for Drew. Looking for the switch. So it'd been time to go.

First, to what seemed to be a renegade doctor's office, someone related to Riis' pack who had examined Drew in the dark basement of a hospital with the help of a human nurse. They had gone there to get the switch out. It seemed just generally smarter to carry it outside of one's body. Maybe lock it up somewhere and bury it.

That's when they'd learned the truth, and the careful future Drew hadn't realized he'd lined up toppled like dominos in a scattered row.

"There's just no way. I'm sorry. The way they put it in, it's essentially impossible to remove without severing his spine completely, possibly risking

extreme damage to the heart..."

So. Panic attack first.

Drew's own anxiety had been easier to deal with than ever before. Perhaps especially because Riis had been practically hyperventilating on the floor beside him, letting out these strange whistling hissing swear-shaped words.

Riis had grabbed him when he ducked down next to him and held Drew, hard, shaking, and Drew'd been suddenly transported to the time in the car after their interview, practically a lifetime ago, when it seemed like all was lost.

It wasn't lost, though, was it?

It was strangely much easier to deal with your own feelings when someone else's shone brighter, warranted more importance.

Then, motel! Slightly more panic attack. Panic attack conversation. Panic attack-fueled sex (not their first time having sex —that had been pretty soon after Drew got back—but the first time they figured out how to actually get a little past confused desperation, which was *thrilling*; they were making *progress*) and then, strange spicy pickle shawarma like thing Riis had run out to get.

There was a TV in their motel room.

They leaned against each other after dinner. Drew had shared all the picklyest parts of his food and Riis was finishing them delicately, looking frankly exhausted. A rerun of some *Star Trek* knockoff came on and Drew sighed, pushing his head into Riis' neck.

Riis shuddered. "Drew," he said, and his voice shook slightly, "that is, you should know, a very... intimate move, for Emni."

"Ooh, this?" Drew nuzzled his head in deeper. Riis made the best sound ever, so he did it again, grinning, thrilled.

"Yes! Yes, that, Drew, you can't... do that in public ever again, do you understand?"

"Ahaha, yeah."

Quiet for a moment. Drew let it rest, just tipping the top of his head against Riis' broad shoulder. When he spoke, it was very quiet. "You said there's... others, like us?"

"Hm? Oh… I mean, not exactly…"

"No, that'd be fucking insane if it was exactly…"

"But. Yes, there are… pairs, like us. Human and Emni." Riis was oddly clipped, distant. "A little like us."

"Who?"

Riis let out a huff. "I don't know them personally, Drew. They… are rather on the outskirts. It's not *illegal* or anything, though there is a movement to make it so. The proposed law is phrased as something to protect those involved. As I previously stated, this… doesn't often have a happy ending. So, yes, there's a likelihood it will be named illegal in the coming years. So, most live in hiding, preemptively."

"Ah."

"…Does that bother you?"

"Oh yeah, definitely," Drew said immediately, "I don't like to break the law. That's going just a *step too far*, darling."

Absolute silence. Just long enough for Drew to become worried Riis was taking him dead-ass seriously, but then, a belting bellow laugh and Riis elbowed him lightly. Drew giggled manically, falling back on the bed, grabbing Riis and pulling him with him. Riis went, and he was a solid weight over Drew, and he peered into Drew's eyes, squinting, and then he shifted, pushing his face down into Drew's neck and letting out that low, reverberating hum of a growl again, and things got really exciting again really quickly after that.

It was significantly less confusing each time. Calmer, too. Already, they had found a familiar, lazy rhythm with one another, though there was still the bright edge of discovery on this side of it.

Afterwards, Drew found himself overbrimming with light and rather breathless.

Riis let out a shuddering sigh into Drew's neck. "It is *so* much easier to smell it on you now that I can actually do something about it," he muttered.

Drew blinked. "Wait, *what?*"

Riis cringed with his whole body. "Eh… I mean. It just. Used to… affect me a great deal. When we were at University. And you…"

Silence. Drew started giggling madly then though, and Riis hid his face with his hands (and Drew's neck) and swore and all was kind of well and good after that.

Until Sister had shown up with the vest.

****

Not to be flat-out obnoxious, but Drew was kind of cool with how things had been going. Riis went out and got the least pickle-like food he could find. He brought it back, where Drew'd be waiting in their dim little motel room, they'd eat and make out like a *lot*, a lot a lot a lot, and then sleep. Rinse, lather, repeat.

Sister evidently thought she was helping quite a bit by bringing the vest.

"So you wear, and—" she whistled "—no light! Light gone! Bye light. No one see switch."

Drew wrinkled his nose, staring down at the vest. It was literally grunt gear, a black bullet-proof vest. "It's a bullet-proof," he said.

"Excellent," Riis said in a breath. "Thank you—" he grumbled, croaked, and hissed.

They tried it on him. It worked; no light. Drew shrugged, grinned. Sister was all but beaming, so he decided to stop being a wallowing little trophy squire intent on being hidden away and just be grateful. "Okay, cool. Wanna go down to the beach?"

"Yes! Beach!" Sister cackled.

"Absolutely not." Riis snapped. "No, what if it *slips*, what if it *comes undone*, what if someone recognizes you even without the light beaming out of your chest? No."

Which is how Drew discovered Riis was just super fucking crazy about him going out, too. Sister widened her eyes at Drew, and Drew widened his eyes back. She cackled and Riis pouted and eventually they went out anyway, Riis acting like a madman bodyguard the whole time.

****

Riis was being anal about the vest again.

The line was back between his eyes, his mouth a tight press of similar focus, and Drew let out a breath that made Riis blink, slow, and lean forward. He adjusted the vest again, trying yet again to tighten it. Drew blew a little more intentionally out this time, right into his face, and Riis blinked quick, startling. Drew giggled.

"This is serious, Drew, honestly," Riis snapped. But his annoyance seemed to nervously melt away as Drew pushed forward and tipped his forehead against Riis' chin, wrapping his arms around his waist, which was, you know, something he was *allowed to do now, hallelujah chorus! Ahhh!* "Drew, we just got it on—"

"Mm. Good, it's not under a lot of clothes. Easy to take off again." Drew murmured against Riis collarbone, and Riis did a full-body shudder that Drew was very proud of.

"Drew… we're going to be late…"

"Hm. For what, anyway? What's a—" he grunted, growled, and hissed "—anyway?"

Riis looked at him very pointedly in a way that contained a tad more than an edge of irk. "A lifemate bonding ceremony. Traditionally done before… well. Anyway. My pack insisted on it."

Drew froze. Backed up.

Riis blinked rather quickly. His mouth was tight again. Drew felt a slow grin spread across his face, though, and Riis blinked a tad slower, squinting slightly, and Drew bellowed, "Our *wedding?* You're telling me this thing is our *wedding?* Why didn't you *say so!* Jeezus, I gotta get dressed!"

Riis let out a huff. "You are a *child.*"

"You better hope not."

"Okay, that's enough of that. Let me fix—Drew, that's barely hiding the light!" Riis grabbed him hard, yanking Drew's shirt off in definitely the least exciting way he'd done so far and beginning to wrestle with the vest again.

****

Spicy curry and strange little sliders next to pickled radish-like cakes and a pudding that was literally relish. The donut-like things he and Riis had made at school, overabundant in the center of the table. Honey wine everywhere.

They were greeted with even more enthusiasm than Riis' pack normally presented them with, Riis going quiet and soft around them, like he did, Drew grinning so hard his cheeks hurt, laughing when Sister made some joke he barely understood, though he could tell by the bright cackle which immediately followed that it had been a joke. Straight Cousin and the crew were even there, as he and Riis were leaving on Straight Cousin's freight as soon as this was over, a future that contained equal amounts of joy and dread as well as an overarching theme of excitement. It was a very shitty honeymoon. It was terrible, and he was so, so excited.

Smalls seemed very happy in the wide low bowl chair thing by the fire. Straight Cousin slapped Drew's back, and all went very quiet in the room for a second, before Riis quickly cut in with, "No no, that's of no concern, trust me, I've learned humans often hit one another like that *affectionately*" and all the humans started laughing.

The smallest of the adult Emni came out then. They were painted blue from head to toe, and smudged blue paint on Drew and Riis' foreheads, spoke in whistling grunts for a long time to a suddenly silent crowd. It took Drew a second to realize Straight Cousin had even splurged on a hyperspace call, and he almost cried out when he saw Amy and Shrink Kanak's faces on the tablet he held facing them, both looking pleased as punch.

"Now, in Standard, for the human Drew," the small Emni said, and turned to them both sharply. "You will share a life together, for all your life. You will live together, and die together, too. You accept?"

"Yes," Drew said immediately. He was practically *vibrating*. Riis, though, hesitated.

He was looking at Drew, and Drew looked back, smile fading. Riis shut his eyes. "Of course," he said softly.

That was that, okay, cool.

Cheers all around.

"This is the part where you go have the first sex," Sister said brightly, and Drew choked on his wine, and Riis, seeming to come out of his funk, laughed. "I am think you already do this."

Riis hissed something at her and she cackled. Drew laughed, and then went over to Straight Cousin, who shook his hand like he'd personally arranged this marriage and congratulated him before presenting the tablet, where a grainy Amy and Shrink Kanak were whooping and hollering something similar. For a while he just basked in this, but looking up, realized something: Riis was gone.

A very uncomfortable swoop.

"I'll talk to you later, yeah? Thanks…" He handed the tablet back and started around the crowd, searching, but coming up short. Most folk were distracted by the feast, some kids playing a game in the center of the fray as well that was causing some amusement. It wasn't until he caught Sister's eye that she gestured quickly behind herself, back towards the stairs that he realized where he had to look.

He took the stairs slowly, carefully. Came upon the door, beads breaking the light into lines of shadow before the dark of the room, and said softly, "Riis?"

Riis didn't look up at him. He was sitting straight, legs curled under him on his squat couch, staring at the wall.

Drew slowly came inside. Sat, and tipped his head against Riis' shoulder. Riis sighed, but immediately opened his arm and held him there, tightly. "It's going to be a lot of change from here on out," Riis said softly.

Drew breathed. Stared for a moment at the familiar fixtures— the rug, the dresser, the neatly made bed. "Yeah," he said softly. Shut his eyes. Yeah.

"We will not be able to stay in one place."

"I know."

"It will be a lifetime of running."

"Riis… I'm sorry."

"…What?"

Drew squeezed his eyes closed, hard. He felt Riis' hand come up to his face, though, and a delicate claw came down between his eyes and he opened them, looking up. Riis blinked slowly at him, seeming confused.

"I'm sorry," Drew spoke softly. "I, like, doomed you."

Riis stiffened. His grip on Drew tightened.

"Not like that," Drew added quickly. "I'm not saying I'll leave you, 'cause I won't. I meant running. Running forever, like—"

"I do not at all mind running forever," Riis said softly. Quiet, for a moment, and then he spoke haltingly, rather quickly, as if to get it out like ripping off a bandaid, "And most likely, you will indeed leave me. It's simply... too late for that to not hurt anyway. So."

"I won't!" Drew said immediately.

Riis rolled his whole head—an insane interpretation of an eye-roll, it seemed—and Drew couldn't help the mad laughter that came up in him, and he would literally *never leave Riis, how could he...*

"You speak like a child, sometimes. You do not know. An Emni knows things like this. We only feel this way once. Humans are not like us. You are incapable of knowing if you'll ever leave me, because it is a future you have not yet visited."

Drew stopped, a tad stumped on this twist of language. Thought for a moment about the best, most honest thing to say. Finally spoke, "I mean, yeah. Yeah, I guess you're right. I don't know if I'll still feel this way, like, years and years from now. It feels *insane* to suggest I won't—" he added quickly when Riis stiffened, "—but uh, yeah. I can't know, I guess. But I do know I'll never leave you."

Riis tilted his head, staring blankly at Drew. "Is that not the same thing?"

Drew laughed. "Now *you* don't know what you're doing at all."

Riis let out a huff, looked away. Drew rested his head on Riis' shoulder. "I know exactly what I'm doing," Riis finally said softly, "I know every unwise concession I have ever made, and I find myself quite incapable of regretting any of them, foolish though that may be."

Drew let out a breath. "You talk so nice," he said, and then felt utterly ridiculous. Riis snorted. "Anyway," Drew continued quickly,

"I'm saying I won't leave you. I can promise you *that*, okay? I won't. Like, yeah. We'll both grow. We'll both change. Maybe me more than you, whatever. But to the bitter end, even if I don't end up feeling exactly this way forever, there's still… like, a mark. A mark of you in my life," he shut his eyes as Riis turned to him, heart beating quick, wanting to say it right, "knowing you will still be one of the most important parts of my life. I can promise that. You'll always be you to me, and therefore important. And I *can* promise you that, Riis. I can."

Quiet for a long time. He snuck a glance, opening his eyes in a squint. Riis was squinting back, softly.

Eventually, they would rise. Rejoin their party, get patted on the back and hugged and congratulated some more. For now, though, there was just the quiet. Quiet, and the familiarity of Riis' room, both of them breathing in the space before all that was to come after.

Call to

Action!

Enjoyed this book? Hated it but reached
this point anyway? Felt strongly at all?
Reviews make my world go round. Please
leave a review on Goodreads/Amazon/
Wherever your funktastic little heart desires!

Awknowlegments

This story's been living in my head for a long time.

I'm not quite sure what made me finally take it from playlists and scenes in fanfictions I was writing and do it its full, deserved justice of being its own thing. But these characters have been with me a long time, Drew especially.

I'd like to thank so many people.

Starting from the beginning, I'd like to thank my Mom and Dad, for being crazy and funky and so, so loving. The lake, for being electrifying and creative and good. My friends for encouraging this every day of my life, even when I was at my worst. Drugs, for bringing me to my knees.

I'd like to thank Starlingstory for becoming the one story that rules all others in my mind, despite never being finished. I'd like to thank Starlingstory for never being finished. It gave me the urge to write something.

Thank you to Naomi, best sister in law a boi could ask for. Thank you to Teen and Aarin, beta readers from beyond the pearly gates. Thank you Meridian for taking me on credit, making the best cover, seriously just digging into my head and pulling out the light. Thank you Willow, for polishing my prose and cheking me on my punctuation. This story would be word vomit without you, girl.

I'd finally like to thank Mr. Williams, my middle school Creative Writing teacher, for telling me I was talented but lazy, and needed to actually do the work.

I loved that.

Olly Dee

Olly Dee is an agender, neurodivergent parent in recovery residing just outside Philadelphia in a small, strange house. They share their life with a husband, a child, a fetus, two cats, and one lizard.

Curious? Learn more about them and what they do at www.ollydee.com